THE SISTER OF...

With her husband ... rtime, Hilda travels w... y with his six sisters. E... oreau house. Five of th... oldest, Pauline, who controls them all through intimidation and blackmail. Their father's will left Pauline in control of the family fortune, and only a marriage can break the trust. Now Hilda finds herself pitted against Pauline to get hers and David's share of the money.

In spite of their fear of Pauline, the sisters put up a united front to the world. Then one night, Pauline is found murdered by a knife from the family kitchen. Now secrets are being revealed, and Hilda finds herself in the middle of it. So it comes as no surprise to her when she finds the sisters all pointing their finger at her as the prime suspect!

Mary Collins Bibliography
(1908-1979)

Novels:
The Fog Comes (1941)
Dead Center (1942)
Only the Good (1942)
The Sister of Cain (1943)
Death Warmed Over (1947)
Dog Eat Dog (1949)

Crime Stories:
Sirens in the Night (*Street & Smith's Detective Story Magazine*, April 1943)

THE SISTER OF CAIN

Mary Collins

Introduction by Curtis Evans

STARK HOUSE

Stark House Press • Eureka California

THE SISTER OF CAIN

Published by Stark House Press
1315 H Street
Eureka, CA 95501, USA
griffinskye3@sbcglobal.net
www.starkhousepress.com

THE SISTER OF CAIN
Originally published by Charles Scribner's Sons, New York, and copyright ©
1943 by Mary Collins. Reprinted 1950 in paperback by Bantam Books, New
York. Copyright renewed January 26, 1971 by Mary Collins.

Reprinted by permission of the Mary Collins estate. All rights reserved
under International and Pan-American Copyright Conventions.

"Never such devoted sisters..." © 2025 by Curtis Evans

ISBN: 979-8-88601-129-6

Text design by Mark Shepard, shepgraphics.com
Cover design by Jeff Vorzimmer, ¡caliente!design, Austin, Texas
Proofreading by Bill Kelly

PUBLISHER'S NOTE:
This is a work of fiction. Names, characters, places and incidents are either
the products of the author's imagination or used fictionally, and any
resemblance to actual persons, living or dead, events or locales, is entirely
coincidental.
Without limiting the rights under copyright reserved above, no part of this
publication may be reproduced, stored, or introduced into a retrieval system
or transmitted in any form or by any means (electronic, mechanical,
photocopying, recording or otherwise) without the prior written permission
of both the copyright owner and the above publisher of the book.

First Stark House Press Edition: February 2025

"NEVER SUCH DEVOTED SISTERS..."

Mary Collins' *The Sister of Cain* (1943)
by Curtis Evans

I looked from one face to the other, searching desperately for some sign of guilt, the mark of Cain, anything that would end this frightful, bloody massacre that had taken place in less than a week....

Mary Collins' fourth mystery novel, *The Sister of Cain*, was published in October 1943, a year after *Only the Good*, reprinted by Stark House in 2022. Like many a suspense thriller before and after it, *Cain* is concerned with decidedly odd dwellers in a decayed family mansion. In *Cain*, these strange denizens are the six weird Moreau sisters, who together reside in festering animosity in San Francisco at an ominous Gothic Revival abode, crenelated like a castle and located on exclusive Russian Hill. The author, who herself grew up in San Francisco in the 1910s and 1920s, based the setting on a real city mansion, built in 1852 and known locally as Humphrey's Castle. A memorable rendering of the decaying old house, reputedly then the oldest still standing in San Francisco, appears on the cover of the novel's American hardcover edition. Sadly, despite efforts to save it, the "castle" was demolished in 1948, just a few years short of its centenary.

Narrator Hilda Moreau is the bride of the lone male Moreau sibling, David, who is far away from home fighting in World War Two. Pregnant with David's child, Hilda has come to stay with his sisters at the Moreau mansion, but what she finds there makes her want to turn heel and head back whence she came to good, old Cleveland, Ohio. Dominated by and hating their tyrannical eldest sister, Pauline, the Moreau women seem primed for murder from the moment of Hilda's arrival. And, sure enough, Pauline soon is found stabbed to death with a kitchen knife in her bedroom. Nor is Pauline's death the final fatal event that will take place at the Moreau mansion during Hilda's deadly stay.

Pauline Moreau turns out to have been quite a bad apple indeed (no one misses her except her scheming maid, Nanette), but truth be told,

Hilda finds that the whole Moreau orchard bears rather strange feminine fruit. There is twenty-year-old Rose, whom the other sisters, all older, insist on treating like a child (they all call her "Baby"); Marthe, who seems down-to-earth but is really a dissembler; Elise, a dipsomaniac; Anne, a doctor whose initial friendliness to Hilda soon gives way to hostility; and sex-starved Sophie, who is more desperate than ever to land a husband now that she has hit forty. All the sisters, it seems, had motives to murder Pauline—as did several other ladies!

Dedicated by Mary Collins to her fellow San Francisco native, the prominent feminist novelist Gertrude Atherton, *The Sister of Cain* is an interesting crime novel. With the exception of a police detective, Lieutenant Cassidy (Irish, naturally) and a lawyer friend of the family (not Irish), all the major characters—and suspects—are women. In addition to Anne Moreau, the doctor, there are a woman lawyer and a woman psychiatrist. Additionally, Hilda before her marriage was a schoolteacher; and a wealthy matron complains bitterly that one of her maids plans to leave her to take up war work as a welder. "Wendy the Welder" was famously photographed for *Life* in October 1943, the month *Cain* was published.

Social detail in *Cain* frequently is fascinating. Although Hilda as mentioned is pregnant (albeit not "showing" yet), she smokes cigarettes with distressing frequency. When the police detective discovers that Hilda is "expecting," he promptly drops her from his list of suspects in the murder of her sister-in-law, presumably on the theory that a mommy-to-be is incapable of harming anyone (secondhand smoke aside). In real life the author, herself nearing the age of forty, was pregnant when she wrote *Cain*; and she gave birth to her only child, Jeffrey, in February 1944.

In its day *Cain* was categorized as an HIBK (Had I But Known), "feminine anxiety" novel, but Hilda is too self-aware a narrator for true HIBK. She even expressly disavows such an idea—"I certainly could not see myself behaving like the heroine of an HIBK mystery plodding around in the dangerous dark," she declares at one point—though in classic fashion she does manage while egregiously snooping to get herself clonked on the head a couple of times anyway.

Hilda is an appealing character with, at times, rather an unusual way with words. "I was so starved for human companionship that I would have welcomed a cannibal woman clad in a G-string," she declares early in the novel. Like her sisters-in-law she does not hesitate to sling around swear words: readers will find that "bitch" and "hell" are common expletives in *Cain*. The mystery plot is quite interesting too and there is a single good physical clue, one which in reading I did not pick up on, alas!

Mary Collins' fourth mystery novel, which was broadcast on NBC's Molle Mystery Theatre radio program in 1944, was well received by reviewers, just like the author's earlier essays in fictional crime. "Murder novels have long delighted in rundown family houses with at least one despicable retainer and a variety of simmering hatreds," observed Dorothy B. Hughes in her rave review of the novel in the *Albuquerque Tribune*. "Mary Collins places this one high on the list. Her Moreau family fringes on the psychopathic.... The atmosphere creaks and chills and the mystification is thorough.... Its hold is never halfway." Similarly, an anonymous reviewer in the *Oregon Daily Journal* enthused: "Mary Collins could put gooseflesh on a statue with her skill at creating morbid situations. This is a murder story of almost terrifying suspense in the atmosphere of a dilapidated San Francisco mansion."

With a slight feminist edge to her review of *The Sister of Cain*, Acadian children's book author Mary Alice Fontenot advised in the Crowley, Louisiana *Post-Signal* that "in spite of this unusual predominance of feminine characters in a mystery-fiction story, masculine readers will find it every bit as exciting as Ellery Queen or Perry Mason, and may even learn a little about feminine psychology...." And that, surely, today is as worthy a quality in fiction as it is in life.

—November 2024

···

Curtis Evans received a PhD in American history in 1998. He is the author of *Masters of the "Humdrum" Mystery: Cecil John Charles Street, Freeman Wills Crofts, Alfred Walter Stewart and British Detective Fiction, 1920-1961* (2012), *Clues and Corpses: The Detective Fiction and Mystery Criticism of Todd Downing* (2013), *The Spectrum of English Murder: The Detective Fiction of Henry Lancelot Aubrey-Fletcher and G. D. H. and Margaret Cole* (2015) and editor of the Edgar nominated *Murder in the Closet: Essays on Queer Clues in Crime Fiction Before Stonewall* (2017). He writes about vintage crime fiction at his blog The Passing Tramp and at Crimereads.

THE SISTER OF CAIN
Mary Collins

To Gertrude Atherton

The characters and incidents which follow are entirely fictional. The "Moreau House" is fictional only where I have described it as shabby and dingy. Actually it is a charming period piece, and I am eternally grateful to my good friends, the Giffens and the Morrisons, who allowed me to use their home as a setting for these murderous goings-on.
M. C.

CHAPTER 1

"This is it, lady," the cab driver said over his shoulder. He swung his yellow taxi at right angles to the sidewalk. "I can't see no number, but the place next door is 980 so this must be 986 here on the corner."

I slid across the leather seat and struggled against gravity to get myself ungracefully out of the cab. I'd had my heart in my throat for a large part of the drive from the Ferry Building to my destination. The steep hills of San Francisco are a cause for good, healthy fear to one used to the gentle curves of Ohio.

As the cab driver got out my four bags, I pulled out a bill, and then took a good look at the house. It sat back thirty feet or so from the street, grey, grim and precise in its angularity. The four-squarishness of the house was only slightly relieved by a huge, droopy tree—I thought it was probably eucalyptus from the pictures I'd seen—a rather colorful lot of geraniums and purple stock behind the picket fence, and a tangle of vines on the flat veranda roof. The flat roof of the house was trimmed with a wooden battlement. Right square in the middle of the roof was a jaunty little cupola which gave somewhat the same effect as would a small, giddy hat worn by a serious old woman.

The cab driver held open a wooden gate which looked frivolous with its Victorian curlicues in the middle of the straight, uncompromising pickets, and I stumbled along behind him down a rough stone path.

We went up a flight of seven or eight crooked wooden stairs which led to the veranda that ran across the front of the house, and I punched the doorbell.

"Old house, ain't it, lady?" The cab driver put down the bags and fished out a grimy handkerchief with which he wiped the inside of his cap before replacing it on his baldish head. I wondered idly how in God's name anybody could perspire in the damp, foggy wind of a September day in San Francisco. I was shivering under my print dress and light wool redingote.

"Yes," I said. "Very old. It's the oldest house still standing in San Francisco, I believe. Built in 1852."

Then we waited. After a reasonable length of time, I punched the doorbell again, thinking that my husband's family was certainly not straining itself to give me a royal welcome.

The paneled door was pulled open abruptly. A very old woman, dressed in a black dress and an apron definitely guilty of "tattle-tale grey," glared at me out of sharp little black eyes set in pouches of wrinkled skin.

"I heard you," she snapped in a quavery voice. "You're Mrs. Moreau?"

"Yes," I said, trying not too hard to keep anger and sarcasm out of my voice. "Will you show the driver where to put my luggage and tell Miss Moreau that I'm here." I was tired after jolting across the country for four nights in a second-class train. It had been perfectly all right with me that my husband's sisters didn't all traipse down to the Ferry Building to meet my train which was four hours late anyway, but I had expected something a little warmer in the reception line when I actually arrived at the house.

"I'll take the bags," the old woman said. "Miss Moreau had to go out. She said for me to show you to your room."

I paid the cab driver and tipped him generously.

The door banged behind me, and I stood looking around the hall. In front of me a steep flight of stairs rose to the second floor. The hall was dark and smelled of dust improperly removed from ancient Brussels carpet. All the doors opening off the hall were closed, and on my right I saw myself in an enormous mirror heavily framed in carved rosewood—a hatrack thing full of jabbing brass hooks and carving and streaked red marble.

"Are none of the other sisters home?" The maid had started up the stairs ahead of me carrying my two largest bags. I picked up the two smaller ones reluctantly. I didn't care much about carrying anything.

"Miss Moreau will be home pretty soon." The maid's voice was flat and final, and I could hardly bring myself to shout that I, Hilda Moreau, had arrived and wanted to meet my husband's family, so I followed her up the stairs and down the hall to the front of the house.

The old woman flapped the door open and walked ahead and banged down the bags. "The bathroom's at the end of the hall opposite the stairs," she said.

As the daughter of a small-town lawyer, I had not been used to a retinue of well-trained, decently mannered servants, but this woman was really a bit too rich for my blood.

"What's your name?" I said snappily.

"Nanette," the old woman answered. "Lunch is at one. I'll tell you when Miss Moreau gets home." Then she marched out of the room, banging the door behind her.

I sat down on a hard, uncomfortable little rosewood chair and threw my hat on the floor and bawled unashamedly and without restraint. It was bad enough to have my charming, affectionate, intelligent husband gone to the wars—I knew his ship was somewhere in the Atlantic and that's all I did know—but to have to come clear across the country to this steep, cold, grey, alien town and into this horrible old cold house without so much as a word of welcome after four sleepless nights and days.

Then I managed something in the laugh line. I have always been ashamed of self-pity.

I blew my nose decisively and mopped my eyes. It would never do to meet David's family looking unnecessarily unattractive. Besides, the room in which dear Nanette had deposited me was interesting. It had flowered wallpaper that was definitely cheerful and white woodwork and rather attractive cream silk curtains trimmed with ball fringe. There was an enormous rosewood bed with a headboard that ended only six or eight inches below the ceiling, a monumental bookcase filled with dusty-looking old school books, a vast, elaborately carved bureau topped with grey marble and assorted Victorian chairs. In a shallow alcove, there was a very attractive white marble fireplace with a coal fire laid in a small iron grate.

I lit it and watched the flames curl around the newspaper and catch the kindling. Maybe I was disobeying house rules in lighting the fire, but I didn't really care. If this was the kind of house where one had fires only when ill, I couldn't be blamed for taking care of myself and while I had little hope that the small fire would ever really warm the room, I could at least warm my hands at its cheerful heat.

I lit a cigarette and blew the smoke at the fireplace and watched it tangle with the smoke from the kindling and wind up the chimney. These Moreaus were six or seven mysteries in my mind. David, apparently taking his family for granted, had merely told me their names, their ages, and whether they were blonde or brunette. He'd been away from them a good many years, at school and later at his teaching job at Western Reserve where I'd met him during a summer session which my school board had requested I attend. I knew, of course, when I married him a few weeks after Pearl Harbor, that he had a reserve commission in the Navy, but I'd still been grateful for the eight months of our marriage. When he was ordered to active duty in the Atlantic, it had seemed wise to both of us that I come to San Francisco to his family. I had no family—not even an aunt or an uncle—and David had said that while he didn't want me to live with his sisters—I planned to take an apartment—he'd feel more comfortable if he knew that there was someone looking after me. Of course, I didn't bother to tell him that I was quite capable of looking after myself and had done so since I was graduated from college. I kept still because David seemed to enjoy himself in the role of protective husband and myself in the role of clinging little wife. I rather enjoyed it myself. Being a cherished wife is an infinitely more satisfying career than that of school teaching, and I am perfectly willing to take on anyone who says it isn't.

I called a mental roll of the Moreau family. Pauline, 51; Sophie, 40; Doctor Anne, 35; Elise, 34; David, 32; Marthe, 25; Rose, 20. Pierre Moreau had had three wives to produce this family so overweighted with daughters. The first wife had borne him Pauline. The second one had done considerably better, having produced all of them except the last two who were accounted for by the third and final wife. A year after the death of wife number three, Pierre had died, too, and Pauline, the eldest daughter, had continued in her role of mother-sister.

The little coal fire threw off a surprising amount of heat, and when semblances of circulation had been restored to my hands and feet, I threw my cigarette into the fire and stood up. I'd change my clothes and get ready for this formidable mess of sisters-in-law.

I opened my fortnighter where it lay on the floor and knelt down to take out my shoes which were snuggled into their cotton-knitted bags. I decided on my good dark red wool dress and black suede pumps, full of the knowledge that the dress was excruciatingly becoming as well as very costly.

Suddenly I turned around on my knees. My door had been knocked on, opened and shut quietly, all in the well-known twinkling of an eye. A woman stood a foot or two inside my room.

"Hello," I said getting up off the floor. "Which one are you? Sophie?"

The woman quickly put a finger up to her lips. Her pink-and-white-powder-and-rouge face bore lines of anxiety.

"Shush," she said in a whisper. "Yes, I'm Sophie. Pauline's out, and she said we weren't to talk to you until she did, but I couldn't wait. How do you do?" She held out her hand, so I shook it.

Her hair, obviously bleached, was elaborately arranged in dozens of rather messy-looking little curls. Her fussy-looking powder-blue dress, trimmed with row upon row of tiny lace ruffles, might have been good on a young girl of twenty who didn't care about looking smart. It was decidedly awful on Sophie, but I was so starved for human companionship that I would have welcomed a cannibal woman clad in a G-string.

I smiled and wished I'd had time to get properly dressed. Sophie undoubtedly spent a lot of time "getting herself up," as my mother used to put it.

"Well," I whispered, "I'm glad you came in anyway. I've been thinking maybe I wasn't welcome."

"Oh, no, not at all. It's just that Pauline wanted to talk to you first. But please don't tell her you've met me. Just pretend we're strangers when we meet downstairs. Pauline's gone to bring Elise home." Her eyes darted furtively around the room, and she walked to the front window and looked out into the street. "When we see them drive up, I'll go back to my room."

Well, well, I thought, the good Pauline obviously scares the pants off of Sophie. I wondered just what to expect when it came time for me to transact my business with Pauline.

"Elise is the sister that's next to David, isn't she?" I asked. Sophie bobbed her head yes and continued to look apprehensively out of the window. "Where's Pauline bringing her home from?"

"The sanitarium. How's David?" she whispered.

"Fine—when I saw him a month ago in New York. I haven't heard from him since." It was no fun at all to talk about David. It brought my constant, nagging worrying too close to the top of my mind for comfort. "Has Elise been ill?"

"Yes." Sophie swung around from the window and gave me a good long look. "Your clothes are very plain, aren't they? Do you think men really like such simple things?"

I smiled feebly and shrugged my shoulders. I should hope to God they do, I thought. "David does," I muttered. "He likes my clothes very much."

"Well," she said, smiling and showing teeth that were just faintly buck, "of course you were a school teacher, so I suppose that accounts for it, but my friend tells me he likes women to be more feminine."

I swallowed. Had I married into a lunatic asylum? It certainly sounded like it.

Sophie nearly jumped out of her skin as a car door banged in the street. "It's them," she hissed and streaked out of the room.

I looked out of the window and watched two women come down the path until they disappeared up the porch stairs. Both of the women wore black, and I couldn't tell which was which looking down on them, so I turned back to the business at hand—getting dressed in my un-feminine clothes. Hoping desperately to see something of the family, I went down the hall to the bathroom. The old house might well have been deserted except for the faint murmur of voices that drifted up the stairs.

I had just finished checking on my stocking seams when there was a peremptory knock on my door, and that old charmer, Nanette, stuck her head in to say that Miss Moreau was home and would I come downstairs.

I followed the maid downstairs manfully resisting all impulses to kick her extensive posterior and was ushered into that flower of Victorian art, the front parlor. The room was full of mahogany sofas, women, pale blue striped wallpaper, heavy gold framed mirrors, women, Aubusson carpet, horsehair upholstery, huge gold cornices and lambrequins around the windows, and women.

I stood in the door feeling dizzy and foolish. I was almost faint with joy when one woman emerged from the group and came toward me with a warm, heartening smile on her face. I thought then and still do that she had the most expressive eyes I'd ever seen in my life.

She did not, thank the Lord, kiss me, but she put her arm across my shoulder and turned me to the rest of the audience. "Isn't she lovely?" she said in a warm, rich voice that matched her eyes. "Aren't we lucky that David sent us such a nice sister?"

I swallowed. It didn't seem possible that this really genuine graciousness could follow in the wake of my strange, inhuman reception. Pauline was *human*, tremendously so.

My fine new friend was tall and thin without being bony. Her short, curly black hair had beautiful white streaks growing from either temple, and the molding of her facial bones would have been the delight of any sculptor. Her hands were very long and thin and capable-looking, the nails strong and faintly pink without any polish at all.

The silly little tears that clouded my eyes so suddenly made it hard for me to think and act even reasonably intelligent.

"We're so glad you're here, Hilda. First I'll try to straighten us out for you, and then at lunch you must tell us all about David." Her right hand tightened on my shoulder as she gestured expansively with her left. "That very pretty child is Rose." She was pretty, too, with her soft, shiny brown hair and infant's skin and wide-set blue eyes, but her young mouth seemed slightly tight and nervous. "The next is Marthe who's very amusing and makes us all laugh." Marthe grinned, and I knew from her expression that she'd probably be good company. "Sophie." I bowed and smiled and felt like an idiot, but I did not give away Sophie's guilty secret. "Elise, the family beauty." And she was, almost ethereally so. In fact, she looked very much like Gertrude Lawrence. And such a figure!

There were two females left. One was a nice, plain, sensible-looking, rather stocky woman. The other was a very small, wiry woman with old ivory skin and black, black eyes and equally black hair worn in bangs. Her thin magenta mouth was twisted in an expression of sardonic amusement. Decidedly not my cup of tea. When I'm feeling all sentimental and full of love, I want others to join in and not look at me as though I were something escaped from a home for feeble-minded children.

"Janet Holmes is that nice, dependable person. She shares an apartment with me next door." The long thin left hand swooped through the air.

The little black and ivory woman stood up. "For a woman of science, so-called, you are shockingly sentimental, Anne. Shall we go in to lunch?" She walked past us and stood in the door. "I am Pauline Moreau—if you are interested."

My friend was Anne, the one who'd starved and slaved to put herself through medical school. The nasty little black piece was Pauline, and she was the one I'd have to deal with.

My hand as I put it up to my forehead felt like a fish straight from cold storage.

CHAPTER 2

My first meal in the Moreau house could best be described as a labored performance. Pauline, with her exit line, had reduced young Rose and middle-aged Sophie to a state of cowardly dejection. Elise's lovely curving eyebrows curved even higher so that her face bore, throughout the meal, an expression of vast amusement.

My friend Anne and her friend Janet Holmes worked valiantly to manufacture conversation, and I fed them all the idiotic questions that Middle Western tourists can be depended on to eject.

They told me that San Francisco was always foggy and cold in summer but that it was supposed to warm up in September, that the clanking noise I heard outside was made by the cable in Hyde Street and that it was perfectly safe to ride on the cable cars.

I told them that David was in good health as far as I knew and that his ship was somewhere in the Atlantic. We dealt momentarily with the subject of nationwide gas rationing, the Solomon Islands, the war in Russia, and the selfishness of the Farm Bloc.

Halfway through the roast chicken, we got back to the subject of San Francisco.

"Do you think I'll have much trouble finding a small apartment?" I asked.

Pauline spoke directly to me for the first time. "You intend to take an apartment?" Her thin mouth pulled back tightly as she spoke.

"Yes," I said, "of course. I thought David told you in his letter."

"Apartments are pretty scarce, Hilda," Anne said kindly. "You'll probably have difficulty, but there's plenty of room here for you in the meantime."

I smiled back at her. "I met a nice woman on the train, a Mrs. Graham. She said she'd help me." I turned to Pauline. "She wants to call on me. I hope that's all right with you."

Pauline's Gallic blood was demonstrated by an elaborate shoulder shrug. "A great many people in San Francisco would like to call at this house. They're very curious."

I had not the slightest desire to placate my husband's half-sister, nor did I feel like explaining myself, but I did. "As a matter of fact, Mrs. Graham had never heard of the Moreaus or their old house. I think she was merely being gracious."

The sullen maid took away the plates and brought the dessert. The cooking in the Moreau house was excellent, and, I believed, probably French. At least it tasted like things I'd read about, and it was entirely different from the plain, Middle Western food I was used to. Sauces and strange flavors and fruit and cheese for dessert.

We finished our lunch and went back to the parlor for coffee which Pauline poured from a large, interesting-looking pewter pot. The cups were pretty little pink Haviland things that looked as though they'd been bought when the house was built.

Sophie gulped half her coffee and then set the cup down on the tray with an alarming clatter.

"Good Lord, Sophie, must you break the cup?" Pauline's voice was an unpleasant snap. Sophie's face was an ugly purple under her heavy makeup.

"I'm sorry, Pauline, but I'm in a hurry. I was just getting ready to excuse myself. I must keep my engagement."

Anne's dark eyes were watchful. She put her cup down on the marble mantel slowly, deliberately.

"What engagement?" Pauline asked.

Sophie took a deep breath, swallowed, and licked her lips. "Mr. Brown is taking me to dine with his sister and brother-in-law. That's why I didn't eat much lunch."

"Really, Sophie, you're being very rude to Hilda. Go telephone Brown at once and tell him you can't come. I'm amazed at you."

I emitted a strange noise that was intended to be a light laugh. "Of course you mustn't break your engagement on my account, Sophie. I'll be here for ages. Please go ahead."

Pauline switched around in her chair. "Really, Hilda...."

I wanted to hit her. Her habit of drawling out the word "really" as though we were all idiots who couldn't understand the obvious was maddening.

Anne stepped forward. "Yes, Pauline, let Sophie keep her engagement. Of course Hilda won't mind."

Pauline's black eyes narrowed just faintly. "Sophie will telephone her friend, won't you, Sophie?"

The poor bleached blonde was torn into little pieces. And I distinctly saw tears in her eyes. She gulped and spoke quickly. "But, Pauline, Sunday afternoon is the only time he has. He has to open the store again at eight o'clock, and we've been planning this for weeks."

"Really, Sophie, we needn't argue, need we? Go upstairs and telephone—at once."

Sophie rushed out of the room, her face blotchy and red with disappointment and anger. I was simply incredulous.

Pauline turned to Anne. "Don't look at me as though I were a brute, Anne. You know as well as I do that it's horrible for Sophie to be making a fool of herself with the corner druggist at her age."

Anne's eyes were dark and cloudy. "Brown's a perfectly decent sort, Pauline, and he seems very fond of Sophie. Besides, there was no reason to embarrass her in front of the rest of us. However . . ." She, too, went in for Gallic shrugs.

I walked over to Pauline to get my cup filled. I wanted desperately to think of something to say, something preferably inane that would break the tension, but Pauline seemed to be enjoying it.

She smiled in her habitually unpleasant fashion. "You see, Hilda, my sisters do not always choose their men friends wisely. Even our little Rose made a foolish mistake, didn't you?"

Rose's baby face seemed to crumple before my eyes. If someone had suddenly hit her very hard, she could not have looked more pathetic. I decided right at that moment that I would get out of the Moreau house the next day, that I'd go to a hotel if I couldn't find an apartment. My own parents lived in pleasant harmony all their lives, and my marriage to David had been peaceful and filled with good nature. The atmosphere that Pauline created was hideous and deliberate as well.

Elise stood up. "Perhaps you'd like to see something of San Francisco this afternoon, Hilda. Marthe still has a little rubber left on her tires. She could take you and Rose and me for a ride."

Marthe's wide mouth broke into a grin. "I'd be delighted to play Greyhound Tour, Hilda. My car is a '33 Chevvie, but it runs—with coaxing."

"Elise is not going out, Marthe. She has to rest." Pauline stood up. "Come on, Elise. You know what Breton said."

Elise stood up, yawned, and stretched her long graceful arms back so that her dress was pulled taut across her shapely breasts.

"Gawd, yes, I know what Breton said." Her rich, husky voice was dull and flat. I wondered what was wrong with her health as she certainly didn't look like an invalid. Her skin was clear and unlined, the whites of her eyes almost blue, and her chestnut hair shining and vital. It was a pleasure to watch her move her beautiful, well-coordinated body.

She sauntered out of the room in Pauline's wake, and Marthe and Rose and I busied ourselves with lighting cigarettes. Rose's face seemed slightly less disintegrated, but her soft, babyish mouth looked hurt.

Janet Holmes, who had told me at lunch that she was a lawyer, stood up. "Well, I have work to do, so I must go along, but when you girls come back from your ride, come over to the apartment for a cocktail."

Pauline came back into the room at the tail end of Janet's speech. "So you're plying my sisters with liquor, Janet?" Her voice was light, but not convincing. "Really . . ."

"Yes, Pauline, I am, and I'll ply you, too, if you'd like to come."

"No, thanks. I must stay with Elise."

Anne ground out her cigarette. "Incidentally, Pauline, I've arranged for Doctor Henry to see Elise on Wednesday."

Pauline swung around on her heels. "You're not taking Elise to that woman, Anne, and that's final. I asked Breton if he knew anything about your Doctor Henry. He doesn't think much of her—or any of the rest of the *psycho* people."

In a gesture of infinite patience, Anne put her hand up to her head and smoothed back her hair. "Pauline, of course Breton doesn't think anything of Doctor Henry. He doesn't want Elise to get well. He wants her to go right on in the same old way so that he can keep her in his sanitarium at fifty dollars a week six months out of the year."

Pauline's mouth was clamped in a firm tight line as Anne spoke. "Really, *Doctor* Moreau, aren't you being rather unethical? Breton knows what's wrong with Elise, and so do I. She needs to be watched, constantly, and that's all she does need."

The fine roast chicken had turned to a dull, leaden lump just below my ribs. What was this, anyway? Anne's face had flushed to a delicate apricot.

"But, Pauline, she's no better off than she was five years ago. Breton doesn't help her, and I'm convinced that she can be cured. She has brains and . . ."

Pauline interrupted her with a gesture. "You're wasting your breath, Anne. You know what happened when I let you take her case. She was worse than ever."

"Yes, I know that." Anne's voice was harsh with emotion. "I couldn't do a damned thing for her, because I'm her sister, and I love her, but Doctor Henry could help her. You've no right on earth to refuse."

Pauline sighed loudly. "Anne, Doctor Breton is in charge of Elise's case. Do you want the County Medical Society to hear about your efforts behind his back? I think not."

I looked for a good big hole to jump into, and there was none. Anne turned up one of her long, thin hands in a gesture of complete defeat and walked out of the room.

CHAPTER 3

I lay in my huge, top-heavy bed shivering with cold—the sheets were distinctly damp from the foggy air—and with exhaustion. I had never in all my life spent such an afternoon and evening, and with each convulsive shiver, I strengthened my determination to get out of the Moreaus' house very early in the morning.

The fear and bitterness and hatred that Pauline seemed to engender by the very fact of her existence had, I thought, culminated in a stormy scene with Sophie which took place outside my door right after I had come upstairs to bed, but I was wrong. There was more to come. I shivered with fear for myself, too, finally, as I had by that time a very good idea of what to expect in my own business dealings with David's sister.

In the afternoon the two younger girls had taken me for a ride around the city in Marthe's chugging old car. I'd gasped at the views, the Bay with its superb bridges, the skyscrapers shooting up from the tops of steep hills, the horticultural achievements of the Golden Gate Park, built, Marthe had told me, on bare sand dunes, the grey streets crammed with uniformed men, and the ominous arrows pointing to air raid shelters.

The cocktail interlude in Anne's and Janet's apartment next door had been the only bright spot in the day aside from my sightseeing tour. The apartment was furnished with sleek but simple modern furniture, and in delightful contrast to the house next door, its four spacious rooms were full of light, gay colors and an atmosphere of really gracious hospitality. But Pauline had managed to cast her black shadow over our little gathering by telephoning after we had been with Janet and Anne a bare five minutes to demand that we drink up quickly and come home for supper. I, thoughtfully and deliberately, took my time finishing my drink until I saw that Rose and Marthe were becoming restive.

Neither Elise nor Sophie appeared to eat cold chicken and salad with Pauline and Marthe and Rose and me. We sat at the table in stony silence after my attempts to comment on our drive had met with cynical eyebrow liftings from Pauline.

When we had finished Pauline finally deigned to speak.

"Rose," she said, "you wash the dishes tonight. Nanette's knees are bothering her. I told her to go to bed."

"I'll help," I said, infinitely preferring a few minutes in the kitchen with Rose to spending my time with Pauline in the parlor.

"That's not at all necessary," Pauline said quietly. "Our guests don't do the housework, you know."

"Well," Marthe said, "Nanette didn't wash my clothes, so I have to if I'm going to go clean to work. I'll keep Rose company."

"There's no reason why Nanette should do your things, Marthe. You may work in the daytime—because you choose to—but you've plenty of time in the evenings."

"I'd give my right eye to know what we pay that old hag a hundred dollars a month for, I would," Marthe said. "She does less work every day of her life. Rose told me she even makes her fix the vegetables now."

Pauline's thin mouth looked cruel. "Nanette has served me faithfully since the day I was born. You're strong and young. She's not."

Marthe may have been strong and young, but she had told me something about her job as secretary to the personnel manager of one of the war-booming shipyards, and I had a pretty good idea that she was tired at night, all of which was none of my business. Of course, Pauline bitterly disapproved of her sisters working, and David alone had made it possible for Marthe to get her business training and finally a good job.

As Pauline's words ended, I distinctly heard the thud of the front door closing. I looked at Pauline to see if she too, had heard.

"Maybe that's Anne," I said hopefully. "The front door closed, I mean."

Pauline walked ahead of me to the hall and quickly opened the door. Standing behind her, I was just in time to see Sophie scramble nervously onto a Hyde Street cable car and disappear up the hill. Poor Sophie. When she got home, there would be hell to pay, but apparently she had thought her escape was worth the future indignities at Pauline's hands.

Pauline closed the front door and walked slowly down the hall and went into a room which I hadn't seen before. It extended across the left-hand side of the house and had a small alcove jutting out toward the street at the far end. The entire room was paneled in beautiful dark brown wood with fine burling in the center of each panel. There was an elaborately carved mantel and shelves on either side. The Victorian side chairs were upholstered in needlepoint of a pale beige background with pastel flowers. A graceful, carved mahogany sofa was covered in old rose and gold damask, and another large rocking chair was covered in pale green and beige brocade. A coal fire burned gayly in a large grate. It was a beautiful, mellow room.

"How lovely," I said. "I've never seen wood like this. What is it?"

"Redwood burl," Pauline said with a faint overtone of enthusiasm. "My father built this room on for my mother as a present when I was born. Unfortunately she didn't live long to enjoy it."

The woman ran one of her little ivory hands possessively along the carving at the back of the sofa. She pulled down the skirt of her extremely smart, well-made black dress, and I thought, privately, that Pauline had paid a pretty penny for said dress. The other sisters had decent enough clothes, but theirs looked as though they'd been chosen with good taste in the Budget Shop of a large department store. Pauline's was something turned out by a fine couturier, or I was crazy.

An old marble-topped table cut down to coffee-table height stood in front of the sofa. I helped myself to a cigarette from the Vaseline glass jar on the table and lit it. Then I walked over and stood in front of the fireplace warming the backs of my legs.

Pauline had picked up part of the Sunday paper and seemed to be enjoying it. I stood looking down at her thoughtfully for some minutes. I'd only known her for six or seven hours, but I understood for the first time a great many things about my husband that had puzzled and confused me for months.

He never spoke of his sisters or his old home except in the most superficial way. He'd told me a little of the history of the Moreau family and their old house—that Paul Moreau, a ship chandler, had built it in 1852 of a cargo of white oak timber sent around the Horn and abandoned by the crew which had gone to the gold fields, that his father Pierre Moreau had been born in the house in 1856, and that his sister, Pauline, had outlasted his father's three wives and had looked after all the children.

I knew at last why David had seemed, during the eight months that we spent together after our marriage, almost dazed with happiness. I knew why he had told me that I must not live with his sisters but merely near them. I knew that all his life until he got his teaching job in the Middle West he had lived in a cold, unfriendly atmosphere created by this bitter, domineering woman. I knew, too, that all the days of my life must be dedicated to proving to David that families could be happy and harmonious together, that life could be lived in love and not in hate, and that my first step in helping David must be to force Pauline to give David his share of his father's estate.

"Pauline," I said quietly and with a good deal of false courage, "I think you know that David wants me to discuss his affairs with you. This seems as good a time as any."

She looked up quickly from her paper.

"And why, Hilda, should you discuss David's affairs?"

I smiled patiently and was very angry that my mouth trembled involuntarily. "Because David isn't here to do it. That's why."

She looked up at me, her eyes ink black with resentment. I was glad that I was tall and standing up and that she was short and sitting down. It gave me a small advantage which my twenty-six years compared to her fifty-one didn't.

"I shall discuss David's affairs with *him*—after the war. Not before."

"Very well," I said. "That leaves me no choice. I shall have to use my power of attorney and a lawyer."

She stood up abruptly. "You wouldn't dare.... Really."

"I'm afraid I would," I said. "I had hoped, naturally, that we could settle this thing amicably, but if you force me to do so, I'll have to take other steps."

I knew very well that Pauline was killing me at that moment in her mind. I watched her nails dig into the palms of her little claw-like hands.

And then the telephone rang.

She looked at me sharply and then quickly walked out of the room and into the blue parlor where I had noticed a telephone on the big desk just inside the door. I breathed deeply. I had probably won the first round, but I knew, of course, that I could not spend the night in the Moreau house. I'd have to go upstairs in a few minutes and pack my things and go to a hotel. There was too much animosity between Pauline and me to stay under the same roof together.

Apparently my subconscious mind had been listening to Pauline's telephone conversation. I could feel myself frowning in puzzlement.

She had said to someone, "No, she isn't here.... No, she is out of town and can't be reached.... I don't know when she'll be back. Not for some months anyway."

Now what? As far as I knew, Sophie was the only "she" out of the house, and she certainly had not gone out of town. If my guess was correct, she had been en route to her pharmaceutical Mr. Brown when she hopped on the cable car, so Pauline's lie couldn't have been invented for Sophie's suitor. Well, just one more bit of Miss Moreau's sweetness and light, I supposed.

Pauline came back into the room. She stood looking at me for a long, silent minute. "I don't care to discuss this matter further tonight. Tomorrow I'll show you the books. I've been very patient with David. Apparently I must be patient with you." Then she turned and went upstairs.

All right, I thought, I'd give it another whirl tomorrow which, grimly enough, meant that I'd have to stay all night. In the meantime, I'd join the girls in the kitchen and enjoy a little decent human companionship.

Rose was busy rubbing hand lotion into her rather battered young hands which looked as though vegetable paring and strong soap were not strangers to them.

Marthe was singing a slightly bawdy song in a lusty voice as she bent over a small washtub in a laundry room opening off the kitchen.

"Pauline's gone upstairs," I said. "Now that the work's done I thought

I'd join you."

The kitchen was a large, gloomy inconvenient room, and I was very glad indeed that I didn't have to prepare three meals a day in it. Maybe there was some excuse for Nanette's knees, after all.

Rose smiled cordially out of tired, hurt, young eyes.

"Fine," Marthe shouted, "I'm nearly finished anyway. Make some coffee, Rosie. I'll contribute the remains of my wine cellar—a quarter of a cup of rum."

We sat around the large center table drinking our coffee and talking desultorily. The two girls had never ventured so much as a single word concerning their older sister, but I decided to take the bull by the horns. Of course, there was the danger that I might run into fierce, unreasoning loyalty, but I'd take a chance.

"I think Pauline pulled a fast one a few minutes ago," I said, lighting a cigarette.

"That's not news," Marthe said. Only the gleam of humor in her eyes kept her face from having an expression of complete bitterness. "What now?"

"She told somebody that 'she'—whoever that meant—was out of town for some months and couldn't be reached. On the telephone, I mean. I don't think it was Sophie's beau, because Sophie whipped up the hill on the cable car a little while ago. Is Mr. Brown's drugstore in that direction?"

"Yes, it is." Marthe nodded thoughtfully and turned to Rose, and I nearly fell off my chair.

Rose's face was flat, greenish white, her eyes round, her mouth loose, uncontrolled.

She reached quickly across the table for her sister's arm and gripped it with violence. "Marthe. Marthe. Do you think . . . ?"

"Could be, baby," she said, standing up. "We'll find out. Come on."

"But *how?*" Rose said, struggling awkwardly out of her chair.

"We'll go over to Anne's. I know how. I work for a living."

Not even Pauline's finest terroristic technique could have stopped Marthe at that moment. I followed the two girls out of the back door, down the stairs and out to the street. We ran quickly up to the apartment house entrance, and Marthe leaned heavily on the doorbell. The buzzer released the front door, and we dashed down the hall to Anne's apartment at the back of the building.

"The telephone. Quick," Marthe shouted and pushed Anne out of the way.

"All right. All right," Anne said. "What's up?"

"More skullduggery from Pauline, I think," Marthe said as she sat down at Anne's blonde wood desk and dialed 211.

Rose slumped weakly into a chair, and Anne and I watched and listened to Marthe.

"Operator," she said, "did you have a call for Miss Rose Moreau at Tuxedo 1707 a short time ago? . . . Well, I'm not sure where it would come from. Wait a minute." She looked up at Rose. "What's the name of that place, baby? Raleigh, North Carolina?" Rose nodded hard. "Raleigh, North Carolina, Operator. All right, I'll wait." She put her hand over the mouth piece. "It'll take a few minutes for her to find out."

I told Anne rather hesitantly what had happened. I didn't particularly like myself in the role of trouble-stirrer-upper, but she received the information with merely a quiet "Damn Pauline! If she did . . ."

Marthe's face suddenly lit up. "Yes, yes," she said quickly, "that's it. Lieutenant William Everett."

Rose, completely overcome, put her head down onto her arms and sobbed very loudly.

"Now, baby," Anne said, patting her little sister's shoulder, "pull yourself together. You can't talk to him if you're bawling your eyes out."

"But, Operator, I'll wait," Marthe said. "I know the report said she'd left town, but she came back unexpectedly. She's *here* right now. You find him."

Marthe let out a long whistle and leaned back. Then we waited and waited and waited.

"Pauline said he didn't want me," Rose wailed, "and when he called up, she lied to him."

Anne shushed her and continued to pat her on the back, but from the expression on the faces of both Marthe and Anne, I felt that Pauline was going to get hers in time.

"Well, call the camp," Marthe said emphatically. "What if it was a public telephone? You can find him at the camp if you try. This is very important."

Poor little Rose. Her man friend whom she'd chosen so unwisely—according to Pauline.

"All right," Marthe said into the receiver, "I'll wait right here. You get Lieutenant Everett, and I'll get Miss Moreau, and I won't hang up."

Rose had stopped her first vigorous sobbing, but tears still poured from her eyes. "We . . . we were engaged, Hilda," she said jerkily, "and he had to go back to that camp for training and when he got his commission, we were going to get married, but Pauline didn't like him and all of a sudden, he didn't write anymore, and I wrote and wrote to him. Pauline said I didn't have any dignity...." Her voice ended in a wail.

"Good. Good!" Marthe shouted. "Put him on.... Here, baby, they've got him."

Rose weaved unsteadily over to the desk and sat down. "Oh, Bill . . .

Bill, what's happened?"

Anne and Marthe and I left the living room and walked quickly down the hall to Anne's cheerful bed-sitting room, so that Rose could display proper emotion unobserved.

"Listen, Anne," Marthe said between tightly clenched teeth, "if Pauline did what I think she did, this is the end."

Anne's dark eyes were black with sorrow. "I know, I know, Marthe. It's ghastly."

I felt superfluous and decidedly in the way, but there seemed no point in my walking back through the living room and out of the house so I tried to occupy myself by looking at a long row of framed photographs on the wall over a chest of drawers. The photographs were the Moreau children, starting with Pauline and ending with Rose. They seemed to have been taken when each child was about sixteen, with the exception of Pauline's photograph which showed her in perhaps her late thirties.

But there was something wrong—too many photographs. There was Pauline, then Sophie still naturally blonde. The third photograph wasn't anybody I'd met.

Marthe's eyes looked blankly into space, her face set and bleak with anger.

I pointed to the third photograph. "Who's this, Anne? I haven't met her."

"That's Berthe, Hilda. She's dead."

"Oh," I said, "then there were seven girls and one boy. What a family!"

Anne smiled sadly. "You were an only child, weren't you?"

I nodded. "When did Berthe die? David never even mentioned her."

"A long time ago, Hilda. Fifteen years at least."

The door opened and Rose stood before us, her right hand clutching her throat nervously.

"I think I'll kill Pauline," she said flatly. "I think I'll kill her."

Anne moved forward quickly and folded the young girl in her arms. "Rose, Rose, you mustn't, darling. Nothing that Pauline could do to you would be worth all this hate."

It took a long time to get the facts straight. At first Rose couldn't talk, and when she could, she sobbed so that her words were incoherent.

For weeks past, it seemed, Bill Everett had telephoned, written and wired to Rose. Nothing had come through to her. Pauline had done her work efficiently, and the damage couldn't be repaired. Rose couldn't go back to North Carolina and marry her young man and have even a brief war marriage. It was too late. Bill Everett was on his way to foreign service, and he didn't know where he'd go, or when or if he'd get back.

CHAPTER 4

Rose lay in Anne's bed, staring up at the ceiling, her eyes wide and blank. She looked like a human being with no sensitivity to anything except deep, inner pain, and she refused to acknowledge the existence of the sedative which Anne tried to give her.

Marthe and I went into the living room, and Anne soon joined us.

We sat in silence for a few minutes after we had lit cigarettes. That female Hitler, I kept thinking. That female Hitler who loves destroying lives and torturing and dominating, and *why*?

Marthe's voice jerked me out of my reverie. "There's only one thing to do, Anne. I'll take Rose and get out of the house. I've been hanging onto my salary pretty carefully. I can look after her. We can't stay there after this."

Anne looked thoughtfully at Marthe. "You can't take her unless Pauline lets you. At least not for another seven or eight months. She's still under age, and Pauline's her guardian."

"Oh, God, I'd forgotten that, and that fiendish bitch will keep her, and I'll have to stay with her." No girl of twenty-five should be so filled with frustration and bitterness, I thought, listening to Marthe.

We talked for a long time, pointlessly and fruitlessly. There was no way to undo Pauline's actions, no way to help little Rose out of her agony.

"Why does Pauline do such things? Why is she so determined to maim people's lives—her own sisters' lives?" I asked.

Anne's eyelids dropped wearily. "She isn't, Hilda. You must understand that. She's perfectly sincere in everything she does. She's been responsible for all of us since we were babies, and she was a young girl. When she prevents a marriage or refuses a certain kind of treatment for Elise, she really believes that her course is the wise one."

I could feel my mouth twisting in puzzlement. "But can't she ever, under any circumstances, listen to anyone else? Is her opinion the only possible right one? I really can't conceive of such . . . well, self-righteousness."

Anne shrugged. "She's had people to back her opinions up. Doctors, lawyers, bankers, family friends."

"But what was wrong with Rose's fiancé? Why didn't she like him?"

"Bill Everett was a poor young man with a very uncertain future. That's perfectly true, you see." Anne sighed. "Pauline also has an exaggerated idea of this family's importance. We had a lot of money at one time, and our social position was faintly important. Pauline simply doesn't like the idea of coming down in the world. She's proud. She has her standards, even if we've come to feel that they're out of date."

Marthe looked up from her gloomy contemplation of the floor. "When Anne wanted to study medicine, Pauline almost died. It was unladylike, disgusting. As for my working in an office and especially a shipyard..."

I rubbed my forehead. It simply didn't seem possible that the same standards of conduct which had been in style when the Moreau house was built were still being applied to the lives of women in September of 1942. I smiled to myself. Pauline must have been horrified when David married a career woman and a school teacher at that.

"Well," I said, "we might as well go to bed. I'm tired, to put it mildly."

Anne gave me a long, searching look. "Yes, you've had a bad day. Do you feel all right?" I nodded. "You stay in bed tomorrow morning," she continued. "That train trip and this excitement aren't particularly good for you, you know."

I could feel my face reddening, so I turned quickly and walked out after brief good nights.

My room felt like a crypt, and the water with which I filled my hot water bag was anything but hot. But I went back to my room determined to brave my vast clammy bed. I had just managed to push up a window which promptly banged shut again until I discovered the little metal rods in its frame. Then I stood looking into the street. Long, sad wisps of fog trailed through the eucalyptus tree in front of the house. Far off on the bay, a mournful horn blew. Da-dum, Da-dum, it said over and over again. Its notes were the two that start the *Love Death* in *Tristan*, achingly, infinitely nostalgic.

The world was a sad and dreary place for me just then until I forced myself to remember that I was not alone, that all through the night all over the earth, millions of women were missing their husbands and sons and lovers.

Between the notes of the foghorn, I heard the click of high heels on the sidewalk and then the creak of the gate. Beneath the shadows cast by the streetlight, I saw Sophie's nervous, rather flabby body stumbling down the crooked stone path. Then I heard the quiet closing of the front door. I prayed hard that Pauline was safely asleep—she hadn't appeared when Marthe and I came back from Anne's apartment—and then I listened to the gentle creakings of the old house disturbed from its first light sleep.

I sighed heavily. Somewhere a door opened, and Pauline's voice rang through the house.

"Sophie!"

Right outside my door, I heard Sophie mumble, then Pauline's footsteps came down the hall to join her within good listening distance.

"You went out, didn't you?"

I loathed the cowardice in Sophie's answering voice. "Yes, yes, I did."

"I told you not to, didn't I?"

Sophie's voice clouded over with tears. "Pauline, Pauline! Don't! You're hurting me."

I was almost, but not quite sick. Physical violence, too. I stood there paralyzed, unable to move, torturing myself to listen to the revolting performance in the hall. I felt, too, that Pauline must surely know that I could hear and was glad.

"I told you not to go, didn't I?"

"Yes. Yes, you did, but I don't care. You can't hurt me anymore, Pauline. Harold Brown and I are going to get married. I'm going to leave here, Pauline."

Then Pauline laughed, bitterly and without joy.

"Oh, no, you're not, Sophie. I'm not going to let you make a fool of yourself and all the Moreaus. You're not going to marry any little corner druggist, and some day you'll be glad that I didn't let you!"

"Please. Please, Pauline. *Please*."

"*No!*"

There was a long pause after the flat, firm finality of Pauline's last word.

When Sophie finally spoke, I heard despair, real, complete, infinite despair.

"Berthe, you mean?"

"Yes."

Sophie screamed. "You wouldn't! You *wouldn't!*"

A door banged jarringly. Then footsteps receded down the hall in the direction of Pauline's room at the back of the house.

I whistled. Then I ran quickly across the room and got into my big bed. I pulled the covers tight around me and buried my head in the pillow. What a way to live. What a way to live. Quarrelling, hating, violence on all sides. I am not a very religious person, but I reverently, at that moment, thanked my Maker that I had never lived in such chaos and did not have to in the future.

I could get my little apartment and make some friends and see only the nice members of the Moreau family. I was lucky, lucky, *lucky*.

If I could, in the meantime, just get warm and go to sleep, I'd feel a whole lot luckier.

The tepid warmth of the hot water bottle finally thawed my feet and the sheets, in my immediate vicinity, had about dried out. I was beginning to relax by quarter-inches, and the possibility of sleep was becoming less remote.

I was suddenly jerked back from near oblivion by a series of dull, heavy bangs. I sat up and listened. The pounding seemed, strangely enough, to be coming from my clothes closet.

Struggling into my robe I opened the closet door and listened. Thud! Thud! Thud! Not on the wall nearest me, but somewhere on the other side of the closet.

"Pauline! Please get Anne for me. Please do."

Elise's voice, anguished and muffled, came through the closet wall.

Of course, Elise's room was between mine and Pauline's on the right-hand side of the house, the east side.

Bang! Bang! Bang!

But if she had the strength to pound that hard, why in God's name didn't she go out to the telephone?

"Pauline! I can't sleep. I can't sleep. I'm nearly insane. Please get Anne. She'll give me something."

Her voice was full of suffering. It was horrible to listen to. Ordinarily her voice was rich and low. Now it had become shrill. She was almost, but not quite screaming.

The pounding and the pleading went on for minutes while I stood in the closet door. When I'd had enough I went out to the hall and down to Elise's door. I knocked, but she didn't hear me above the clamor of her pounding and yelling.

I tried to open the door. Then I saw it. A bolt. A strong, brass bolt on the *outside*.

I was still gazing in horrified fascination at the bolt when Pauline's door opened and she came into the hall. "What seems to be the trouble, Hilda?"

I swallowed. "You're asking *me?* My Lord," I shouted above Elise's continuing cries, "what's the matter with Elise?"

Marthe, tousled and bedraggled from interrupted sleep, came out of her room. "We'd better get Anne, Pauline. I'll call her." She started for the telephone.

"You'll do nothing of the sort, Marthe. Elise has been pampered quite long enough. She's going to be on quite a different regime from now on. She'll stop her racket as soon as she learns that it's useless."

Pauline drew her handsome padded brocade robe more tightly around her and started back to her room. "You two had better get back to bed. It's cold."

Through the bolted door came the sound of pitiful sobs. Then I distinctly heard the sound of one of the heavy old windows being pushed up.

"Anne! Anne! Help me!"

Elise was screaming out the east side of the house in the direction of

Anne's apartment, and unless Anne had suddenly gone stone deaf, she'd hear.

Pauline's mouth, minus its magenta lipstick, pursed into a hard, straight line. She pushed me away from the door, unbolted it and went into the room. Marthe and I stood in the hall, watching carefully.

Elise's beautiful face had turned plain. It was lined and blotchy and unlovely. Her hair was stringy as she ran her long, thin fingers through it. She walked jerkily across the room, supporting herself on the backs of chairs and the edges of tables. Her body jerked convulsively under her thin nightgown.

"I've got to sleep, Pauline. I've got to sleep. I can't stand this."

Her room was furnished with the same heavy Victorian furniture as mine. Fascinated, I watched a light curtain blow back from the window. There were bars on that window. Big, black, iron bars.

I clutched at Marthe's arm for support, but she turned quickly at the sound of the front door banging shut.

Anne ran up the stairs, carrying a small black bag in her left hand. We stepped aside quickly, and she went into Elise's room and shoved Pauline out of the way.

She held Elise's left wrist in her own right hand and looked closely at the large, efficient strap watch on her own left arm. Then she smiled with deep sympathy.

"It's all right, Elise. You'll be all right, darling."

Pauline stepped forward. "Are you going to give her something?"

Anne nodded hard. "Of course I am, Pauline." She held back the covers on Elise's big bed. "Come on, now. Get in. I'll fix you up in no time."

"Anne, you are *not* going to give Elise any more dope. I won't have it."

Anne turned on Pauline, her eyes glinting purposefully. "She's been given a sedative every single night of her life at Breton's Sanitarium. She's going to have one right now if I have to knock you down to give it to her."

Pauline shrugged her shoulders and walked out of the room. "See to the door, Marthe, when Anne's through doping our sister, will you?"

I wondered idly if Anne would mind very much doping me. I needed it, heaven knows.

I knew, too, that I'd have to know what was wrong with Elise or I'd never go to sleep.

"Marthe," I said quietly, "what's the matter with her? Elise, I mean."

Marthe shook her head slowly from side to side. "She's an alcoholic, which is a polite way of saying she's a drunk." Her shoulders moved in a shrug under her rather dingy blue flannel robe. "And God knows I don't blame her."

CHAPTER 5

The sound of iron clanking alongside my bed wakened me Monday morning. I turned over to see the maid, Nanette, building a fire in the little grate in the alcove. I watched her light it, hold a sheet of black metal over the opening for a few minutes, and then stand up. The fire was burning well.

"What time is it?" I asked.

The old woman swung around, and to my undying amazement smiled grimly. "Ten-thirty, ma'am. Miss Moreau says you're to stay in bed. I'll bring your breakfast in just a few minutes."

Would wonders never cease?

After the horror-filled night, I was being treated like a welcome guest, but not without reason, I felt sure. Maybe Pauline just wanted to keep me out of the way while she thought up some new method for torturing her sisters. In any case, I was glad to stay in bed. I was still tired, and I dreaded the effort of looking for an apartment and the coming battle with Pauline.

The old house was quiet, almost ominously so. There were no homely sounds of family activity such as ringing telephones or whining vacuums or slamming doors. And I noticed that Elise's door was still bolted as I passed it on my way to and from the bathroom.

Nanette brought me a good breakfast on a nicely appointed tray and a newspaper which I read as I ate. It was Labor Day, so there were extensive editorials about labor's part in the war effort. The President was talking about stabilizing the cost of living. Nothing striking had happened to change the picture in Russia, China, or the Pacific. I turned back to read a human-interest story, a Navy casualty list for Northern California men, and something about Mr. Kaiser and his ships. Finally I turned to the Want Ad section. There were only eight apartments listed, and my heart sank. Five of them were large—with three bathrooms and a doorman—which would, of course, be far too expensive for me. The other three were two-room jobs at $25 and $27.50 a month, and they would undoubtedly prove, at that price, to be dingy affairs on the wrong side of the tracks.

Well, it would have to be a hotel for the time being. I'd certainly had all of the Moreau brand of hospitality that I wanted. Poor Sophie. Poor Rose, and poor Elise. No escape for them, but there was for me, and I'd take it as soon as possible.

There was a knock at my door, and Pauline came in. Her face was mat cream with brown circles around her eyes. Her magenta mouth was tight with strain, but her hair was carefully combed, and her black tailored suit impeccable.

She smiled—not warmly, of course—but it was a smile. "How do you feel this morning?"

"Much better, thanks," I said. "Anne gave me a bromide before she left last night. It helped me to sleep."

"That's good," she said. She took a deep breath, and then spilled out her words. "I'm sorry you've had such an unfortunate introduction to David's family. You must think very badly of all of us, but everything seemed to come to a head yesterday. I was nearly crazy myself."

The about-face was interesting, but I didn't trust Pauline's attempt to be gracious.

"It's all right," I said. "I'm sorry I interfered—about Rose, I mean—and I think it's only fair to tell you that I'm leaving here as soon as I can find someplace to go."

She looked at me sharply. "Just as you like, Hilda, but when you're dressed, will you come into my room? I think we'd better have our talk."

"Yes," I said, "I will."

Pauline's big room at the back of the house was charming, with a wonderful view from a hexagonal bay window that jutted out at the left. It was furnished as a sitting room with a small mahogany sleigh bed along one wall. The walls were papered in a luscious pink striped paper, and the hangings and slip covers were a grey chintz with a white design interspersed with moss roses. It was much less shabby than the other rooms.

Pauline sat at a big writing table in the bay window.

"Come over here," she said. "I've got the books spread out where you can get a look at them." The table was covered with business-like ledgers filled with heavy yellow sheets and little green lines. The writing was small and black and neat, just like Pauline.

I looked out the window.

"That's quite a view, isn't it?" I said. The bay, grey under grey fog clouds, spread out before us. There was a pair of opera glasses on the window ledge.

"Yes," she said, "it is. We have the glasses there for the girls. They like to look at the ships. We often see very exciting things these days."

I sat down in a small mahogany armchair opposite Pauline, and then I slowly lit a cigarette. I'd let her do the talking to begin with.

She sat looking out the window for some minutes. Finally, she turned around and began to speak.

"Of course, Hilda, I must admit to begin with that I simply cannot understand David's action in sending you out here armed to the teeth with legal documents. Force isn't the kind of thing I'd expect David to use. Naturally, I think you must have influenced him to do this thing. You can understand that, can't you?"

I nodded. "Yes, but I didn't influence him. It was entirely his own idea. He felt that he needed his share of the trust and that he should have it. When you wouldn't do anything by mail, he said I'd have to take over."

"Did he show you the letters I wrote him?"

"No, he didn't. But I'll tell you this much, Pauline. He was very angry with you."

Her mouth tightened. "Very well, Hilda. I'll have to see if I can make you listen to reason. Do you know the terms of the trust?"

I nodded. David had explained the setup to me shortly after we were married. His father, Pierre Moreau, had left his estate in trust for his children with Pauline as sole trustee. She was to manage the trust, make investments, and spend all income according to her own discretion, until such time as the children should marry. Immediately after the first marriage in the family, the trust was to be dissolved, its assets sold, and the proceeds divided equally among the children.

"There are several reasons, Hilda, why I can't dissolve the trust at this time. I explained them very patiently to David, and I simply cannot understand why he persists in making trouble for me." She spoke of David as though he were only a naughty little boy stealing jam from the pantry.

"And what are your reasons?" I snapped.

"To begin with, if I have to sell the real estate and the securities at this time, we'll have to take a ruinous loss. In addition to that, I think it would be sheer madness to turn money over to the girls. They're absolutely incapable of looking after themselves. I've got to be able to keep this house and make a home for them."

"Even if they don't want to stay here?"

She stood up and went over to the window. Her straight little back expressed irritation far more loudly than words could have. Then she walked back, sat down and leaned across the desk.

"I know very well, Hilda, that you think I'm a complete brute, and I don't much care, but if you force me to dissolve the trust, you'll be doing a lot of damage. Sophie will marry that ridiculous druggist, and he'll put her money into his shop and lose it. Anne will give hers to some hospital. Elise will kill herself with liquor in six months. Marthe and Rose will blow theirs. There'll be nothing left."

"But, Pauline," I said, with exaggerated patience, "the money belongs to them, not to you. No matter what they do with it, it's *theirs*. You haven't any right on earth to withhold it. You treat them all as though they were half-witted children. They've never had a chance to show whether they were competent or not."

She sighed loudly, and I could see that she was trying very hard to keep rancor out of her voice. "Hilda, I know quite a bit more about this family than you do. Do you know that I've managed this house, and the money, and the girls since I was nineteen years old? My father was a dilettante who knew nothing of business. His father, fortunately, left good sound investments which have kept this large family going, but all my father cared about was having a lot of children and good food and what he called 'fun.' He never did a day's work in his life. He . . . he was a butterfly." She gestured impatiently. "No wonder his children have no sense. But I had sense. Plenty of it. I've done my duty—all my life. And I'm going right on doing it."

I ground out my cigarette. "It may have been your duty, but it's certainly made a lot of unhappiness, Pauline."

She snorted. "Happiness? How happy do you think these girls would be if they didn't have a roof over their heads? How happy do you think Rose would be if she'd married that young upstart and been left a widow with a baby on the way three months after their marriage?"

My face felt hot and uncomfortable. "I think, Pauline, that she'd be very happy, because she'd have had a few happy weeks or months to remember. And babies, even war babies, can bring a lot of happiness."

Her eyes narrowed. "So *that's* it."

"Yes," I said, "that's it. That's why David wants me to have the money."

She took a cigarette out of the box on her desk, lit it, and exhaled a long grey cloud of smoke. "I wondered why you didn't go back to teaching."

I kept still, miserable with embarrassment and with Pauline's disapproval and disinterest.

"Look here," she said, turning one of the ledgers around so that I could see. "Here's an appraisal of the trust made two weeks ago. The valuation on this place is probably too high, because the house is worth nothing, and nobody's buying land they can't build on." I looked intently at the figures as she pointed to them. "But the total assets at the present time come to $102,534.62. The inheritance taxes would take something from that, but before taxes, the amount for each of the seven heirs would be about $14,000." She snapped the book shut. "Not enough for anyone of us to do anything. You can't live on the income from $14,000, you know."

"I know that," I said, "but with David's insurance and a little money I have from my parents *and* the fourteen thousand, the future wouldn't look too bad for us if something did happen to David."

She looked thoughtfully at the end of her cigarette. "Why don't you do this, Hilda? Live here with us, and if something does happen to David, then we can take steps."

"No, Pauline," I said very distinctly. "I will not live here. Frankly, I don't like the atmosphere, and I'm afraid that the dissolution of the trust is out of my hands anyway. If you don't voluntarily petition the court for dissolution by the first of October, David has instructed a lawyer to do it."

All the pseudo-friendliness disappeared from her face. Her small pointed chin jutted with fury. "Why, you dirty little gold digger. Do you mean to sit there and tell me that my own brother would do a thing like that unless you put him up to it? Get out of this room. Get out!"

I got up. "Yes," I said, "and I'll get out of the house, too, just as soon as possible. And as soon as this business is settled, get out of the town, too, and go back to my friends in the East. David sent me out here, because he thought you'd be happy about the baby. So that I could at least have some *family* around, but we both made a horrible mistake." I'd started to cry, to my intense disgust, and I could scarcely see where I was going.

Halfway to the door, Pauline caught up with me and took hold of my arm. "Stop, stop," she said. "I'm sorry for what I said. I just don't see why you can't understand *my* position. You and David are being horribly unreasonable. I'll see what can be done about it."

"All right," I muttered, "but I'm still leaving."

I went downstairs and started calling hotels on the telephone. I must have called fifteen to get the same answer from everyone—no rooms available. Maybe tomorrow. Pauline came in while I was telephoning and told me which ones to call. "You don't want to get into something in the Tenderloin," she said.

I finally had to admit defeat. San Francisco was jammed full of service people, shipyard workers, and government employees, and the housing situation was hopeless. I'd have to stay right here in the Moreau house until one of the hotels had a vacancy and called me. I was *sick*.

When I went back up to my room, both Sophie and Elise were in it. They were making my bed.

"Good heavens," I said, "you needn't do that. I just wanted it to air."

Elise was once more a magnificent woman, and not the tragic, bedraggled figure of the night before. She had on a simple, blue wool dress that was intensely becoming. But Sophie's eyes were red-rimmed. Her whole body drooped under her fussy pink house dress, and her curls—all five dozen of them—had not been carefully combed.

"It's all right," Elise said, smiling. "You certainly had quite a time meeting the family yesterday, didn't you? I'm not too proud of my performance last night, but now that you know about my little weakness,

I can be frank. That damned Breton pumped me full of phenobarbital every night for five weeks, and I'm afraid I'm a dope addict now."

I laughed feebly, amazed that she could take her "little weakness" so calmly. "How's Rose?" I asked.

Sophie gestured toward the east side of the house. "Still over at Anne's."

"And still threatening to bump off our dear sister," Elise said. "And who could blame her?"

Pauline called to Sophie from downstairs, and Sophie skittered out of the room obediently.

"Get anywhere with Pauline?" Elise asked, her eyebrows high.

"Well, I don't really know," I said. "Actually, there isn't much she can do. After all, David's married, so she has to dissolve the trust under its terms."

Elise smiled wryly. "We were all pleased to death when David got married. We thought it would mean freedom for all of us, but we should have known better. And you can bet your last nickel that Pauline won't give up without a struggle even now."

"But there's nothing else she can do," I said, slumping into a chair.

"No? Well, she can have me committed, for one thing, and I don't imagine David would like that much. Blackmail—of a sort—is nothing new to Pauline."

I was never so shocked in my life. Pauline Moreau would threaten to lock up her sister in order to keep her brother from making what she considered "trouble" for her.

"She'd really do that?" I gasped.

"Why not?" Elise said blandly. "I'm what's called a habitual alcoholic. She can get me committed any time, and if David forces her to fork over his money, she'll just tell him that she can't very well turn me loose with several thousand dollars, that I'll have to be protected from myself. David, of course, wouldn't like that." She stretched her arms above her head and looked out the window. "I do believe the sun is actually going to come out. No, my girl, the only time Pauline will ever let go of that money is when she's dead."

Dead. Dead. Pauline dead. I shook my head to clear it of its morbid thoughts. And then I sighed.

"Elise," I said slowly, "you're unquestionably one of the best-looking women I've ever seen in my life. Why aren't you married? You must have had plenty of men around you."

She grinned. "What man in his right mind wants to marry a drunk?"

I gulped. "But why are you, as you put it, a drunk?"

She grinned again. "I wish I knew. Anne says it's because I've been dominated by Pauline and never allowed to grow up. When I first learned about alcohol, it was swell. It made me confident and gay and sure of myself. And, you know, one thing leads to another."

One thing leads to another. Yes, I could see that.

"But before you started drinking too much, you must have had a lot of men friends," I said.

She shoved a long thin hand through her hair. "Yes," she said, "but I was shy, and I never liked any of them very well. Little boys are such hideous bores, so I learned about the joys of the bottle. By the time I met a really un-boring, grownup man, my alcoholism was pretty well established." There was a cold blue shadow of remembered pain on her face. "He had sense enough to know that an alcoholic doesn't make much of a wife."

"Did Pauline tell him that?" I asked, with a flash of insight.

"Of course she did. It was her duty—so she said."

Everything Pauline did was justified by the word duty. No matter what aching unhappiness she caused, she would do her duty.

"Listen, Hilda," Elise said, leaning toward me, "you must be half sick at learning what kind of a family you've married into, but don't worry. I'm the only one that's really a mess. Even poor old Sophie'd be okay if she could get herself a husband. And we're not really candidates for the madhouse."

I laughed. "Of course not. I'm not worried. And I *know* David's sound."

"You're darned right he is, and of course, he was able to get out. Pauline couldn't very well refuse to educate the only man in the family."

I sat quietly thinking about David for a few minutes. Elise picked up the newspaper and started reading it. Outside, a pale sun shone, and a brisk wind rattled the leaves of the big tree. The house was quiet except for the sound of the newspaper moving in Elise's hands.

I turned to her to say something about the sunshine. The paper lay on the floor, and her face had turned blue white. She looked as though she'd fainted. I was terrified.

"Elise, what's the matter?"

She shook her head silently. Then she got slowly out of her chair and walked out of the room, looking weak and ill.

CHAPTER 6

Elise had come down to lunch looking white and shaky, and when Pauline asked her what was wrong, she had muttered noncommittally about a headache. She was obviously under strain of some sort and had at last pushed her plate away nervously and announced that she was going upstairs to rest.

She had been bolted into her room. Pauline had gone downtown on the cable car immediately after, Sophie had gone to her room, and I to mine. I had taken off my clothes and got into bed so that I could really rest, and after I had read for half an hour, my eyes got heavy, and I slept until after five.

By that time, Pauline was home, and when I had dressed, I found her in the wood-paneled room downstairs talking to Anne and Sophie. A few minutes later Marthe had come in, looking tired from her day's work.

She flopped into a chair, dumping her hat and bag on the floor. "Gad, Pauline, I'm dead. Is there a drink in this place? If not, I'll beg one from you, Anne."

Pauline's mouth tightened. "It's a big help to Elise to have you going around here reeking of liquor. In fact, I sometimes wonder...."

Marthe stood up. "Yes, I take an average of four or five drinks a month, so I'm a drunk. Nuts." She walked out of the room and went upstairs.

That was when Pauline had followed her upstairs and found that Elise was gone.

We heard her quick footsteps on the stairs, and she burst breathlessly into the sitting room, heading immediately for Sophie who reacted characteristically by cowering into her chair.

"Sophie!" Pauline snapped. "You let Elise out of her room. Where is she?"

"No, no," Sophie wailed. "I didn't. I didn't. I haven't seen her since lunch."

Then the hunt started. We tore that old house to pieces, from the cupola on the roof clear down to the huge, gloomy basement that clung to the hillside in back. We opened closets and wardrobes, we even looked behind large pieces of furniture. There was no sign of Elise anywhere.

Anne went over to her own apartment and came back to say that she wasn't there. And momentarily Pauline became whiter and tighter with rage. She finally turned to me.

"Hilda, someone let her out of that room. You're such a dear sympathetic little creature. Did you do it?"

I glared back. "I didn't," I snapped, "but if she'd asked me to, I would have."

We all stood in the middle of Elise's room, looking helplessly around us. She simply couldn't have got out of that room unless someone unbolted the hall door. There were no secret passages, and the bars on the windows were still blackly grim. "How about Nanette?" I asked at last.

"Nanette would never do such a thing. She knows all about Elise," Pauline said. "She's also fanatically loyal to me. My God!" She sat down on the edge of the bed and banged her little claws nervously on the footboard.

Marthe backed out of Elise's closet. "Her hat and coat are gone—the navy ones, I mean."

"Did she have any money?" Anne asked.

"Of course not," Pauline said, "unless she managed to *steal* some."

She went into her room and came back almost immediately. "She didn't get any from me. Really...."

I went into my room and looked in my bag which lay on top of the big bureau between the two east windows. I sighed hard. My coin purse was empty, and I'd had about twenty-five dollars in cash. My travelers' checks were still intact.

I called to Anne to come into my room and pointed to my bag. "There's about twenty-five dollars gone out of my purse," I said.

Anne shook her head sadly from side to side. "Poor Elise," she said.

Then I told her how Elise had behaved in my room in the morning. "Does she all of a sudden get an uncontrollable urge to go on a bender?" I asked.

"I don't know, Hilda. She might have. I talked to her this morning, and she seemed quite calm and even fairly cheerful. I told her I'd take her to Doctor Henry if I had to strangle Pauline to do it, and she said that was fine and that she really did want to get well. I don't see what could have happened to set her off." She shrugged elaborately. "Well, Pauline will find her, but I'm afraid she'll be in pretty bad shape. She's had three or four hours to get going and plenty of money to spend."

"But, Anne, how in God's name did she get out of that room? Somebody must have let her out."

Anne looked at me very sadly. "Sophie is a little sly, Hilda. She's had to be. She might have done it."

As Anne spoke, I saw the screwdriver in the chair where Elise had sat that morning. It was pretty well stuffed down behind the cushions, but the handle stuck out.

"Look," I said, "what's this doing here?"

I handed Anne the large, efficient-looking screwdriver. To my infinite amazement, Anne opened one of my windows and stepped onto the flat roof that extended six or eight feet out to the side. I followed her across the roof down to Elise's windows. She touched the heavy iron bars on the first window, but they were tight, undisturbed. Not so those on the second window. Three of them came away easily, their screws loose in the holes.

"She did this once a long time ago," Anne said slowly. "Did you go to sleep this afternoon?" I nodded yes. "Then she probably went out through your room when you were asleep. But I wonder when she unscrewed the bars."

We went back into my room and called to the family to tell them of our discovery. Sophie's eyes were round with amazement and excitement. "She was in here in Hilda's room when I came up from lunch. She must have just come in the window. It was open, and I shut it because it was cold."

"You see, Anne?" Pauline said. "She can't be trusted for one single minute. Here we spent a lot of money getting her sobered up, and the first chance she got, she broke out. Really...." She groaned. "Now I'll have to spend more money to find her." She flounced out of the room.

"Money to find her?" I said. "What does she mean?"

"She has a private detective who scouts around and finds Elise—when necessary." Marthe's mouth was set, grim.

Dinner was a gloomy, dismal performance, with Nanette obviously reluctant to serve people who had upset her Miss Moreau. She hovered over Pauline trying to anticipate her wishes and ignored the rest of us.

After dinner, Marthe went over to Anne's to bring Rose home as Rose had agreed to come if she didn't have to see Pauline.

Pauline shut herself into her sitting room upstairs, and I stayed downstairs with Sophie playing Russian bank. Anne had said that she'd go to a couple of Elise's favorite hangouts in the North Beach district and see if she could find her.

If the atmosphere of the Moreau house had been bad the day before, it was worse that night. Sophie and I had started on our second game when Anne came back to report no trace of Elise. She went upstairs to tell Pauline, and Sophie and I sat, dumbfounded, to listen to the tail end of a loud quarrel.

"You can't lock Elise up in a place like that," Anne shouted from the head of the stairs. "She'd *die*. I'll see you in hell, Pauline Moreau, before I'll allow it."

Then she stomped out of the house, banging the door behind her.

Sophie and I made an effort to go on with our game. I stopped her four times, and she stopped me twice on perfectly simple, obvious moves.

The next loud bellowing came from Marthe. "Pauline, you promised to leave Rose alone. You've done enough. If you come in here, I won't be responsible...." Another loud bang of a door.

I stood up jerkily. "Good Lord, Sophie. How do you stand it?"

She looked up at me, her face sagging and even a bit stupid. "All families quarrel, Hilda."

"Nonsense," I said, grabbing a cigarette, "not like this. I'll go mad if I don't get away from it. I'm as nervous as a witch. Why in the name of heaven don't you elope with your Mr. Brown? You're over age. Pauline couldn't stop you."

She licked her lips nervously. "Pauline won't let me get married," she said almost in a whisper.

I sighed irritably. "What are you? A woman or a half-witted child? Pauline won't *let* you!"

Sophie stretched her hand out to pick up her cards. I watched it fascinated. It was a long hand, wrinkled and lined, with nails that were far too long for good taste. The nails were painted from base to tip a nauseating shade of coral pink. The hand shook violently and dropped the cards.

"As long as Pauline lives, I'll be an *old maid*."

She put her head down on the card table and sobbed. And I felt inadequate and stupid and embarrassed.

When I went upstairs to go to bed, I stopped at Pauline's door to ask if she'd heard anything from the detective who was looking for Elise. The telephone had rung from time to time during the evening, and Pauline had been answering at the extension on her desk upstairs.

"No," she snapped. "She's being very cagey this time. She hasn't gone to any of her usual places."

The fury and impotence that surged through Pauline Moreau's little body showed very plainly in the lines of her face and the trembling of her hands.

I turned away to go to my room. The next time I saw her she was dying, still furious, still impotent.

CHAPTER 7

It was after three when I wakened, cold, depressed, achingly lonely. The *Tristan und Isolde* foghorn was wailing down on the bay. My hot water bag was almost offensively tepid. I turned away from it, and then hastily turned back to my former position. The sheets beyond were villainously cold and damp. I tried making myself smaller, huddling in a little mound, but that, too, was hopeless. I simply could not get warm, and to stay awake worrying about this madhouse from which I'd chosen a husband was simply unthinkable.

It must have taken me five minutes to nerve myself to get out of bed and go down the hall and fill up the hot water bag. My flannel robe was clammy, and my mules felt like frozen iron, but I tried to cheer myself by believing that possibly the water would be hot and that a cigarette in the middle of the night was always a comfort.

With a lighted cigarette dangling out of my mouth and almost blinding me, I picked up my hot water bag, opened my door and started down the hall. The light was still on in Pauline's room as I could see from the crack under the door.

Shivering, I knocked. I might as well find out if Elise had come back.

There was no answer to my knock. Pauline must have fallen asleep with her light on. I turned away. Then I turned back. I'd heard something, some sort of noise. I opened the door. The cigarette and the hot water bag fell to the floor unnoticed, and I was across the room in one leap.

Pauline, still dressed in her tailored suit, lay upon the floor in front of her big writing table. The light from a large table lamp beat down into her face, her eyes round, wild, beseeching. One leg was drawn up awkwardly under her, and she was trying desperately to pull herself up onto her left elbow.

"My God," I said, "what's the matter? What can I do?" I got behind her and held her in my arms. I realized that she was trying, desperately, to speak.

"What is it? *What is it?*"

Nothing came from between the magenta lips except a long whistling sound.

Her head fell back onto my arm. And I saw the bubbles. Little bright red foamy bubbles trickling over the magenta lips down onto her chin.

I shouted. "Marthe! Sophie! Marthe!"

Several long years passed while I sat there on the floor waiting for someone to come. And I learned something about terror, too. I was afraid to let go of my burden, and afraid to stay where I was. Pauline's weight on my arms seemed to be getting greater with each passing second.

"Marthe!" I screamed desperately.

"I'm coming. I'm coming. What the hell?"

Marthe's face was blank, sleepy, without understanding.

"What's the matter with her?" she said quietly.

I shook my head, violently. "I don't know. I don't know. Look at the blood on her chin. Get Anne. Please. Quickly."

Sophie and Rose came to stand in the door while Marthe telephoned to Anne. Their faces, too, were blank with amazement.

I was still afraid to move, so I sat until at long last Anne came with her little bag.

She walked purposefully over to Pauline and me. "You can get up, Hilda," she said, reaching for Pauline's wrist.

I pulled myself erect in spite of knees that sagged and buckled. We all stood in a little circle watching Anne. Pauline's eyes were still wide open, round, staring. Anne pressed one of the eyeballs. Nothing happened.

There was no sound in the room except someone's heavy breathing. I jumped slightly at a scraping sound from the window. A vine had blown across the pane.

Anne looked up at us, her face dead white, her huge dark eyes blazing. "She's dead," she said quietly.

A sort of communal gasp went up from Sophie and Rose and Marthe and myself. But we had no words.

Anne turned back to Pauline and with long gentle hands felt around under her clothes. She finally stood up. "Help me carry her to the bed, Marthe," she said. "I can't see anything here."

"Hadn't we better call the police, Anne?"

The words burst like an explosion in the midst of our waiting silence. Marthe spoke them.

Anne's sensitive mouth was twisted in amazement. For the first time, I noticed that she wore her street clothes. "Police? Why?"

Marthe gestured toward the large writing table in the bay window. "Under the table. Look."

We looked.

A butcher knife with a blade fully twelve inches long lay under the table. Its blade was wet.

"Good God!" The words jerked from between Anne's lips. She walked slowly toward the door, and then she turned back.

"Wait," she said. "Listen to me. Listen carefully."

We waited, listening. The room seemed to pulsate with fear and a kind of morbid excitement.

The silence was shattered by the sound of the front door being banged back. There was a dull thump of something falling.

Quickly, eagerly, we crowded to the head of the stairs. I think we were all glad, somehow, to get out of that room that held Pauline and the terrible knife.

Down in the hall, half over the threshold, Elise lay on the floor face down. Anne ran quickly to her and turned her over. "Quick, Marthe," she shouted, "help me."

Silently, we watched them carry Elise upstairs and into her room. She was out cold, insensible, and reeking of liquor.

"Bring me my bag, Rose, quickly." Anne's voice was urgent. "Marthe, help me get her clothes off. Hilda, open the windows."

In an astonishingly short space of time, Elise was in bed, undressed, and had been given a hypodermic, and we were all back in the hall outside Elise's carefully bolted door.

"Now listen to me, all of you," Anne said in a voice that was quiet but decisive, "Elise will sleep for seven or eight hours, and we must, under no circumstances, let the police get at her, do you understand?" Four night-clothed females nodded in chorus. "You know as well as I do," she continued, "that there's no grief in this house over Pauline's death. We've all wished her dead a thousand times, and I'm half glad it's come." I was shocked, somehow, but I could understand the logic of her speech. "The only thing I regret is the way she died. It'll make more trouble for every single one of us. That's why I've fixed Elise so she can't talk." She pounded one long hand into the palm of the other. "That's why not one of you is to answer one single police question unless Janet Holmes is present. Do you understand? We're in for a lot of hell. We can make it less if we keep our mouths shut."

The busybody, law-abiding school teacher in me woke up. "You mean you'll condone *murder*, Anne?"

She turned swiftly to face me. "We don't know if it's murder, or who did it, Hilda. We'll keep our mouths shut and let the police do the investigating. I'm not going to see my sisters pilloried until we know more about this."

We all jerked around at a sound from the bottom of the stairs.

"Shall I call the police, *Doctor* Moreau?"

Nanette. Pauline's loyal old friend stood in the hall below. My heart leaped in anguish. The sinister, black old witch had heard every word Anne had said.

CHAPTER 8

"Now, Mrs. Moreau, as I understand it, you went down the hall to fill your hot water bag and you saw the light on in Miss Moreau's room. Is that right?"

"Yes," I said, for the ninety-first time, "that's right."

The policeman's name was Lieutenant Cassidy, and I was number one on his questioning list. We sat opposite each other at the round, marble-topped table in the blue front parlor. The policeman was very calm, his voice quiet, without emotion. His eyes were dark blue and very deep set below heavy, wiry black eyebrows. They were very tired, unbelieving eyes, I was sure, and I never talked to him at any time without a deep-seated feeling of nervousness and a compulsion to talk too much in order to convince him.

"Then you knocked at the door, and you heard a noise?"

I nodded.

"What kind of a noise?"

I shut my eyes and tried hard to reproduce the sound in my mind. Although we'd all been given a chance to dress after the police came, and I wore a suit with a Brooks sweater, I was still cold. I felt damp clear inside and very, very tired.

"It was a kind of scraping noise, I think. From what I know now, I think it was her foot scraping across the floor as she pulled it up under her."

Cassidy nodded. I looked quickly across the room at Janet Holmes who sat, stolid and serene, at least outwardly. I wondered if she had any idea how often the ice had been thin beneath me as I talked to the policeman. I had no way of knowing, of course, whether or not Nanette had talked to him, and I had said nothing of the strange scene in the hall when Marthe went back into Pauline's room while Nanette was calling the police.

I was almost afraid to think about Marthe for fear the unbelieving homicide detective might somehow manage to read my mind.

"What did you think was wrong with Miss Moreau when you saw her there on the floor?"

I started. "I've told you. I had no idea on earth. I didn't see the knife and there wasn't any blood until it came from her mouth." I was even colder. "I thought she was ill—heart or something."

"So you shouted for help, and one of the other sisters called Doctor Anne Moreau from next door, right?"

"Right."

"And—" he consulted a note on a piece of paper, "Miss Marthe Moreau saw the knife." He pronounced it "Marth," and I wanted to correct him, tell him it was "Mart."

"Now tell me again who was in the house when this happened."

I put my icy hands up to my face and was surprised to find that my face was hot. "As far as I know, Marthe, Sophie, Rose, the maid, and I were the only ones in the house when I found Pauline. Then, of course, Doctor Anne came."

The blue eyes were disconcertingly direct. "Why didn't you search the house, Mrs. Moreau?"

"I don't know," I said. "I really don't. We were all so shocked that we weren't very bright, I guess."

"Did you think of suicide?"

I shut my eyes and lied. "Yes, I did, but I didn't say anything, of course." Pauline was the last woman on earth to commit suicide, but I'd let the man think what he liked.

"And the maid wasn't there when you found the body."

"No," I said, "we were all in the upstairs hall talking. Then she called up to us, but she seemed to know what had happened. She must have been in the lower hall for some time listening to what we were saying."

He stood up and walked over to the fireplace and stretched out his hands to the blaze that came from the coal grate. I was very glad to learn that he was human enough to feel the early morning cold. Then he came back to the table. "How did you happen to wake up, Mrs. Moreau? I mean, did a noise waken you?"

"I don't know. I don't think so. I think it was just being cold. You see, I've just come from a hot Middle Western summer. I feel the dampness terribly. I don't like a lot of blankets, and I knew I'd never get back to sleep unless I got my feet warm. That's why I decided to fill the hot water bag."

I was babbling again.

"Marthe, Sophie, Rose," he said, looking at his scribbled paper. "Which one is the drunk?"

"Elise," I said snappily. "She came back after we found Pauline."

"How'd she get in?"

"With her key," I said. "She had it in her hand."

I was churning inside. I'd managed to avoid mention of Elise up until this time, but apparently Mr. Cassidy had seen her, dead to the world. While the rest of us had waited for the police, Anne had warned us not to say anything about Elise, but as long as Cassidy knew about her, there was no point in even trying to lie.

"Mrs. Moreau, *look at me.*"

I looked very hard, trying valiantly to keep my eyes from wavering.

"The knife came from the kitchen of this house. Every door and window downstairs was tightly locked. Unless Miss Moreau killed herself, somebody in the house did it. Of course, it's always possible that she let someone she knew from outside into the house, and they did it, but I don't think so. The doctor says she was probably stabbed after two o'clock in the morning. I don't think she'd let in an outsider, make it possible for him to get the knife, and then give up without a struggle. Do you?"

My eyes had long since wavered. "I don't know," I murmured. "I don't know."

He snorted in quiet irritation. "Oh, come now, Mrs. Moreau. You've been in this house for two days. You know these people. Surely you must have some idea about why Pauline Moreau was killed."

I shook my head. "No. No."

I looked across the room at Janet Holmes' stocky figure. Her face was flat, impassive. She said nothing. Apparently my answers, so far at least, were satisfactory and not incriminating.

Cassidy stood up. "All right," he said, "you may go. Don't leave the house, please, and I'll have to ask for your fingerprints."

Janet stood up and put out her cigarette. Her short, compact body was full of strength, her short hair neat and unfussy. She exuded competence. "Why the fingerprints, Lieutenant?" she said quietly.

"There're prints on the knife, Miss Holmes. Only a couple, and they're not very clear, but we'll have to have prints from everyone in this house."

Janet turned to me. "You don't have to do this if you don't want to, Hilda."

"It's all right," I said. "I'm not afraid. I never handled that knife in my life." But I was afraid, terribly so, and not for myself. I was afraid for some one of the Moreau sisters who had finally rebelled in such frightful fashion against Pauline's tyranny.

Then, as I rolled my fingers carefully, according to instructions, on an ink pad and finally on a heavy white card, I felt better. Marthe had gone back into the room where Pauline had died. She had defied us to follow her, and she had closed the door. I was willing to bet a whole lot that Marthe had wiped off the handle of that knife. Of course, if Cassidy were to be believed, she had missed a couple of fingerprints, but they weren't very good, and perhaps would not be good enough to incriminate their owner.

I was a little shocked at my anxiety to keep anyone in the Moreau house from paying for killing Pauline, but something had happened to my law-abiding soul. I'd seen too much of Pauline's cruelty toward her sisters. I had come to feel that her killing was not murder, but merely the assassination of a tyrant. The world would make a saint of anyone who assassinated the Axis tyrants. I felt that something of that sort should be done for Pauline's killer.

Later, of course, I changed my mind when I saw the killer's efforts to push the blame for the crime onto innocent shoulders, but on that first morning after Pauline's death, my principal feeling was to try to protect these Moreau sisters who had already had far too much suffering at their half-sister's hands.

When the fingerprinting was finished, I started to leave the front parlor. I heard Cassidy give orders for the maid to be brought in next. Janet and I exchanged long, slow looks. I walked out.

At the end of the front hall, there was a small dressing room with lavatory. I headed for it, and when a man in the hall asked me where I was going, I said, bluntly and defiantly, that I was going to the bathroom. "Do you mind?" I asked.

The poor man blushed and turned back toward the front door. The first part of my plan for eavesdropping was successful.

In the dressing room I clanked the plumbing unnecessarily loudly. While the water was still roaring in the pipes, I opened the door a crack. The policeman still had his back to me.

I slipped quickly through the door and across the hall and into the back parlor which was shut off from the room in front with big double sliding doors. I tiptoed quietly across the room, shivering with cold and apprehension, and stood with my ear glued to the door. I had to know what Nanette told the police. She, I was certain, would probably undo all our efforts to protect the family, and I wanted desperately to know just what her story was.

I was right. She was hard at work making trouble for us.

"*Of cou*rse one of them did it," she rasped. "They all hated her. They were in and out of that room all night quarreling and fighting and making trouble for Miss Moreau. I heard them before I went to bed and even after I heard shouting."

"What time did you go to bed, Miss La Touche?" Cassidy's quiet voice came through the door very clearly. Miss La Touche. What a name. She sounded like something from burlesque.

"Midnight I put my light out. I went downstairs right after dinner."

"You could hear clear down there at the bottom of the house two stories below?"

"I could."

She was lying, of course. The windows in Pauline's room had been shut tight, and with the foghorns blasting on the bay, Nanette could not possibly have heard quarrelling which hadn't been loud enough to wake me.

"Did you recognize the voices that were quarrelling?" There was a long pause.

"I heard Marthe and Sophie and Anne. Rose, too."

The woman's English was usually perfectly correct, but for the first time I heard a strong touch of French accent in her voice. Probably emotion and excitement caused it.

"Which was the last voice you heard? Whose, I mean?"

There was another long pause. I wanted terribly to sit down as my knees were watery beneath me, but I didn't dare drag over a chair, and I *couldn't* leave the door.

"I don't remember."

I don't remember. That was what she said. She didn't dare to say anything else, I suppose.

"Try and think."

Silence. I eased myself down onto the cold parquet floor. I couldn't have stood up another minute.

"Why did they hate her?"

Loud snort. "Because she tried to make them do right—all her life. She worked always to take care of them. They were all ungrateful and troublesome."

"But what specific things do you mean?"

Another snort. "That idiot Sophie wanted to marry the druggist. Madness. The little one Rose wanted to marry a poor little soldier. Elise—always drunk. Anne insisted on being a doctor. Such a thing for a member of the Moreau family. And then that new one, Hilda, she wants to make Miss Moreau give her money. She says she will make a suit in the law courts. Imagine!" The accent was really coming to the surface. "They are bad—all of them. I have been in this house for fifty-two years, before Pauline was born. When her mother dies, I take care of her. When she is seven years old, her father Pierre Moreau marries again. Children, children, children. Five with the second wife. Two more with the third, and such wives. Not at all serious. But *Pauline* is serious. Always she runs the house and looks after the children. When the father dies eighteen years ago, she looks after the whole thing. Trouble. Trouble always."

Cassidy was certainly getting the works, but so far nothing definitely incriminating for anyone. Just a few motives.

"But you still can't tell me who was quarrelling with Miss Moreau at two o'clock this morning?"

Pause. "No! But perhaps later I can think. But, I will tell you this much. Somebody came in the kitchen. I heard her. I think she came to get the knife, yes?"

"What time?"

"One-thirty. Two. I am not sure. But I heard footsteps in the kitchen."
"But you stayed in your room?"
"Yes—until I hear the door banging and more shouting. Then I get up and dress and—" dramatic pause "—I hear them in the hall talking. All of them. Anne, that Hilda, Rose, Sophie, Marthe. They are planning to lie to the police. I hear that Anne say she is glad Pauline is dead, but no one must tell the police anything. Then that Hilda says something about murder. And I know that one of them has killed her and they will all lie." Her voice ended in a sob and she continued to cry for a good long while.

"Lieutenant Cassidy, I think that before you swallow this whole, you'd better talk to some of the others." Janet Holmes was speaking, and I was very glad. She sounded so calm and sensible that Cassidy must surely attach significance to what she said. "You see, Nanette disliked everyone in the house except Pauline. You could hardly call her testimony unbiased."

"Bah!" Nanette shouted through her tears. "That one. The friend of Anne. No better than the rest!"

The telephone rang then, and I heard Cassidy snap into it.

"Miss Holmes," he said at last, "do you think that Pauline Moreau was the type of person to kill herself?"

"I have no idea. She might have if something troubled her sufficiently, but she was, well, secretive. I couldn't say."

"*Jamais!* Never!" Nanette snapped.

I prayed then—hard. Sincerely, too. Please, God, make it suicide so that we'll all be free. So that these poor creatures can be happy and live like decent human beings for the first time in their lives. *Please.*

"Why, Lieutenant?"

"There's something very strange about this," he said. "Her prints are on the knife, only hers. But the knife went in at such a strange angle . . . I wonder."

"Where? Where was the wound?" Janet's voice was urgent.

"On the left side. It penetrated the lung, liver and spleen. She died of internal hemorrhage. The lung was collapsed, completely." His voice was puzzled. "Was she right or left-handed?"

"Right. Right-handed always. I know," Nanette said.

"Well, then, if she inflicted that wound on herself, she did it with her left hand. But I can't understand why."

I could. From what I knew of Pauline, she could have done it. If the prospect of losing her power was too horrible to face, and if she decided that death was preferable, what better gesture than to kill herself in such a manner as to make it look like murder, to inflict the ultimate suffering on her sisters?

Or had Marthe gone into that room, wiped off the knife, and put her dead sister's hand on it to make the prints?

    I'd heard enough. And I was afraid, dreadfully so. The house had always been sinister and unhappy. But now it was worse. All that sadism and unhappiness had boiled up to the top. Ghastly, unhealthy, infinitely tragic.

CHAPTER 9

The day dragged on with maddening slowness. Outside, the city was blanketed with a fog so heavy that I could not see the trees across the street. I felt as though we were shut off in time and space from the rest of the world.

All of us were alone in our rooms forbidden to see each other or to communicate in any way. Some time after noon Nanette, chaperoned by a policeman, brought me a tray. The omelet was cold and the tea tepid, and in any case, I felt no need for food.

There were policemen in front of the house, and a few curious neighbors walked slowly past. Down on the bay the foghorns still moaned, and the cable cars banged and rattled up and down the hill.

Inside the house there were footsteps and masculine voices and the occasional slam of doors.

Sad. Sad. Sad. And mysterious and lonely. I wondered if, outside our little circle of fog, there were friends who would hear of Pauline's death with sorrow. I wondered if the other sisters had friends who would come offering help in time of trouble.

Back and forth. Back and forth. From chair to bed to window. Poor David and his tragedy-laden family. It would probably be a long time before he knew what happened, but I didn't want him to learn first from a newspaper. I tried to write a letter, and after a long time, I gave up. There was nothing I could tell him except that his sister was dead and that no one knew just how—suicide or murder.

In the middle of the afternoon I stuck my head in the hall and asked permission of the policeman doing guard duty to take a bath. He nodded yes, and I went down to the bathroom and soaked for a long time in good, hot comforting water. As I lay there, I heard a long-continued murmur of voices coming from Pauline's sitting room.

When I had finished bathing and was decently covered by my warm flannel robe, I went to the door of Pauline's room. Cassidy was sitting at her desk looking through her papers. Other men were examining other parts of the room.

"Have you learned anything more?" I asked. "It's pretty nerve-racking to sit all alone and wonder what's happening."

Cassidy stood up. "Come in, Mrs. Moreau. I was going to send for you in a few minutes anyway."

I sat down at Pauline's desk opposite Cassidy, and I was agonizingly uncomfortable. My chair stood on the spot where I had found Pauline dying twelve hours before. I shuddered obviously.

"You mind coming in here?" Cassidy asked.

"No," I said, "it's all right. I'm nervous, naturally, but I'll have to learn to control myself."

He nodded. "Mrs. Moreau, Miss Holmes explained the financial setup to me—all about this trust that Pauline Moreau managed—and I've been going over these books. They seem to be in order, but we'll have an accountant look at them, of course. What I'd like to know is what you intended doing to get your share and how Miss Moreau felt about it."

"She felt very angry," I said. "In fact, she was furious. She wanted to continue to control the money, and when I told her that my husband was going to go to court, she didn't believe me."

"I see. Then you had a pretty disagreeable interview with her?"

"Yes, I did, but then toward the end, she seemed to feel a little better about it. She said for me to stay here for a while and maybe we could work something out without lawsuits and such."

He turned in his chair and looked out into the wall of fog beyond the window. "This trust is the damnedest setup I ever saw in my life. Old Moreau certainly must have had a lot of faith in his daughter to give her this much power with no strings tied."

"I think he must have been crazy as a loon," I said. "I told my husband months ago that I thought it was not only foolish but dangerous to let one person control the lives of an entire family. You see, my husband told me how his sister, Anne, had to work her way through medical school and borrow money, because Pauline refused to let her have any of the trust income for her expenses."

Cassidy said "uh-huh," and then he turned his cynical blue eyes on me full blast. "In fact, Miss Moreau's death benefits everybody in this family, doesn't it?"

"Benefits? I hardly think so. You can't call a mysterious death a benefit when it piles up a lot of suspicion and suffering, can you?" I was shaking with anger. "Anyway, do you think she was murdered, or did she kill herself?"

He waited for a maddening five seconds. "I think she was murdered, Mrs. Moreau. I think she got those prints on the knife when she pulled it out of her side."

I swallowed. His explanation was logical, if unwelcome. He tossed a sheet of paper across the desk to me. "Read that. It's dated yesterday. I don't think Miss Moreau had any intention of letting you people get your hands on a nickel of that money."

Slowly, reluctantly, I picked up the letter and read it.

It was headed "Sunday night."

"Dear David—
"As you persist in making things very difficult for me, I shall have to put an end to this nonsense, once and for all. I have explained to you very patiently my reasons for refusing to dissolve the trust at this time. Your effrontery in sending that young chit whom you saw fit to marry armed with legal documents is simply the last straw. If you allow your suit to come to court, I shall have Elise committed to a state institution. I don't think even you would do that for money. What is more, your wife—"

With hands that trembled maddeningly, I put down the letter. I couldn't talk. There was nothing to say. Pauline had said it all.

"I found this under the blotter, Mrs. Moreau. I think she put it there when somebody came in, and she never had a chance to finish it. Her murderer didn't know she was writing the letter, or I'm quite sure I never would have found it."

I was jerked out of my shock when one of the other men walked over to the desk. "There aren't any keys in this room, Boss. There just aren't."

Keys. What did they want with keys?

"All right," Cassidy said, "you've done the downstairs. You'll have to try the bedrooms."

"Why keys?" I asked.

"We're looking for safe deposit keys. She's undoubtedly got a box someplace. We want to see it."

I shifted in my chair. Then I stood up. I didn't want to talk to that man anymore. I wanted to lock myself in my room and stay there until he decided who had murdered Pauline. Then I wanted to go home to Cleveland and never see the Moreau house or the city of San Francisco again.

There was a sudden commotion in the lower hall.

"You take me to the policeman at once," a decisive female voice said. "Persecuting these poor girls. I never heard of such cruelty—as though they haven't had enough."

A very well-dressed, plump, middle-aged woman loomed up in the upper hall. Her round pink and white face topped with grey curls was pursed in anger, but she looked *wholesome*—and nothing else in the Moreau house was.

She marched down the hall and into Pauline's room.

"Are you this Cassidy?" she said. "Your man told me you wanted to see me, and I heard on the radio that Pauline's dead, thank God, and about time. I do hope you're treating the girls decently. God knows they've had enough trouble at that woman's hands."

I didn't know whether to shriek with laughter or to put a muzzle on the woman. She plumped herself down in the chair which I had just vacated, dumped her sable scarf and bag on the floor, and pulled off her gloves. Her fat pink and white hands were decorated with magnificent diamonds and sapphires. Then she swung around in her chair, took a look at me, and got up, with a nice warm smile creasing her fat cheeks.

"My dear child," she said, advancing upon me, "you must be Hilda. What a *ghastly* thing for you to run into. Are you all right? Are the others all right? Are these policemen being kind to you?" I gasped. "I'm Gladys Oxney," she continued. "I've known these people since before they were born. I was an intimate friend of Pierre and Adele Moreau. You *poor* dears."

She enfolded me in a well-padded, perfumed embrace, and I was very close to tears. Then she dragged me over to the couch and pulled me down beside her and continued to pat me on the knee. She also continued to talk. Poor Cassidy never had a chance from the second she got into the room. She took over.

"My husband's Judge Oxney, and he's coming over here as soon as he can leave his chambers, so you'd better behave yourself, young man. Will you please hand me my bag? I think I need a cigarette. Thank you. Now you want to know about those damned notes, don't you? Well, it's really very simple. Just another case of Pauline's lying and treachery." She paused just long enough to hold her lighter to my cigarette and hers. "You see, young man, Anne's as proud as Lucifer. She wouldn't let me *give* her the money for medical school and traveling to those places where she interned. She insisted on signing *notes* for it. Then one day Pauline came and paid them all off, and naturally I gave her the notes. Then after Anne came home, instead of paying *me* out of her miserable little salary, she had to pay Pauline. I don't know how she made her do it, but she did, and I never *could* get the notes back after I'd endorsed them to Pauline or some such fool thing. My husband was *furious,* but Pauline pretended to have a change of heart about Anne being a doctor, so there you are." She stopped five seconds to draw breath, then she went on. "Anne's been paying and paying and *paying* for years, and she's *never* been able to get money enough together to set herself up in her own office. She's assistant to some heart man, you know, who just pays her a wretched little *pittance*. The judge and I have been *begging* her to let us lend her enough money to open her own office. She's a marvelous doctor anyway, but with all the men gone to war, she'd have a really *decent* chance. But, no, she's too proud. She had to pay Pauline first."

She smiled at Cassidy and patted me.

"I see, Mrs. Oxney. Well, thank you very much. I guess that's all I need to know. I'm awfully sorry to make you come over here." Cassidy was actually red in the face. I'll bet he was sorry to learn that he'd summoned a judge's wife to his presence.

"I would have come anyway," Mrs. Oxney said. "Now, tell me all about this. How did Pauline die? It said 'mysteriously' on the radio. And where are all the others?"

Cassidy plunged in with both feet. It was the only way. If you gave Mrs. Oxney two seconds, you'd never get a chance to talk.

"We have reason to believe that Miss Moreau was murdered, Mrs. Oxney."

"*Murdered!*" she shrieked. "Good Lord. Where? How? Who did it? I never heard of such a thing. Imagine, a member of the Moreau family getting herself murdered. How horrible."

Cassidy leapt in again. "She was stabbed with a knife from the kitchen some time after two o'clock this morning. In this room. We don't know who did it—yet."

Mrs. O. clutched my leg until it hurt. It took the announcement of a murder to silence her effectively.

"Good God!" she said softly. "Well, she asked for it, Lord knows." She turned her plump face to me, her blue eyes round, amazed. She swallowed. "Robbery, or something? Burglars, I mean." There was a strong false note in her voice.

Cassidy shook his head. "No, ma'am. No robbery. It was done by some member of the household or by someone known to Miss Moreau whom she let in from outside. There was no sign of illegal entry and no struggle. It was someone she knew."

Mrs. Oxney gulped again and clutched me. Then she stood up. "I can't believe it. I simply *can't*. Where are the others?"

Cassidy looked her right in the eye. "I'm very sorry, Mrs. Oxney, but I can't let you see the other sisters just yet. I've got to ask some more questions and finish my investigation in this room. Your husband will know that I'm only doing my duty. It has to be this way."

She walked over to pick up her scarf and bag. Cassidy got ahead of her, picked them up, and handed them to her. She opened her handsome bag, tore a piece of paper out of a little black leather note book, and wrote on it with a little gold pencil.

She handed the note to me. "My dear child. That's my telephone number. Call me the very *minute* I can come over here. My husband and I will do everything we can. Is Janet Holmes here?"

I turned to Cassidy. I'd forgotten all about Janet.

"Do you know where she is, Lieutenant? I haven't seen her since this morning."

"She had to go to court this afternoon, Mrs. Moreau. She'll be back." Mrs. Oxney squeezed my arm. "Janet's awfully good. She'll help you a lot, and I'll have my husband see her." She walked slowly out of the room. "Pauline. Murdered. I can't believe it."

And I knew, and I'm sure that Cassidy knew, that Mrs. Oxney *could* believe it, and that all her protestations had been a bad case of overacting. The whole latter half of the interview had been staged from start to finish.

CHAPTER 10

I was nearly dressed when I saw the envelope lying on the flowered Brussels carpet over near the hall door. It hadn't been there when I left my room an hour or two before to take my bath.

I picked it up slowly and turned it over. Plain, heavy, white. Then I opened it. It contained two little white pills and a little scrawled note. "See that Elise gets these. *Very* important. You know what to do."

Anne, undoubtedly. I gritted my teeth. Anne wanted me to climb in and out of windows and walk across the roof and give these pills to Elise so that she'd be unable to talk for a few more hours. I could understand Anne's wishes, but I didn't especially relish the risk I'd take at being caught by the police.

When I had finished dressing, I opened one of the side windows and looked out. I could see no one in front, and hoped that I was similarly invisible to the men standing in the front garden. Of course, anyone looking out a west window of the apartment house would see me very plainly and would undoubtedly rush to the telephone to report to the police. Well, I'd have to take my chances on that.

I stepped over the low window sill onto the tarred roof and walked rapidly over to Elise's second window. Yes, the bars were still loose. I shivered taking them down. The wind was blowing cold from the ocean, but there was not much fog left, and there were long streaks of blue sky and brittle sunshine. I laid the bars, all three of them, down very quietly on the roof, and stepped quickly into Elise's darkened room.

The room was deadly quiet without even the sound of breathing. It smelled stuffily of whiskey fumes, and I winced at the thought of the beautiful Elise's excesses. No woman as elegantly made should have had such an unfastidious habit.

When my eyes had got used to the greenish gloom that filtered through the shades, I walked over to the bed.

Elise looked up at me, her huge eyes bloodshot, the skin around them puffy.

"Have you come to ask me to take the pledge?" she said quietly. "I saw you wrinkling your nose."

"Shush," I said. "You must be very quiet."

"Okay," she whispered. "What's up?"

I sat down on the edge of the bed in order to be nearer. I scarcely knew where or how to start. "When did you wake up?"

"An hour or so ago. I can't get up. My head will break off at my shoulders if I do. Will you bring me some water?"

"In a minute. Don't yell or make a sound, Elise. Do you understand?"

She smiled as though it hurt her. "You're being very mysterious, my pet. I'll be quiet."

"Pauline's dead."

She started violently and pulled herself up from the pillows. Then she dropped back, soundlessly, her lips parted in amazement. "When?" she breathed.

"This morning. Sometime after two. She was murdered, Elise, stabbed."

She put one of her long, thin hands over her mouth. I noticed that her hand was dirty, muddy.

Then I told her as quickly and briefly as possible about Pauline's death. "You came in just after she died. You passed out, and Anne gave you a hypo. I've come to give you some more pills. We don't want the police to get at you. Do you understand?"

She nodded hard, her muddy hand still pressed tight against her mouth.

"Where did you go yesterday, Elise? Can you tell me?"

"No," she whispered. "I drew a blank. I'm sorry about your money. I had to take it. I do remember that."

"It's all right," I said. "I'll get you the water."

There was a small lavatory opening off Elise's room. I filled a glass after I had let the water run in a small, silent trickle, and I gave it and the pills to Elise. "Take both of them," I said. "They'll put you out again."

Then I turned her pillow and straightened the fine, soft wool blankets and turned down the sheet. I brought her a wet cloth for her head and opened the window in the lavatory and raised the shade in front of the window that still had its bars intact. I turned away from the window at the sound of a sharp whisper and walked back to the bed.

"Hilda, who did it? Who killed her?"

"We don't know. The police think somebody in the house, Elise. There's no use beating around the bush."

"*God!*" She struggled up on her elbow, and the wet washcloth fell into the pillow. "Hilda," she whispered, "Hilda, maybe I did it. Maybe I did. I don't know where I was or what I was doing. Maybe I killed her. I've wanted to often enough, God knows."

I pushed her back on the pillows. She was getting hysterical, and I was afraid she'd yell any minute.

"No," I said very decisively, "you couldn't have. You weren't here."

Long, silent sobs tore at her body, and big, heavy tears streamed from the corners of her eyes. Her mouth was twisted in agony. "I've been lying here waiting for Pauline to come in and give me hell. She's dead, and I'm glad, glad, glad. But somebody will suffer for it, terribly," she muttered.

"Elise, you must be quiet. You'll have the police in here, and you mustn't talk to them until you feel better." I wiped her face with the washcloth. "Now, try to let those pills work and go back to sleep. I hated to do it, but I had to tell you so you'd be warned."

She held onto my hand, and I wanted badly to get out of her room and go back to my own, but I was afraid to leave her until she calmed down. In her state she might so easily yell her head off.

She had stopped crying, and I could feel her relaxing slowly under the blankets. The room was airing out, too, and I thought irrelevantly that it would be an attractive place with its rose and white wall paper and handsome mahogany furniture if it weren't for its tragic inhabitant.

"Who did you think did it, Hilda?"

I jerked around. "I don't know, Elise. I have no idea. Pauline certainly asked for it, but it doesn't seem possible that either Rose or Marthe or Sophie could...."

"Rose! That baby. *Never.*" She pulled herself upright and I groaned inwardly. I'd started her off again. "Listen, Hilda, they mustn't do anything to the girls. They *mustn't*. Listen, if I told them I did it, they'd just lock me up, wouldn't they? I'll be locked up someday anyway. I'll tell them...."

I put my hand over her mouth and with all the force I could muster pushed her back on the pillow.

"You'll do nothing of the kind. Now, shut up. With Pauline out of the way, you'll have a chance for decent treatment and you'll get well. The Oxneys will look after the girls' interests. You keep your mouth shut." I held her down for a good long time, and gradually she stopped struggling. I sat there in an agony of impatience until I felt her relaxing once more. Finally her eyelids drooped heavily. The medicine was taking effect.

I crawled back into my room with a deep sigh of relief, and slumped into a chair. If my baby didn't turn out to be a miscarriage or a monster, it would be no fault of the Moreau family.

At eight o'clock Tuesday night, Janet Holmes was allowed to summon all of us to the wood-paneled room downstairs for a conference, unchaperoned by the police, although I had a pretty good idea that the detectives were not far off.

As we drifted into the room, one by one, Janet managed a sort of serious smile for each of us. She stood with her back to the fire, and I went over to a chair on her left as near to the warmth as I could get.

Anne was already in the room when I came downstairs. Her face was so worn and ravaged that she was almost unrecognizable. She looked as though she might be suffering from some hideous, painful, incurable disease, and even her clothes looked worn and shabby. She was distressingly nervous and paced around the room picking things up and putting them down and lighting cigarettes until I was ready to scream.

"Thanks for getting those pills in to Elise, Hilda," she said with a feeble smile. "You told her what happened?"

I nodded. "Yes. She took it pretty hard. She thought she might have done it herself. As she said, she'd drawn a blank. Didn't know where she'd been or anything."

Anne walked away from me to speak to Rose and Marthe as they came into the room. Anne put her long slender hand under Rose's trembling young chin and raised her head. "How are you, baby? All right?"

Rose nodded dully. She looked like a baby, to be sure, with her soft infant's hair and her woolly pink bathrobe, but no baby, except one with a bad case of colic, would have had such a sad, tired little face.

Marthe, dressed in an old blue sweater and skirt, came over to me. "For Lord's sake, give me a cigarette. Rose and I ran out hours ago, and that lunkhead cop in the hall wouldn't help us out at all." I gave her the cigarette and looked into her face as the glare of the match shone into it. She looked surprisingly calm, or at least outwardly controlled. She sprawled on the floor in front of my chair with her long legs stretched out in front of her, and her very long shoulder-length bob swept into my lap. I put my hand out to touch her hair. It was wonderful hair, shining and alive and thick.

Sophie was the last to arrive. She wore a fussy pale green negligee that was hideously unbecoming, but even in this crisis, she had been careful to apply a generous portion of make-up. She tottered to a chair and melted into it as though her legs had ceased to function. Her eyes darted wildly around the room, and she put her hand up to her mouth as though she had to suppress a scream. I noticed that her nails were no longer talons. They were bitten off short. I shuddered.

"You'd better call Nanette, Anne," Janet said from her place in front of the fire. "I want her here, too."

Nanette came, after quite an interlude. She stomped into the room and over to Janet. "Why do I have to come in here?" she snapped.

"I'll take that up later, Nanette. Sit down, will you?" Janet indicated a chair. Then she gave her thick tweed jacket a yank, took a deep breath, and started in. "I would be not only unkind, but stupid if I minimized the seriousness of the position you are all in. The police have permitted me to talk to you, and I'm going to tell you something of what they know to date. Of course, it's not only possible, but probable, that they know a great deal more than they've permitted me to learn. They'd be fools to tell me all their secrets, and they're not fools. This man Cassidy who's in charge of the case seems to be a very intelligent and able man."

"He's a brute," Sophie moaned. "He's a brute. He nagged and nagged and nagged at me."

"That's his duty, Sophie," Janet said with only a little impatience in her voice. "I'll tell you first that the police think that Pauline was murdered and that it was done by someone well known to her. It was either someone already in the house or someone whom she let into the house. And, of course, it had to be someone who knew the house well enough to be able to find the knife, and there were no signs of a struggle."

"But what about those fingerprints on the knife, Janet? Pauline's, I mean." It was Marthe who spoke.

"They have good reason to believe that Pauline marked the knife when she pulled it out of her side, Marthe. In fact, Cassidy says he can prove it."

"Hell," Marthe said with quiet finality. If she'd put those fingerprints on the knife, I could well imagine her disappointment at the turn of events.

"Now, Nanette," Janet said turning to the old woman, "you've talked very freely to the police. You've told them that everyone in the house hated Pauline and that they all went into her room some time during the night last night and quarreled with her, separately and in a body. For your information, Cassidy knows that you're lying and that you could not possibly have heard a quarrel from the basement." The maid's face got whiter as Janet spoke. "The only way you could have heard people quarreling in Miss Moreau's room was by coming upstairs. Is that what you did?"

"No, I did not. I stayed in my room. But I heard quarreling from midnight until two." Her fat old body trembled like jelly. Her anger was a tangible thing.

"All right, Nanette," Janet snapped. "If you heard quarreling and recognized the voices, whose voice did you hear at two o'clock this morning?"

"I don't remember," she said. And then she smiled a travesty of a smile. It was grisly.

Marthe pulled herself up onto her knees and swung around to face Nanette. "You're lying through your teeth, Nanette. You didn't hear any quarreling from midnight until two for the simple reason that Pauline wasn't in her room then."

The room stirred with excitement. "What do you mean, Marthe?" Janet asked.

She stood up on her two feet and shrugged her shoulders. "I went in to talk to Pauline at a little after one. She wasn't there. The lights were on, but she was gone. I hadn't been able to sleep, and I wanted to talk to her.

When I didn't find her, I went back to bed."

"Well, well, Marthe, this is very interesting. Why didn't you tell the police this morning that you were awake after eleven o'clock?" Janet's voice was irritable.

"I couldn't see any reason for incriminating myself. That's why." Marthe walked over and sat down by Rose and took her hand. "Rose was in bed asleep. I looked to see."

Rose and Marthe had two connecting rooms at the back of the house on the west side of the hall. Rose's opened onto the hall, but Marthe's was beyond, so that she had to go through Rose's room in order to get into any other part of the house.

"And you didn't look in any other part of the house for Pauline, Marthe?" She shook her head. "Nope," she said, "I didn't. I knew she was probably out, so I went back to bed."

"Out?" Anne asked. "Why would Pauline be out at that time of night? You know she never goes out, or rather went out."

Nanette stirred uneasily under Marthe's direct glance.

"Ask Nanette about that. She knows more than I do," Marthe said, "but I know that Pauline went out lots of times after we were all supposed to be in bed. She used to come in the side door on the porch, the one that opens into the front parlor. Then she'd go through the back parlor into the hall and leave her things in the dressing room and sneak upstairs."

"Good God," Anne gasped. "*Really*, Marthe?"

"She's making that up," Nanette snapped. "It's not true."

Marthe's eyebrows raised to a new high. "Yeah, sure, and sometimes you'd wait up and give her coffee in the kitchen at four in the morning."

"But where do you suppose she went?" Janet asked.

"As I said before, Nanette probably knows. I don't."

Janet swung around purposefully to face the maid. "Now, Nanette, you tell us what you know. You've got to. This puts an entirely different face on everything that's happened. Pauline might have come home with someone who followed her into the house. Was she mixed up with some man?"

"Miss Moreau was a very fine woman. She was not mixed up with a man, and she did not leave the house at night. Not last night or any other night." Nanette had dragged herself erect and was preparing to leave the room. "That one, Miss Marthe, she is a liar. Always. Now she tries to protect herself. She says things about Miss Moreau, and Miss Moreau is dead and can't prove . . ."

Marthe walked over to Nanette and put her hands on her shoulders. "Look at me, you old hag." Nanette tried to pull away from her, but Marthe hung on and shook, hard. "Pauline paid you a hundred dollars month, and you weren't worth twenty. Four years ago she was going to send you back to France on a very small pension. You didn't want to go, but she kept you, and what's more, she doubled your wages. You used to get fifty a month, and for four long years you've been getting a hundred." The words jerked out of Marthe with rhythmic regularity. "You had something on her, didn't you? You were covering up for her, weren't you? Pauline was stingy as hell. She didn't pay you a hundred dollars a month because you were her old nurse."

The old woman finally jerked out of Marthe's grasp. She breathed deeply and said something in rapid French which I couldn't understand. I caught only a few words which sounded something like "Vous avez fait"—"You have done."

Then she marched steadily out of the room.

I gasped for breath. Marthe stood blankly looking into space, her face the color of thin milk.

"What did she say, Marthe?" Janet said firmly.

Marthe shook her head. "Nothing. Nothing. She just said I was a terrible liar. But everything I said was true. Really."

"How did you find all this out, Marthe?" Anne's voice was weary. "About Pauline, I mean."

Marthe walked over to me and gestured for a cigarette. I gave it to her, and she lit it. She took her time about answering. "I've come in pretty late myself a few times. One time Pauline was just ahead of me, and when she didn't say anything the next day, I got suspicious. Before I started to work, I used to read most of the night, and Pauline couldn't see my light and didn't know I heard her, but I did. I was going to follow her some time and see where she went." She grinned sadly. "I was dying to get something on her. I thought it'd help all of us."

"But you never did, Marthe?" Sophie was wildly excited.

"Nope, worse luck." Marthe went back to sit by little Rose who sat dumb and frightened inside her pink robe. "Your feet cold, baby?" She pulled her little sister's feet up on the couch and tucked the robe around them.

"Marthe, look at me." Janet spoke emphatically, and Marthe looked up at her blandly. "Are you telling the truth?"

"I am," she said.

"Well, this puts an entirely different face on the whole thing, doesn't it? Pauline's life was probably more complicated than any of us thought. I wonder what we'd better do."

"Tell the police about it, I suppose," I said. "They may be able to find out where she went." A sudden thought made my heart leap in excitement. "Listen, her keys. This afternoon the police were looking for her keys.

Maybe somebody came in the house with her last night and took her keys after she was dead. Maybe that person—male or female—will come back."

"Why?" Janet said. "Murderer revisiting the scene of his crime, or something?" She smiled in a deadly superior manner that caused little chills of irritation to vibrate all over me. In fact, Janet's intelligent detachment was bothering me a lot more than I wanted to admit out loud.

"I don't know," I snapped, "but why take the keys if they weren't to be used again?"

Anne stopped her restless pacing. "We'd better tell the police—about Pauline's nocturnal wanderings, I mean. Let them worry about why the keys are gone." She started toward the door.

"Wait, Anne," Janet said. "Let's not be hasty about this. Pauline's being out of the house at night may have nothing to do with the murder."

"But Good Lord, Janet, why take a chance? Can't you see that this development brings another element into the case? It means that the suspects aren't confined to this house alone?" Anne's voice was urgent, worried.

"Anne, you've asked me to represent your family in this investigation. I'm afraid you'll have to trust my judgment if you want me to continue to do so." Janet wasn't calm anymore. She was excited and angry, and I couldn't imagine why. "I'm doing my best to protect your interests, but I'll have to do it in my own way. Do you understand?"

She was speaking directly to Anne, but every face in the room was turned toward her. Marthe's was white and cynical, Rose's white and wondering, Sophie's white and frightened.

"I want you to know, Anne, that I think you're making a great mistake in keeping Elise doped." Janet didn't sound at all friendly. "The police are naturally anxious to question her, and they've told me that they consider your action in doping her extremely suspicious."

Anne shrugged wearily. "Listen, Janet, Elise would collapse under a police questioning right now. I'm not only her sister, I'm a doctor. It's my duty to protect her, but if you insist on exposing her to questioning, I'll let them talk to her in the morning. She doesn't know anything anyway."

"Anne, where were you last night? You weren't home."

Janet's words caused slightly less excitement than a Japanese air raid would have.

Anne's eyelids dropped down over her eyes for a long half minute. When she raised them, her expression was blank and sad. "You're quite right, Janet. I wasn't home. I was out looking for Elise."

"Where did you go?"

"Down along Columbus Avenue to all the usual bars."

"Did anyone see you?"

Anne shook her head slowly. "Probably not, Janet. I'd just look in the door, and if she wasn't there, I'd go to another one."

"You didn't take your car, did you?"

"No, I didn't." Anne's voice could scarcely be heard. "I walked. I couldn't sleep anyway, and I thought the walk might help. I came home after all the bars closed at two. I suppose I got in about two-thirty. I just sat in my room, thinking and worrying until Marthe called me."

Janet managed a sort of disgusted smile. "This isn't the story you told the police, you know," she snapped. Apparently her legal ethics were winning over the ties of friendship. "You put me in a very embarrassing position this morning, but I'm *not* going to alibi you."

Sophie squirmed in her chair. Her eyes were sly and crafty. "Then Anne won't be able to alibi you, either, Janet, will she?"

The woman lawyer swung around on her flat, sensible heels. "Why should I need an alibi, Sophie? What possible connection could I have with this case?"

Sophie stood up and drew her dreadful green negligee around her soft, droopy figure. "You can answer that better than I can, Janet. Well, I was asleep in my room after eleven o'clock until Hilda yelled and nobody can prove anything else, so now I'm going to call Mr. Brown." Halfway to the door she turned back. "I can get married now, and none of you can stop me."

Sophie was very pleased with herself. And no wonder. She'd left a room seething with excitement and anger and suspicion.

CHAPTER 11

Lying in bed that night I tried to do a little orderly thinking. With the possible exception of Rose and Elise, nobody in the Moreau house or in the apartment next door had an alibi. Sophie, Marthe, Janet, Nanette, and I were in bed, although I was the only one whose word I was willing to trust. Rose was in bed, according to Marthe who could be counted on to lie for her young sister whenever necessary. Anne was wandering around the streets, and Elise was, too.

That took care of the Department of Alibis for the crucial time which was probably two to three o'clock on Tuesday morning.

All the Moreaus, including myself, wanted money, and although my lawsuit would probably have brought about the same result, Pauline's death meant that the dissolution of the trust would be much simpler and would certainly not involve threats of commitment to insane asylums.

But the real motives, I felt, were much stronger than a mere desire for money. There was enough hate locked up in the maidenly bosoms of the Moreau sisters to cause a dozen homicides. Anne's professional career had been thwarted if not ruined by Pauline's funny business with the Oxney notes. Rose and Sophie had been prevented from marrying their own true loves. Elise had been badgered and terrorized for years and her possible recovery prevented by her elder sister. Her marriage had been prevented, too. Marthe, quite obviously, just plain hated Pauline and was devoted to Rose.

There was certainly something fishy between Nanette and Pauline if Marthe were to be believed—and I thought she was—and it seemed to me quite possible that Nanette had chosen her own kitchen knife for a lethal weapon. The old woman was lying like mad in an effort to implicate the family, and if, for some reason, Pauline had suddenly decided to discontinue Nanette's extravagant wage, the maid could very well have decided to discontinue Pauline's existence.

If Sophie wasn't just strewing red herrings around for the fun of it, Janet Holmes had reason to hate and fear Pauline, and Janet's refusal to tell the police about Pauline's possible outside interests was highly suspicious to me, although she had been able to convince both Anne and Marthe that nothing should be said until she had time to make her own investigation. "After all, Anne, it may help us to have a little information that the police don't have." Then she had smiled in a very friendly manner, and I could have hit her. "You must trust me, you know, if I'm to help you."

Well, after all, she and Anne had been friends for years, and I suppose Anne would have been foolish to distrust her all of a sudden, but I didn't like it, at all.

But the most astonishing phase of the whole affair was the tacit agreement among the Moreau sisters that they should protect each other, innocent or guilty, and that no one should be expected to pay for having committed a murder.

I had seen very clearly during the evening's conference that the sisters didn't give information except when it implicated others. Marthe had talked freely about Pauline and Nanette's deal about the wages, and Sophie had been perfectly willing to cast suspicion, albeit very nebulous suspicion, on Janet. I had the feeling, too, that if they had anything on me, they'd certainly tell it. Fortunately, they didn't have, and I would certainly make it very clear to Mr. Cassidy that I had had nothing to fear from Pauline at any time, that getting David's money was an automatic performance which would be arranged by lawyers and judges and certified public accountants.

I felt somehow that I really had less to fear from the police than I did from my husband's sisters. Well, there was nothing I could do. I'd tried to get them to tell the police about Pauline's behavior in the night, and I'd also hinted rather broadly that it might be a good idea to get hold of Judge Oxney and ask for his advice. I might just as well have kept my mouth shut. I was quietly ignored, so I'd left the room and come upstairs to bed, and now I'd have to go to sleep if I were to have any strength at all. The night before had been a total loss for sleeping.

Pauline, Anne, Sophie, Rose, Marthe, Janet, Nanette. Over and over again. Motives, alibis, times. Pauline....

I looked out on another cold, foggy morning. The *Tristan und Isolde* foghorn moaned drearily, and water dropped with monotonous regularity from the leaves of the big tree down onto the sidewalk. Well, at least I'd slept, and I could get warm in the tub.

When I was dressed, I went downstairs in search of breakfast. One of Cassidy's men sat on the bench part of the hat rack, and I was happy to see that someone had lit the gas heater in the hall. Its warmth was reassuring.

The policeman looked at me blandly, and said good morning without enthusiasm.

"Good morning," I said. "That heater feels good, doesn't it?"

"If the inspectors was to see that heater, they'd take it out. It ain't safe, open like that," the gentleman replied.

I supposed it wasn't. It was connected by a rather worn-looking hose to a gas outlet, and there wasn't much of a grill to shield one's skirts from the open flame. But it threw off heat which I considered very important. Marthe and Rose were in the kitchen getting breakfast. There was a nice hot fire burning in the old-fashioned coal range. "This heat is wonderful," I said. "How are you?"

Marthe banged a frying pan onto the stove with unnecessary racket. She still wore her old blue sweater and skirt and grimy saddle oxfords, but she looked as though she'd had some sleep. Rose, too, looked better.

"I'll live," Marthe said. "Nanette's on strike. Says she won't cook for us—the knees, as usual. How'd you like to picket her?"

"Okay," I said. "I'll make myself a banner. 'Don't patronize Nanette. Unfair to organized Moreau sisters.'"

Rose laughed mildly. She looked very cute and young in her yellow angora sweater and brown flannel skirt. "She says we have to bring her her breakfast. I'm looking for the arsenic right now. Isn't she awful? She's such a liar."

"Set the table, baby, and go bellow at Sophie. She'll want something to eat, I suppose."

I helped Rose with the table, and pretty soon Sophie came along wearing a dreadful bright blue chenille robe. I wondered how she contrived to select such unbecoming clothes. I also wondered where they were sold. Then I thought about Pauline's beautiful clothes. Her black dress and her tailored suit hadn't cost one red nickel less than a hundred dollars apiece. The brocade robe she had worn Sunday night was definitely expensive. How had she managed to have such beautiful things when her sisters had nothing?

"Marthe," I said meditatively, "this is certainly none of my business, but didn't it make you sore to see Pauline wearing beautiful, expensive clothes when the rest of you didn't?"

"Her clothes didn't cost so much," Marthe said, waving a piece of toast in the air. "She bought things on sale, and she wore them forever."

"Oh, nuts," I said, "even on sale that black dress of hers would have cost at least fifty dollars."

"Twenty-five," Sophie said. "She showed me the tag. Besides, we all used to look at the books. Most of the income went to keep up the house. Pauline didn't spend so much on herself."

Well, I wouldn't argue with them if they were going to be so insistent, but I knew enough about clothes to know that Pauline had probably pulled a fast one on her sisters.

The hall policeman stuck his head in the kitchen door. "There's a lady on the phone wants to talk to *Mrs.* Moreau. Which one's that?"

"I am," I said. I followed him into the front parlor, wondering who could be calling me. I found out.

"Mrs. Moreau," a nice voice said, "this is Katherine Graham, your traveling companion."

"Oh, hello," I said. "How nice of you to call."

"Well," she said, "I hesitated for quite a while. After all, I know you people are in trouble, and I certainly don't want to have you think I'm a sensation-monger, but I do want to see you."

"Why, of course," I said. "I think you're being very kind. There are probably a lot of people who wouldn't want to have anything to do with us at this point."

"Perhaps," Mrs. Graham said, "but I did so enjoy meeting you on the train, and I think it's perfectly dreadful for you to have to come out here to California for the first time to this kind of a mess, but, Mrs. Moreau, I think maybe I can help you a little. May I come and see you this afternoon?"

Help me? "Of course. Come around four, and I'll give you a cup of tea. If you have any trouble getting in, tell someone to send for me."

We said goodbye and hung up. I shivered. The blue parlor was not only damp and cold. It was a mess with newspapers and cigarette butts scattered around and ashes overflowing the fireplace grate and all the furniture out of place. I went back to the warm kitchen eagerly.

Marthe and Rose looked up. "What's cookin'?" Marthe asked.

I could feel myself frowning. "I don't know," I said. "You know I told you about meeting a Mrs. Graham on the train. Well, she's a nice woman, and I'm sure she isn't just full of idle curiosity, but she wants to come and see me this afternoon. She says she thinks she can *help* me."

Marthe grinned. "Do you think you need help, my pet?"

I snapped, "Marthe, we all need help. You people seem to be principally concerned with preventing the police from making an arrest. But they're not fools. They're not going to give up easily. After all, a murder has been committed in this house."

Rose's infantile face blushed dark red, and her eyes were shiny with tears. "Oh, Hilda...."

Anne interrupted our conversation at that point by coming in the back door. She inquired solicitously as to how we had all slept. "Have you seen Elise yet, Marthe?"

"Yeah. She's still hung over. I gave her some black coffee."

Anne quickly swallowed half of a cup of coffee, put out her cigarette and left muttering something about the damned police, and Elise's condition.

Rose fixed a tray for Nanette. "I'm afraid to take it down to her, Marthe. She's such an old crab."

"I'll do it," I said.

I took the tray, and Rose showed me the door to the basement stairs. It was in the dining room, and the stairs that led down were steep and worn and very badly lighted with one small globe. The air in the great, dusty lower region was even colder and damper than it was upstairs. No wonder the old woman had rheumatism.

The basement was pretty well crammed with the usual cast-offs of a large family. Broken, discarded furniture, wooden packing boxes, rusty bed springs, piles of newspapers, a few dusty garments hanging on a clothes line, trunks, a boy's bicycle, a very interesting old hobbyhorse that might, when painted, be nice for the new member of the Moreau family....

I looked around trying to decide which of the doors and passages might lead to Nanette's quarters. At the foot of the stairs, there was one door leading to the east side of the house. There was another to the north, but beyond the dirty glass panes, I could see trees and shrubbery. There was another wood-paneled door to the right of the north exit. I balanced the tray carefully and opened it.

Astonishingly enough, it opened into a very cheerful, cozily Victorian sitting room with Brussels carpet in gay reds and greens, and heavily framed pictures of nature-not-at-its-best, and big upholstered chairs. The windows were heavily curtained in Battenberg lace and faded red damask hangings. A neat fire was laid in the brick fireplace. I called out, "Nanette, where are you? I've brought your breakfast."

"Here," she snapped back. "In my bed, unable to get up."

I walked across the sitting room in the direction of the voice. In an alcove, there was a comfortable-looking day bed with blankets of good quality. The old servant had three pillows behind her back and a black crocheted shawl over her shoulders. She looked very comfortable. I'd wasted a lot of unnecessary sympathy on her because she was old and had rooms in the basement. Actually it wasn't really a basement as it stood above ground level on the lower slope of the steep hill.

"Thank you," she said sullenly, as I handed her the tray. "I can't lean over to light the fire, so I'll thank you to do it. It's cold this morning."

I lit the fire. Then I turned around to face the woman in the bed. "Nanette," I said thoughtfully, "I know you were devoted to Miss Moreau, but I don't think it would hurt you to help her sisters a little if you can. If you know anything about where Miss Moreau went at night, you may be able to help the police catch her murderer. Why won't you tell?"

She put down the coffee pot and glared up at me. I'd made a bad mistake if I expected help from that quarter.

"Miss Marthe's lying. And if you take my advice you'll keep your mouth shut and not tell the police that story." Her black eyes glittered evilly.

"*Why?*"

"It'll make things look worse for you. The police'll think you're lying to help yourself."

I raised my eyebrows. "I'm afraid I don't need help," I said. "The police know perfectly well that I had no reason to murder Miss Moreau, because I could get my money in an orderly fashion—through the courts."

"*Your* money. You mean *David's* money."

I nodded impatiently. "Well, yes, to be technical, it is David's money."

"But if you weren't married to David, you wouldn't have the money, would you?" She looked me straight in the eye as she spoke.

"But I *am* married to him," I said emphatically.

"*You might not have stayed married to him if Miss Moreau had lived,*" she snapped.

I slumped onto a hassock. I was speechless for a long three minutes while the blood pounded and roared through my body. Apparently Pauline had planned some of her usual skullduggery to use on me.

"What on earth are you talking about?" I said finally.

"Never mind," she snapped. "You know what I mean. You go upstairs and keep your mouth shut. And just remember that if you tell the police about Miss Moreau—Marthe's lies, I mean—I'll tell what I know."

I tried hard to make her explain herself. It was no use. She just didn't open her mouth except to put food in it, and I was in no mood to watch the ugly old woman swab up the eggs on her plate with a piece of toast and lie there carefully munching.

I stood looking around the old basement for a long time. What in the world could Pauline have told the maid about me? My life had been about as innocuous as anyone's could be. I'd grown up in a small town, gone to a good girl's college, and taken up teaching. I'd taught in the small town where I was born, and as far as I knew, my life was so blameless that its dullness quite often irritated me. I'd had the usual assortment of men friends, but no serious love affair until I met David. I'd gone to dances on Saturday night at the country club, the opera and symphony concerts in Cleveland, occasionally, and I'd played a lot of bridge. Since 1939 I'd knitted for the Red Cross, read a lot of books which were entertaining but not improving, and taken two first aid courses.

I'd gone to summer school at Western Reserve for two summers, and during the second one I'd met David. For the first and only time in my life I'd been in love, and very fortunately for me, David had been in love, too. We'd been married in January after the war began as it seemed foolish to wait with David's call to active duty in the Navy hanging over us. My school board had been very understanding about my leaving in the middle of the school year, and the girl who had taken my place was, I was sure, perfectly satisfactory. If Pauline had been able to find anything of a guilty nature in my life, she was a whole lot smarter than I was.

Slowly and thoughtfully I climbed the stairs to the main floor of the house. My back and my head ached, and I felt rotten all over. Nanette's threats, ridiculous as I knew them to be, had upset me. I could hear Marthe and Rose chattering in the kitchen, but I didn't want to see them.

I went into the hall, thinking that I'd tidy up the front parlor which I could at least do in solitude, but I stopped at the back of the hall.

Elise was in the front parlor, shouting her head off.

"Have you never been drunk, my good man?" Her voice carried very nicely. "Have you never had a blackout? Well, then, you've never lived. How in hell do I know where I was?"

I heard Cassidy's voice, which I recognized by its quality, but I couldn't distinguish his words. Unnoticed, I retired to my listening post in the back parlor.

"But I tell you I can't remember," Elise shouted. "I simply don't know where I was. I had *amnesia*. Ever heard of it?"

"Now, Miss Moreau," Cassidy said very patiently, "you certainly must remember leaving this house Monday afternoon, don't you?"

"Very dimly," Elise said. "I know I went out through Hilda's room, and she was asleep, but I don't remember anything after that."

"You don't remember which bar you headed for first?"

"Nope. I'm completely blank."

There was an unbroken silence except for footsteps and the sound of a match being struck.

Something thudded lightly. "This is your shoe, isn't it?" Cassidy asked.

"Right you are, my man. Size 8½ quadruple A. Dirty, isn't it?"

"Yes, it is. We found it out in front of this house in a flower bed. There was also an empty Scotch bottle and marks in the ground to indicate that someone lay there for some time. There's also mud on your clothes, Miss Moreau."

Elise laughed lightly. I blushed. "Well, I probably lay down for a little rest and a wee nippy. Don't you think so?"

"Yes, I do, Miss Moreau. I'd give a whole lot if you could remember *when*. Maybe you saw somebody come in the house while you were lying there or saw your sister let somebody in."

Elise laughed again. "It'd have to be a hell of a lot, Constable. By the time I landed in the flower bed I was undoubtedly deaf, dumb, and blind."

"But you finally got up and opened the front door and came in the house. What made you do that?"

"Probably two reasons. The bottle was empty, and I may very well have been cold—or uncomfortable—on my earthen bed. Wouldn't you think so?"

Very slowly and carefully I managed to open the folding door about one inch. I wanted to see this interview as well as hear it, and I got a good view of Elise through my one-inch crack. Cassidy's back was toward me, but the grey morning light from the west windows shone clearly into Elise's white, rather worn face. Her eyes, though, were very blue, and she looked very lovely in a dull rose fitted house coat. She leaned back comfortably in a big rosewood chair, her long legs crossed. She gestured with a cigarette as she spoke.

"Really, if you want information, I'm definitely not the girl to give it to you," she said. "You know that, don't you?"

"Well, you're not much help, I'll admit." There was a little smile in Cassidy's voice. "You didn't like your sister very much, did you? Miss Pauline Moreau, I mean."

"*Like* her? I hated her guts, my friend. I'm overjoyed at her untimely demise. In fact, we all are, but really," she said, leaning toward Cassidy and looking intently at him, "there isn't a human being in this house that'd have the guts to kill her. She had us much too well under her thumb for any such antics. You look elsewhere for your killer. You'll have much better luck, I'm sure." She put out her cigarette. "I'm pretty sure Pauline had outside interests—she was awfully cagey—and if she blackmailed her family, it's a cinch she did it elsewhere."

"Blackmail, Miss Moreau? What do you mean?" Cassidy said urgently.

"Well, for instance, she told me the other day that if David persisted in getting the trust dissolved, she'd have to have me committed. My brother wouldn't have appreciated that at all. In fact, he's very fond of me, and he would have backed down before he let Pauline lock me up for good." She smiled and showed her lovely white teeth. "That's why I went on that bender, incidentally. I thought I'd better go while I had the chance. But that's Pauline's type of blackmail, you see. Why wouldn't she try it on outsiders?"

"She might have, of course," Cassidy said. "But *who?* I can't find anything in her papers that points to much contact with outsiders. In fact, there isn't anything except a few business letters to brokers and the bank and tax collectors."

She shrugged her shoulders and stood up and stretched with her arms wide. Cassidy would have had to be a very tough cop indeed not to have appreciated Elise's looks at that moment.

"That's your problem, my friend," she said, smiling again. "I'm afraid I can't do anything for you there, either. And if you do find out where I was, would you mind letting me know? I'd love to find out if I had a good time or not."

She waved lightly and walked out of the room.

Good Lord in Heaven, I thought, *what* a woman.

Then she came back. I couldn't see her as she was out of my line of vision, but I could hear.

"You can't tell, you know. Maybe *I* bumped off my dear sister. I could have."

My heart lurched quaintly.

"I know that, Miss Moreau. I know that very well."

Cassidy's voice was very even and controlled and entirely without emotion.

I whipped out of the back parlor and into the hall just in time to see Elise trailing up the stairs, followed by Anne.

"No, Anne," Elise was saying, "no psychiatrists today. I'm much too weary from all that dope. Besides I want to spend the day rejoicing."

"My God, Elise," Anne muttered, "you'll drive me mad."

"Hello, Hilda," Elise said smiling back at me as I followed along behind. "Come in and talk to me. Anne, you'd better go see your patients, hadn't you, love?"

Elise flung off her robe with an exuberant gesture, and fished in a drawer for a bedjacket. She settled herself comfortably in bed.

"Elise, will you promise me to stay at home and behave yourself?" Anne's voice was tremulous and old.

Elise looked at her wide-eyed. Then she laughed. "Poor old Annie. Don't worry, darling. I shall be very good. No more getting drunk. Now that Pauline's dead, I don't have to, and in a day or two, we'll go see your Doctor Henry, and she can make me over. Re-educate? Isn't that it?"

Anne nodded. "That's it, and in the meantime, stop telling the police that maybe *you* killed Pauline."

"He didn't believe me. He likes me very much. I could tell, but he was shocked, too." She smiled and leaned back on her pillows.

Anne went off, and I stayed for some time talking with Elise. She was full of exuberant plans for the future.

"Tell me, Hilda, how can we get our money? Can we just have your little suit and get it right away or will it be tied up for donkey's ages?"

I shook my head. "I don't know. We'll have to ask Janet."

A frown clouded her fine, regular features. "That one. I do not love her. Very shirty and too damned sure of herself. I wouldn't be at all surprised to see her pull a Pauline and make us all whistle for our dough."

"Me, too. Not at all surprised, I mean." Then I told Elise about Janet's refusal to tell the police about Pauline's wandering around at night.

"Ah-ha!" she yipped. "You see. I was right. I knew damned well that Pauline had other fish to fry. I wouldn't be at all surprised if she's been living in sin for lo, these many years." She sighed. "But I can't imagine why on earth any man in his right mind would get tied up with Pauline." She giggled. "Can't you just hear Pauline giving him his orders for the night?"

We both laughed until our eyes streamed. When our amusement was once more under control, Elise managed to speak.

"The hell with Janet," she said. "I think we definitely ought to tell the good Cassidy and let him start hunting around for Pauline's sinful goings-on."

But we decided, finally, that we'd have one more go at Janet before we took matters into our own hands.

"Isn't it simply wonderful to have Pauline out of the way?" she said thoughtfully. "Except for poor little Rosie, of course. Pauline's demise came too late to do her any good. But the rest of us can have a lovely time. We can sell this costly old hole and live in an apartment, and I can get the works from the lady psychiatrist and be a good girl, and you know what, Hilda?"

"No, what?"

"I am going husband-hunting. I am going to get me a simply beautiful, lovely husband, preferably one in the Navy all covered with gold braid."

And why on earth not, I thought. Any man could have a wonderful time with the beautiful Elise in a sober, happy condition.

She looked at me cagily from beneath lowered lids. "In fact," she said slowly, "I've got one all lined up. I just met him the other day, but he seemed intrigued."

I jerked upright. "When? When did you meet him?"

She batted her eyelashes and assumed a very coy expression. "Monday, my pet. I told dear old Cassidy a few well-chosen lies. I met my fine new friend down in Palo Alto. I was calling on a woman who just got herself widowed."

"Elise, for God's sake! Start at the beginning."

She sighed. "It's all very simple. I met the lovely man at my friend's house in Palo Alto, and he brought me back to town, and we had dinner, and then he had to go aboard his ship." She smiled as though reliving something pleasant. "Of course, I was going to come home, and then, I thought, what the hell. One more bender, and then I'll be good forever. He's worth it."

My mind was swimming in a pea soup fog. "But, Elise, I'm not trying to be nasty, but why on earth didn't you just say that you wanted to call on your widow and go? Why all the bars unscrewed and pinching my money and sneaking out?"

"Well, really, dear Hilda. You should have known Pauline better than that. She wouldn't *let* me go out. I had to sneak out, and of course, I'll admit I intended to get stinking as soon as I saw my widow. But I managed to wait awhile, and now, no more. My fine Lieutenant is going to write to me. He's a toots." She grinned.

"Well, *why* didn't you tell Cassidy where you'd been?"

Her eyes were round. "And drag my friends into this pretty pickle? Certainly not. And you keep your little mouth shut, too."

"All right," I said. "Tell me about your man."

She rolled her eyes. "He is lovely. Very large and amusing and cute. I told him I was a drunk. He said I could be cured, on account of I am intelligent." She laughed. "Imagine! Me intelligent. That shows he was impressed. Men always say that women with good figures are intelligent, haven't you noticed?"

I laughed and said yes. We started to talk about the clothes that Elise would have to get before her sailor returned from the sea, but we were interrupted by a great bustle.

The bustle was Mrs. Oxney bent on good deeds.

She came bursting in with two maids in her wake bearing large baskets. I leaned over the stairs and watched her and her retinue.

Marthe and Rose came from the back of the house and Mrs. Oxney kissed them both and talked all the time.

"You poor darling babies, what a dreadful time you're having. Wouldn't you know that wretched Pauline couldn't even die decently without stirring up a lot of trouble? Mabel and Wilma, take the stuff out in the kitchen and clean things up and fix these people a decent lunch." She turned to Marthe. "I do hope you've fired that old Nanette. She's a dreadful old thing. My girls are going to fix the house and see that you eat properly. Where are all the others?"

Marthe plunged bravely in. "Anne's gone doctoring, but the rest of us are all here. Gosh, I'm glad you came. The house is a wreck, and there's nothing to eat, and Nanette's taken to her bed. It must be wonderful to be rich."

"It certainly is, darling. Have you seen the papers? There isn't much in them, really. That man Cassidy says he's not going to make statements to the papers until his case is complete. He says another case of his was wrecked just a little while ago, because too much was printed before he was ready, and my husband says he's perfectly right."

Cassidy was standing in the hall right behind Mrs. Oxney, and Marthe was trying to tell her so without success.

The policeman finally got around in front of Mrs. Oxney and made her acknowledge his existence.

"Oh, there you are," she said. "How are you getting on? Have you found out anything important?"

"I'd like to talk to you for a minute, Mrs. Oxney, if I may." He was being veddy, veddy polite to the Judge's spouse.

"Of course," she said, bustling after him. "My Lord, this place is a mess. It's a good thing I thought to bring my maids. This house is a terrible place to keep up and with only one decrepit old servant . . ."

Cassidy closed the door.

"Marthe," I hissed over the stair railing. "Go in the back parlor and listen. To what they talk about, I mean."

Marthe waved her hand widely. "Smart gal," she muttered and disappeared.

Rose came upstairs, and she and I went into Elise's room.

"Gladys has arrived, and the situation is well in hand, I gather," Elise said. She was frowning. "Gladys, Gladys, Gladys, I haven't seen her for ages, but . . ." She sighed, "Oh, well."

"Is Madame Oxney very well-heeled?" I asked. "Not that it's any of my damned business, of course."

"And how," Elise said. "Simply rolling. I could live like the Duchess of Windsor on what the Oxney spends for clothes. Oh, dear, and I'd look so much better in them." She gazed wistfully into space, then jerked herself back. "And how are you today, baby?" she said, pulling Rose down beside her on the bed.

"Okay, Weez." Then she blushed. "I try to remember I'm grown up, but I forget."

Marthe came streaking up the stairs and into Elise's room. She shut the door and stood in front of it, panting and rolling her eyes. "My Lord," she gasped breathlessly. "Cassidy's down there asking Gladys for an alibi for Monday night. He wants to know why in hell she endorsed those notes over to Pauline instead of marking them paid. What goes, do you suppose? Anne's old notes, I mean."

Elise pulled herself erect. She frowned and put a long, white hand up to her forehead. "Damn!" she said. "I know something, and I can't remember what."

"Marthe, maybe you left too soon," I said. "You should have stayed and heard the rest."

Marthe grinned widely. "Aren't you a one? Eavesdropping in the back parlor! What an idea."

"And a very good one, too. I want to keep track of Cassidy. What did Mrs. O. say about the notes?"

Marthe groaned. "Plenty and strictly nothing. She just prattled on, and said she didn't know the difference between endorsing and marking paid and that the Judge gave her hell and that she spent the money Pauline paid her in riotous living and for Cassidy not to dare to go near the Judge. She's had enough trouble. And she was right at home in her own little bed and hadn't seen Pauline for weeks. Her bed, incidentally, is peach satin and white and gold wood. It bulges, just like Gladys."

Elise made an unladylike sound indicating disbelief. "Gladys is lying, my pets—about the notes, I mean." She turned to me. "Mrs. O. was the Judge's secretary for years and years, and some say that she was more than secretary, if you get my dirty meaning." She leered. "When his pore old wife finally went to her reward, he made an honest woman of our Gladys, and the story is that she writes all his opinions. After all, the old boy must be over eighty. The hell Gladys doesn't know the difference between endorsing and marking paid. She's a smart one."

CHAPTER 12

Gladys spent the rest of the morning giving orders. Her maids dashed through the house with lightning efficiency, and soon all was in the well-known apple pie order with fires burning merrily in all the grates, furniture dusted, beds made, ashtrays washed, bathrooms scrubbed, and rugs vacuumed.

Gladys left at one o'clock to keep a luncheon engagement but she said that we were to eat a good lunch which would be ready at one-thirty and that the maids would spend the afternoon doing anything that was needed. "Just tell them, darlings, and they'll get your dinner, too, and I'll be back later, and if that Cassidy bothers you, be sure to let me know."

Sophie, dressed to the teeth in a dowdy gold creation and too much junk jewelry, was really enjoying herself. "Well, this is something like," she said. "I mean this good service. Now that Pauline's passed away, maybe we can live like human beings instead of church mice."

"On the income from a hundred thousand bucks? Don't be silly," Marthe said. "Do you know what the taxes are on this place?"

Sophie pursed her lips and put down her fork. The Oxney hired help was in the kitchen. "You can't tell, Marthe. Maybe Pauline put too low a valuation on our holdings."

Marthe grinned. "You certainly sound like an heiress, Sophie. How about Mr. Brown?"

"Don't be indelicate, Marthe," Sophie said, with a leer in the direction of the maid who had come in to bring the dessert.

Cassidy had gone about his business, but one of his men was still holding down the hall. After lunch we all went upstairs, and I undressed to take a nap so that I would be fresh and bright to receive my guest, Mrs. Graham. I was again wondering what her proffered help meant when Marthe came dashing into my room.

"Come and look," she said. "There's a whole big bunch of battleships going out."

I got up and put on a robe and followed Marthe into Rose's room, whose windows overlooked the bay. The wind had blown the fog away, and the view was superb. Alcatraz, the famous "Rock," stood out like something on a picture postcard, and an enormous blue-grey battleship was just passing it. To the east, we could see another one, and as we stood watching two smaller ships—probably destroyers—came under the Bay bridge in front of Yerba Buena Island.

"Gosh, aren't they wonderful?" Marthe said, hanging over my shoulder.

"I wish we could get into Pauline's room. The view's much better from there. The glasses are in there, too."

Elise joined us at the window. "Nice little things, aren't they? I wonder where they're going." She gave me a poke in the back, and I turned around and looked at her. She winked a terrific gay wink at me. Her Lieutenant was probably on one of the ships.

"Let's go up on the roof," Rose said. "We can see better there."

I stuck my head into Sophie's room as we passed her door. "Come on up on the roof, Sophie. There's a whole lot of battleships going out."

She was sitting at her desk writing, and she looked up as I spoke. "No, thanks," she said. "I . . . I don't want to."

I shrugged my shoulders and followed the other girls up the steep flight of stairs leading to the little cupola. A door opposite the stairs opened onto the flat roof, which was edged with a wooden battlement, a bit of whimsy on the part of Paul Moreau which had given the house its name of Moreau's Castle.

The wind was blowing what I privately considered to be a gale, but we stood at the north edge of the roof for a long time watching the impressive parade of the great ships. Down at the west end of the bay, there were a number of things floating on the water.

"What are those things?" I asked Marthe. "Those black things."

"Buoys on the submarine net," she said. "See those two tugs?" I nodded. "Well, they pull the net back so that the ships can go through. If you stay here, you can see them put it back."

Beyond the tugs and the submarine net, the great orange towers of the Golden Gate Bridge reached proudly up to the clear, chilly blue sky.

"The tugs'll have to put the net back without me," I said. "I'm freezing to death. Sophie stayed inside. Too cold, I guess."

"She's afraid of heights," Marthe shouted through the wind. "Look down."

I looked and stepped back quickly from the edge of the roof. The drop down three stories to the small back garden was distinctly unnerving.

"I don't blame her," I said and went back to take my nap.

At four o'clock I was dressed and waiting in the redwood-paneled room for Mrs. Graham. I was in a swivet of nerves and had been unable to sleep at all, because the more I thought about Mrs. Graham, the more I wondered what in heaven's name she wanted and how she could help me.

Gladys' maids had fixed a nice tea tray for me, and Marthe and Rose had agreed to give me a clear field for my guest.

With my eyes glued to the clock, I waited. Four-ten, four-fifteen, four-twenty-five, and no Mrs. Graham. I poured myself a cup of strong, cold tea and ate a couple of pieces of brown bread which were smeared with a delicious concoction of marmalade and cream cheese.

I went over to the window and looked out. There were a few people in the street, and a man in plainclothes stood just inside the gate. But no Mrs. Graham.

At five o'clock, I told Gladys' maid that she could take the tray. Apparently my friend wasn't coming. I was sick with disappointment.

Then at five-twenty, she turned up. Cassidy's man let her in very reluctantly, and I had a little argument with him to convince him that Mrs. Graham was a friend and not a member of the press.

The nervous disappointment on my face must have been quite obvious.

"I'm so sorry I was late, Mrs. Moreau," my train friend exclaimed as she came in. "It's just a shame, but my last tire gave out, and I couldn't get a cab for love nor money, and I had to come on the trolley. I know I should have telephoned, but I didn't want to stop."

I smiled shakily and reassured Mrs. G. that it was quite all right.

She was a nice-looking, compactly built woman of about forty. Her hair was grey and beautifully groomed above snapping brown eyes and clear olive skin. Her black suit and hat and sable scarf were extremely smart.

"How awful about the tire," I said. "Can it be fixed?"

She shook her head and smiled wryly. "No," she said. "It's gone." She shrugged her shoulders. "Well, *c'est la guerre*. A little walking won't do me a bit of harm anyway."

We exchanged a few amenities—such as her expressions of sympathy about Pauline—and I offered her tea which she refused, and she commented upon the charms of the room and the age of the house which, apparently, was very great for California.

"I never even knew it was here," she said. "You see, I live away out in St. Francis Wood clear across town, and I grew up in Dolores Street which is in the Mission so I don't know much about this neighborhood."

I smiled grimly and wondered when, if ever, the woman would get to the point. She took the cigarette which I offered her.

Finally, she cleared her throat gently. "Mrs. Moreau, I wonder if you could show me a picture of Pauline Moreau. Of course, I saw the newspaper picture, but I want to be sure before I tell you my story."

"Of course," I said standing up. "Come on in the back parlor. There's a picture of Pauline in there."

We went down the hall, and as I opened the door to my listening post, Mrs. Graham laughed aloud.

"Good Lord," she said, "this is like something out of a book. The horsehair and all, I mean. And I do believe this is a genuine hair wreath, isn't it?"

I nodded. "Yes, I guess it is. This is the photograph of Pauline," I said, pointing to a silver-framed picture on top of the huge ebony piano. Mrs. Graham picked it up in her black-gloved hand and studied it carefully. "Was she a small woman, Mrs. Moreau?"

"Yes," I said. "She couldn't have been more than five feet tall at the most, and she weighed about ninety pounds. She was really tiny, but well proportioned, too."

Mrs. Graham sighed. "That's the one, all right." She put the photograph back. "Shall we go back by that nice fire? Then I'll tell my tale."

We settled ourselves on the rose damask sofa in the living room, and Mrs. Graham began to talk.

"I'll have to bore you with a lot of background," she said, "but this is such a coincidence that I think I'd better. You see, Mrs. Moreau, my husband has a blueprint business away down in what we call the Tenderloin." She smiled. "It's a section of town off of Market Street, and it's full of rather dingy hotels and apartment houses and bars, and office space is cheap there. Because we need a good deal of room for our work, we chose that neighborhood."

"I see."

"I've kept the books for my husband for years. At first I did it because we couldn't afford to hire anybody, and recently I've done it because we just can't get anybody, so I go down there with him nearly every afternoon. You see, we work at night."

She explained that her husband had messengers go around to architects' and engineers' offices late in the afternoon and pick up the drawings to be blueprinted at night so that they could be delivered the next morning.

"We leave the office usually around midnight or a little before, and it was leaving the office that I used to see Miss Moreau, although I didn't, of course, know who she was."

I was throbbing with excitement. I was going to find out where Pauline went at night.

Mrs. Graham gave me a long look. "I hate to be so long-winded, but I can't help it. You see, Mrs. Moreau, the newspaper didn't say a thing about her having been out of this house the night she was killed, but she was. I saw her at about a quarter of twelve, and I saw her very plainly, too. I recognized her from the many other times I've seen her." She shrugged her shoulders. "Of course, I suppose I should have gone to the police with this, and I will, if you want me to, but as long as I knew you, I thought I'd tell you first."

"Where was she when you saw her, Mrs. Graham?" I stood up and went over to the fireplace. I was suddenly cold all over.

"Going into her house."

"Her house?" I gulped. What was Pauline doing with a house in the

Tenderloin?

Mrs. Graham nodded her head very vigorously. "Yes. That's right. At least, I think it must be her house. I've seen her going in and out lots of times, and of course, I've been almost consumed with curiosity to know who she was. It's such a crazy place for a house." She leaned forward. "It's a little, tiny, narrow two-story house away down in the two-hundred block in Leavenworth Street. It's surrounded by these awful hotels and apartments, and our loft where we do our blueprinting is two doors up the street. I've been dying to find out who owned it for years, and occasionally I've even thought I'd go up to the county assessor's office and look at those maps, but somehow I never did. I tell you, I almost dropped dead when I saw Pauline Moreau's picture in the paper and recognized her."

She went on to tell me about the house. It was, it seemed, an exquisite little grey stone building, rather French in design with a door and one window on the first floor and two windows on the second, all of them heavily curtained in stretched curtains. "The house comes right out to the street," she continued, "and those curtains are simply beautiful. They're fine embroidered linen with cut-work and Venetian point insets. The little house looks like a gardenia in a cabbage patch in that neighborhood."

I sat down with a thud. "It's simply unbelievable," I said.

"I know. You must think I'm crazy, but I'm not. I was talking about the house in the office one day, and one of our men told me that it was built originally by some vice king who had perfect taste. It seems that the vice king—I can't remember his name—couldn't stand the thought of living in one of those dingy places down there, but he wanted to keep an eye on his business, so he built the little house about thirty years ago."

I swallowed. "Good Lord. Pauline and a *vice* king!"

Mrs. Graham laughed lightly. "Don't worry about that. She wasn't tied up with the vice king. He died in San Quentin a long time ago. It seems that we had one of our periodic cleanups back in about 1915 and the Barbary Coast and the Tenderloin were presumably closed up. The man who built the little house was caught in the reform wave."

"Well," I said breathlessly, "that's something. Did you ever see anyone else going in and out of the house?"

She shook her head slowly from side to side. "Never. I never saw anyone except Miss Moreau, but of course, there's a back entrance."

Mrs. Graham and I talked for a while longer, although I can't remember to this day what we talked about. My head was simply whirling, but I did manage to thank her for coming to me instead of to the police. "If you don't mind keeping still about this for a day or two, I'd certainly appreciate it," I said. "I'd like to talk to our lawyer first."

That was all perfectly agreeable to Mrs. Graham, and we finally said goodbye to each other at the front door with mutual hopes that we would see each other soon.

I went back into the living room to warm my hands at the fire. In that little house in the Tenderloin lay the solution to Pauline's death, I felt sure.

Marthe came in. "Your friend came, didn't she? What'd she want?"

I debated for several minutes. Should I tell Marthe my juicy bit of information, or save it for Cassidy?

Marthe won.

"She told me where Pauline went at night."

"WHAT!" Marthe's brown eyes were round with excitement. "Really? Where?"

"To her house in the Tenderloin."

Marthe let out a long, shrill whistle. Then she thumped her hand forcefully on the mantel shelf and caused a couple of Victorian vases to jiggle precariously.

"Wow," she said. "Where is it? It's a damned good thing I pinched those keys. Now I can get into the place before the police do."

I nearly fainted. "*You* pinched the keys. My Lord, Marthe. Why?"

"Never mind why. You just tell me where the place is. I've got to get into it."

"Is that what you went into Pauline's room for? The keys, I mean? While we were waiting for the police?"

"Right the first time," she said, jiggling in impatience. "Where's the house, Hilda, my pet? Come on, give."

I suddenly became stubborn. "Nothing doing. You give me the keys."

Marthe swept her hand through her hair and glared at me. "What's come over you? Don't you want to help us? I've got to get into that house."

I made my decision. "Very well," I said. "We'll go together—if we can get out of this house without the police stopping us or trailing us."

She shook her head impatiently. "You're a pain in the neck, sweetie pants, but I guess we'll have to hang together. We can get out of this place all right. I know how. We'll do it tonight after the others have gone to bed." She groaned. "But it'd be a whole lot easier if I went alone. Don't you trust me?"

I grinned. "Nope. We'll go together."

With Nanette threatening me, I thought I'd better look out for my own interests and keep a close eye on the united Moreau sisters. I felt pretty sure by that time that they wouldn't hesitate for two seconds to protect themselves at my expense.

Marthe and I agreed to meet in the basement at some time around eleven-thirty. "There are gates in the back fences. We can go through our yard and clear down to the Winships' and then into Francisco Street. Eventually, we can get down to Columbus Avenue and get a cab in front of one of those nightclubs."

"Okay," I said. "It's a deal."

One of Cassidy's men stuck his head in the door. "Lieutenant Cassidy wants to talk to Mrs. Moreau," he said.

I looked at him. His voice had been cold and detached. I licked my lips nervously.

CHAPTER 13

Cassidy sat at his old place at the round center table. He did not get up when I came in, but merely indicated with his hand that I was to sit in the chair opposite him. His eyes were as unbelieving as I had ever seen them. Cold, blue ice. He had a folded telegram on the table in front of him.

The silence got the best of me. "Well, you want to see me. What's it all about?" My voice shook, and I was furious.

"I want you to tell me, Mrs. Moreau, just exactly how Miss Pauline Moreau threatened you. I want you to tell me what she was going to do if you persisted in getting the trust dissolved." He tapped the telegram lightly.

I gasped. "I don't know what you're talking about. She didn't threaten me. She threatened to lock up Elise, as you know, but as a matter of fact, she said that maybe we could work something out. Those were her words. How could she threaten me?"

My breathing was uncomfortably fast, and I shivered involuntarily. Nanette . . . Cassidy . . .

"I think you can tell me that," he said flatly. "In any case, I'll find out in a day or two, but I'd like to know now." He unfolded the telegram slowly and shoved it toward me. "This was sent to me through the mail. I would like to hear what you have to say about it."

I could almost hear the bones rattle in my hands as I took the telegram. I read it. It was dated Sunday, but delivered Monday morning. It was addressed to Pauline. It came from Cleveland.

"BELIEVE WE HAVE OBTAINED DESIRED INFORMATION ON HILDA BLAKE MOREAU. HOWEVER, OTHER PARTY IS DEMANDING LARGE SUM BEFORE AFFIDAVITS ARE MADE. WRITING YOU AIRMAIL TO ADDRESS REQUESTED. WILL AWAIT YOUR DECISION BEFORE PROCEEDING FURTHER.
       SHANLEY INVESTIGATORS, INC."

My throat was paralyzed for seconds. When I was finally able to speak, my voice was a silly croak.

"But this is crazy. I don't understand it at all. There's simply no information she could get on me. My life is an open book. She was trying to cook something up."

Cassidy's cold blue eyes got colder. "That's your story, is it?" I nodded.

"You know I have only to wait for the letter," he continued. I nodded dumbly again. "And I know it hasn't come yet, because I've had a close eye on the mail box. Now, why don't you come clean?"

I swallowed with great difficulty. "I swear to you that I haven't the vaguest idea what this is all about." I leaned forward. "Somebody sent you that wire through the mail. Don't you realize that was just done to implicate me?"

He snorted silently. "Maybe. But maybe somebody in this house found the wire and is *afraid* of you."

"But that's ridiculous," I said urgently. "Where's the envelope? The one it was mailed to you in. Maybe we can tell from the handwriting who did it."

Cassidy's mouth twisted. "It was tested for fingerprints—there were none—and it was addressed with block printing that doesn't indicate anything anyway."

"But when was it mailed? I mean who could get out of the house to mail it? We've all been penned up here for days."

He shrugged lightly. "There's a mailbox across the street. Somebody could have gone over there at night, and Miss Holmes and Doctor Moreau have been allowed to go about their business as usual."

I picked up the wire and looked at it again. "Address requested." I knew what that meant. It meant Pauline's house in the Tenderloin. Then I made a quick decision.

I had been very close to telling Cassidy about that house, but I couldn't. I'd have to go there and see that airmail letter. Somebody in the Moreau house was trying to give me a good strong motive for murdering Pauline, and if the letter did contain damning information, I simply had to get it and keep it out of Cassidy's hands until such time as the real murderer was caught. The unity among the Moreau sisters was so strong that I knew they'd welcome the chance to throw me to the wolves.

"Listen," I said. "You'll just have to wait for the letter. I can't tell you any more about this than you already know. I only know that I've never done anything in my life that Pauline could use for a threat."

I got up and started out of the room on legs that wobbled precariously.

"The other people in this house have had their motives for a good many years, Mrs. Moreau. The fun didn't start until after you got here, did it?"

The cold and damp had moved clear into the center of my mind and body.

CHAPTER 14

I wasn't safe anymore. I was in the soup with the rest of the family, but I was much worse off than anyone else. I'd seen enough to know that they would all lie and lie and lie for each other, but one of them had mailed that wire to Cassidy in order to implicate me. It could, of course, have been the actual murderer, or it could just as easily have been one of the others working to protect her sisters.

I racked my brain to think of some way of getting into Pauline's house without Marthe. I even calmly contemplated hitting her over the head and taking the keys away from her. She was frantic to get into the house, and I had no way of knowing whether she wanted to get the Shanley Investigators' letter concerning Hilda Blake Moreau or something else that Pauline had on her.

Dinner was, for me, a hideous ordeal. I had to sit there and eat with a lot of women, all of whom were probably my enemies. Anne, Sophie, Janet Holmes, Marthe, Gladys Oxney, Rose, Elise, and down in the basement that horrible old woman. I was grateful that at least she had stayed in the basement and not gone blabbing to Cassidy. She apparently had a good idea of what Pauline was planning for me, and if she'd just keep quiet until I could get hold of that letter, I'd feel a whole lot better. I also had high hopes of being able to find evidence that would point to someone else in the family or to Janet Holmes or Gladys Oxney. In fact, I was ready to fight back with the same weapons that the perfidious telegram-mailer was using on me.

Elise nudged me. "Why so silent, baby? Cassidy do something to you?"

She still looked very handsome and gay, and I quite suddenly hated her. I hated all of them, and I wished urgently that I could say so and storm out of the room.

"No," I said. "I'm tired."

"Your company wear you out?" Sophie said with a nasty, mincing smile on her over-painted face.

"Yes," I said, "that's right."

"But what did she want? Why did she call on you?"

I took my time about swallowing a piece of lamb chop. I also looked at Marthe. Her face was carefully blank.

"To offer sympathy and to invite me to stay with her if I didn't want to stay here," I lied cheerfully. "But I have to stay here."

"Well," Elise drawled, "it isn't such a bad old dump now that Pauline's gone. It could be a lot worse."

Sophie glared at her, and everybody else laughed. Sophie was so damned "genteel" anyway. She'd been trying to act for the last twenty-four hours as though a beloved sister had died a natural death and left a bereaved family behind her. It wasn't very convincing, but I imagined that that was what Mr. Brown expected of her.

My head ached from Gladys' babbling about nothing. The dear kind friend was a pain in the neck, and Janet Holmes' careful detachment was another one. I excused myself early and went upstairs and got into bed. At least I'd be warm and comfortable until it was time for me to get up and go down to Pauline's clandestine menage.

But the hours from eight until ten-thirty dragged by like painful years. I thought and thought and thought about everything that had happened since I'd come into the house, and nowhere among my chaotic thoughts could I find an answer to the problem of who had murdered Pauline.

If only I could get into that house without Marthe.... Over and over again. I knew the street, and I had a vague idea of how to get out of the old house through the basement.

At ten-thirty I dragged myself out of bed and washed my face and then came back to dress in a warm tweed suit and sweater and sensible shoes. I was happy to hear that the house was quiet, and I was fairly sure that everyone else in the place had gone to bed.

I had just lit a cigarette when Marthe, also dressed for the street, popped silently into my room. Her brown eyes were round.

"Listen," she whispered, "the damnedest thing has happened. Somebody's taken the keys!"

I did a mental faint. "Good God, Marthe. When? How?"

"I don't know. I had them hidden in a chimney closet in the basement. I'm pretty sure the cops didn't find them, because it's a very tricky place. You can't see it unless you know it's there, but of course, everybody else in the place knows about it. We've used it to hide things ever since we were children."

I stood up and walked around the room in a frenzy of nervousness and frustration. "Damn," I muttered. "Are you sure they're gone?"

She nodded hard. "I just looked. It makes me sick."

I had a brain wave. "If somebody took those keys, Marthe, she knows about the house. Was anybody hanging around the hall or the dining room while Mrs. Graham was here this afternoon?"

Marthe shrugged. "I don't know. I was upstairs with Sophie until I heard the gate bang after your company left. I don't know who was eavesdropping, if any."

"What are we going to do? I've got to get in that house."

She blinked. "Me, too, sister." She sighed. "Well, tomorrow I'll have to get busy and steal the damned keys back. I could scream. Cassidy's going to find that place in a few days. It's a cinch other people have seen Pauline going in there. Your Mrs. Graham can't be the only one who saw her."

Marthe and I smoked a couple of cigarettes and groaned and cursed fluently. And then I made my plans. I was going to get into the little grey house if I had to batter down the door to do it, and I was going to get into it without Marthe. I had a bad time getting her to get out and leave me, and in order to convince her that I was home for the evening, I had to get into bed again which was a great waste of time. But she finally departed, still cursing, and I got up and dressed in the dark.

I put on my hat and a top coat and a pair of well-fitting leather gloves for correct modern burglarious procedure, and in my big brown bag, I put my flashlight which would not only provide illumination but might come in handy for breaking in a door or two. I tied my oxfords together and slung them over my arm.

Finally, I opened the door to the hall and stood listening with every nerve end in my body. Except for its customary creaking the house was dark and silent. I hung over the stair rail and peered into the hall below. No cop, thank the Lord. But I had no doubt that there was one somewhere around the place, and I'd have to be careful not to rouse him from his rest.

I crept down the stairs without mishap and stood listening. Still silence and the dark. Then I started down the hall in the direction of the dining room. Quite as suddenly I stopped. With iron self-control, I kept from screaming aloud. I had run into the damnable little illegal gas heater, and if my leg wasn't broken, it felt like it.

The heater crashed over on its side, and I stood waiting for policemen to come running and for the lights to go on.

Nothing happened. I rubbed my leg and kept going. I got safely past the turn in the basement stairs and then I stopped to wait again. There was no line of light under Nanette's door, and I knew I'd be comparatively safe if I could just get through the ink-black basement and open the north door without a lot of racket.

Then I stopped with my heart somewhere in the region of my tonsils.

Somewhere across the dusty, untidy basement, there was a stir of sound. A scuttling noise. Then it stopped.

A splinter in the old stairs dragged at my stocking, and I said farewell to nylons for the duration—my last pair.

The scuttling noise came again.

Then I fled terrified to the door and wrenched it open and shut it behind me without any care at all. That scuttling noise had been a rat, I was sure. And I'd rather meet a murderer in a dark basement than a rat any day.

I stumbled and ran across the garden to the battered old board fence. I'd made so much noise that I really had little hope of getting away from the Moreau house, but I had to try. In foggy dampness I went up and down the fence three times before I finally found the gate, and when I opened it, it creaked as though in torture. I shut it behind me and walked over somebody's wet lawn, and then I felt and fumbled some more until I finally found another gate. Wet bushes lashed my face and snatched at my clothes, and my sodden feet felt as though they might easily break off at the ankles, but there was no one behind me.

Safe on the other side of the high board fence, I stopped for breath. The house directly in back of the Moreau's was dark, but there was a light upstairs in the house which I had to pass to get down to the next street. I panted in excitement and nervousness. And then I stopped to put on my shoes. They stuck, and I had to tug and stamp to get them on over my soaking stockings.

The Moreaus' gate creaked. My heart lurched and thumped. Was somebody after me? Or had I left the gate open?

I didn't stop to learn. I ran blindly down a concrete path and then down some steps to a sidewalk. And then I stopped to look around under the pale glow of a dimmed-out streetlight.

I was on a sidewalk which was raised up some twelve feet above the street. Thick, glistening ivy covered the terrace between the sidewalk and the wall, and grey stone balustrades marked steps leading down to the street. To the left was the steep hill on which the cable cars ran. To my right, the terraced sidewalk stretched off into the fog and trees. I chose the right.

I ran as fast and as silently as I could until I was under the shelter of the trees. I stopped to listen. There were no footsteps behind me. Just water dripping off the trees and the dreary wail of foghorns down on the Bay and pale lights shimmering across the water to mark the great shipyards that Marthe had pointed out to me.

I walked on down the sidewalk and down some steps, and then the street turned to the right and went on up the hill. There was a steep wall in front of me, and I had to follow the sidewalk around to the right. When I came to the cross street, I looked at the signs. Chestnut Street. The Moreaus' street. And the street I was on was Leavenworth. Pauline's street. I ran frantically to look at the numbers on some houses up above. Pauline's house was in the two-hundred block. Maybe I could walk.

I couldn't. The houses near Chestnut were marked 2400 and something. And Marthe had said something about getting a taxi down on Columbus.

Down. Well, I'd go down the hill on Chestnut Street and hope to find transportation eventually.

I did. I found a taxi in front of a nightclub and told the driver to take me to the four-hundred block on Leavenworth Street. He undoubtedly thought I was crazy and would, of course, remember me, but there was nothing else I could do.

We bumped around on car tracks past stores and bars and apartment buildings that looked remote and dismal in the dimmed-out city, and then we went through a long, noisy, white-tiled tunnel, and after a while we swung back to the right, and the driver asked me where I wanted to go in the four-hundred block on Leavenworth. I said I wasn't sure and to let me out anywhere in that block.

I paid him and stood waiting until he drove away, after he had looked at me carefully. Then I started to walk in what I hoped was the right direction.

I hadn't gone a half block before a sailor tried to pick me up. I threatened the poor boy with the police, and he shrugged his shoulders and walked on. "But this is no place for a nice girl," he said seriously. "You better let me walk down to Market with you."

"No," I snapped. "Beat it, or I'll yell for the cops."

A half block further on, I had to deal in like fashion with a soldier and then another sailor, and I was getting more and more frantic with each step. If the armed services of the United States didn't leave me alone, my long, crazy trip would be useless, and I didn't know anyway how in heaven's name I was going to get back.

I found the little house easily. As Mrs. Graham had said, it looked like a gardenia in a cabbage patch, snuggled between two tall shabby buildings. Elegant carving ornamented the cornice that marked the top of its flat roof. An elaborate wrought-iron grill covered the glass of the recessed front door and the largish window on the left. Well-polished brass gleamed from the doorknob and a slit for the mail and the doorbell.

I darted up onto the step and rang the bell. Far off in the darkened house, I heard it buzz. I rang two or three times more without result.

Then I examined the door with care. The grill was fine, its bars not more than an inch and a half apart. The glass looked like the very best quality plate glass. I hadn't a chance in the world of breaking it with my flashlight, even if I could get it between the bars, which I couldn't.

With mounting excitement, I walked to the corner and around to the right until I came to the alley which was shadowy and frightening under the feeble light of a streetlamp at the far end.

I found the back door. A narrow, discreet door with a brass plate marked "tradesman's entrance." The brass was unpolished and the little grill that covered a two-foot square piece of glass looked old and rusty. Then I looked more closely. The door was ajar. My throat hammered dryly.

Holding my breath, I pushed the door open. It was inky black inside. Reluctantly and very quietly, I stepped over the threshold. The noise of my heart's beating and my breathing roared in my ears.

Ten thousand pale silver stars broke loose in black velvet. I fell into them.

CHAPTER 15

The stars faded, and a black dawn came. My head ached, and my mouth and throat felt like very dry, old sandpaper. I sat up slowly. My leg hurt and I rubbed it slowly, horrified at the size of the welt on my shin.

It took me a long time to remember where I was and what had happened. I was all mixed up with something about our cheerful apartment in Cleveland, and the basement of my grandmother's house in Chagrin Falls and the hall of the Moreau house in Chestnut Street.

I felt my head gingerly. There was a big lump right on top, but my felt stroller had probably saved me a fractured skull. I hadn't fallen, I knew that. Somebody had hit me. Hard, too.

My brain wasn't much good. It felt mossy and detached as though the blow had separated its various parts. But I was in the silent dark somewhere, and I'd have to find out where, and if I could, I'd have to carry out the rest of my task. There was something important I had come to find. Ah, yes. The detective's letter. "Address requested."

Slowly and painfully I felt around the floor. Cold concrete. My bag. I pulled it toward me. The flashlight. With shaky, uncoordinated hands, I pulled it out of the bag and laboriously pushed at the catch until I got it lighted.

I wasn't, strangely enough, afraid. I was quite sure that whoever had hit me had gone away. Out the back door where I came in.

Back door. Yes, yes, of course. Pauline's back door in the little house. I waved the light around. I was in a little concrete back entrance at the foot of four steps which led up to another door.

I got onto my feet and tested my weaving legs by climbing up the stairs. The door was open. There was a small, well-appointed white-tiled kitchen in front of me.

Then I went back and closed the door to the alley and the kitchen door. This place was too popular, I thought muzzily. Entirely too many people going in and out. I wanted the house to myself.

The kitchen was clean and bare and very, very quiet. I could see that easily with the light from my torch. And there was something very interesting about the window that overlooked the alley. I went closer.

It was blacked out. There was a tight-fitting piece of black beaverboard set into the frame. The stiff, white organdy curtains looked funny against the cardboard. I smiled, and my head hurt, and I was very happy. I could have lights. I snapped on the switch and took a good look around me.

Stove, refrigerator, sink, well-planned cupboards, white-tiled walls, well waxed blue linoleum, white enameled center table. Fine, fine, I thought. Nice and clean.

I found a glass in a cupboard over the sink and a big bottle of cold water in the ice box, and I drank and drank and drank. I felt much better, and my brain began to function in a more orderly fashion.

Someone had been in the house, and had hit me over the head in order to make a getaway. The "someone" was probably a "she" from the old Moreau house who had succeeded in stealing Pauline's keys from Marthe, and I hoped madly that I had succeeded in scaring her away with my doorbell ringing before she had a chance to find what I was after—or better yet, what *she* was after. I felt quite sure that the good housekeeping of which I saw evidence in the kitchen was not done by a servant who lived in the house. The Number One Prowler would, undoubtedly, have roused any sleeper in the place. I felt quite safe. I also felt nervous and hurried.

The swinging door from the kitchen led into a small, windowless pantry. I snapped on the light and paused fleetingly to admire the glass and china on the shelves. Spode Copeland bone china, unless I missed my guess.

The little oval dining room beyond was a gem. Heavy white and gold brocade hangings under a gracefully carved gold cornice covered more nice black cardboard. I snapped on the lights and gasped.

The walls were paneled in white canvas with the moldings picked out in faded gilt. The ceiling was domed and carved and exquisite. Dull blue brocade covered the four exquisite little French chairs set around the small oval fruitwood table. The oval rug was fine Aubusson in pale, pastel colors mellowed with age. It was the loveliest little room of its type that I had ever seen.

Double doors led me into a tiny hall. My luck held. It was blacked out, too. Small blocks of black and white marble made the floor. The light came from a glistening little chandelier. Two pale grey marble consoles flanked the small staircase leading to the upper floor.

The small and very formal drawing room was as elegant and beautiful as the rest of the house. The walls were paneled in pale apricot brocade with a small pattern of gold fleur-de-lis. The small sofas and bergères and cabinets filled with tiny Dresden figurines were in perfect scale. Tiny and elegant, just like their former owner. There were little fruitwood tables and the elaborate taffeta hangings and a pale green and white and gold Aubusson carpet. All the things were so beautiful and so fine that I found myself smiling.

But the rooms were cold and precious and remote. They were quite perfectly proportioned and entirely without heart or warmth. There, too, they resembled Pauline.

Quickly I opened the little marquetry desk. It was as bare of papers as a desk in a museum.

Then I went back to the hall. The box beneath the mail slot was empty. I went up the narrow stairs, my footsteps inaudible on the thick green carpet. The little upper hall had three doors set into the paneled walls. I opened the one near a hand-decorated half-circle console. Without a qualm, I switched on the lights.

A bedroom, all French elegance with its pale blue walls and white satin bed. A tiny fruitwood powder table with its little center mirror propped open. Another little marquetry table laden with bottles of terribly expensive perfume and little Dresden jars of fine-smelling creams and an enameled powder box.

One paneled door led to a closet, the light of which snapped on automatically as I opened it. A wave of delicious perfume whooshed out at me, and I stood gasping at the long rows of beautiful, beautiful clothes. There was a preponderance of cream and powder blue and apricot and pale green satin and literally miles of Alençon lace. Negligees, house coats. Dozens of them for Pauline to wear in her beautiful little house. There were a few beautifully made black things, too. Long crepe and chiffon dinner dresses and a couple of street-length things and safe inside a cellophane bag a dark mink coat.

"Good God! How did she do it?"

I jumped and looked behind me into the little bedroom. Then I grinned. I had spoken aloud, and no wonder.

It was fine to stand there in openmouthed amazement looking at Pauline's things, but that wasn't what I had come for.

I walked across the room, carefully skirting a rose and blue brocaded chaise longue and opened the other closet. Then I really gasped.

A good strong smell of tweeds fanned my face. Before me hung a long row of male garments. Tweeds, gabardines, black broadcloth, and camel's hair, all of fine quality. Fine enough to have been made by a good tailor.

I reached into the first coat that hung in front of me and turned a breast pocket inside out and read the tailor's label.

The coat had been made by Jameson & Sons of Los Angeles, California, for Mr. John Hamilton on October 29, 1940.

Mr. John Hamilton.

And who was Mr. Hamilton, and where was he, and how long had Pauline known him and . . .?

Dazed and weak, I turned away from the closet and marched purposefully into the hall and opened the second door.

A super ultra little bathroom with a half dozen luxurious fixtures crowded into a small space. They were of an outmoded type, but none the less elegant against the white marble walls and floor.

Door Number Three was it.

It opened into a small room with plain white walls, a linoleum floor, another black boarded window, and two large dark green metal desks. Filing cabinets lined one wall. A covered typewriter stood on a stand near one of the desks. Three—count them—telephones stood on the other desk.

And strewed from one end of the room to the other were papers. File drawers gaped open and spewed forth papers. Papers of all colors, sizes, and shapes. Typewritten, printed, and handwritten. Pink, blue, green and white.

I picked up a long, narrow pink paper. "SOLD," it said, "Merrill, Lynch, Pierce & Cassatt, 5,000 Newport Industries, price 8½, December 30, 1940." The extension read "$40,625.00, net credit, $39,439.00." In an oval at the lower left-hand corner was typed the legend, "Moreau Trust, c/o, Miss Pauline Moreau, Box 427, Ferry Post Office, San Francisco, California."

I itched to take off my gloves so that I could really feel my way about, but I'd read enough mysteries to know better. I went over to the desk. A manila folder was tumbled open.

I picked up a piece of legal sized paper. "Appraisal, Moreau Trust, July 31, 1942." Bonds, bonds, bonds, stocks, stocks, cash on hand, real estate, Hamilton notes. I read on and on and on, trembling to see the total on the next page and half afraid to look.

I did finally. It was typed very neatly and underlined with two lines.

"GRAND TOTAL............................$5,172,436.97"

I sat down. I had to. *There were over five million dollars in the Moreau Trust.*

And up on the corner of Chestnut Street, Pauline Moreau and her sisters lived in a cold, inconvenient old house with one decrepit servant and wore clothes from the budget shops of department stores and drove old cars and starved for an education.

Grinding my teeth in anger, I looked around the room.

The person who slugged me had messed up this room, and, I was afraid, might very well have taken the letter I came to get. I'd have a fine time in the midst of all these papers, but I'd have to look through them and find out something about the Moreaus and their trust and the mysterious Mr. Hamilton.

I started on the appraisal folder in front of me. It told me very little except that the Moreaus had five million dollars.

The long, narrow colored papers were all confirmations from brokers concerning the purchase and sale of securities, but as I piled them up neatly, I took a more careful look at one of them. In the oval, there was a different typewritten name. It read, "John Hamilton and Pauline M. Hamilton," and above it was a rubber-stamped legend, AS JOINT TENANTS WITH RIGHT OF SURVIVORSHIP AND NOT AS TENANTS IN COMMON.

Pauline was married to the man!

I went over to the file drawers and frantically pawed through rows of manila folders. Back through the years they marched. Clear back to 1927. The folders contained business letters to banks, insurance companies, brokers, and real estate firms, many of them addressed to John Hamilton and quite a number of them to Pauline M. Hamilton.

If Pauline Moreau hadn't already been taken care of by someone else, I would have strangled her then and there with my bare hands.

"The bitch," I muttered venomously over and over again. "The bitch."

She had been married for fifteen years. She had controlled millions....

I almost screamed aloud in frustration and wild, unleashed hatred.

Then I went back to work. I found the drawer that contained the monthly appraisals of the Moreau Trust and of the Hamilton account. With widening eyes, I watched the growth of that trust from something in the neighborhood of three hundred thousand dollars in 1927 to its recent five million. Through the Depression years, there were increasingly large sums of cash on hand and something about "short sales." I knew little enough about the stock market, heaven knows, and David's efforts to explain a short sale to me had met with dismal failure, but I knew enough to know that in a falling market, you sell short, and I knew that the market had fallen from 1929 through most of 1933, and the Moreau Trust had sold.

The Hamilton account was very small potatoes. It contained only about a million dollars, but it had started with a paltry fifty thousand. By comparing appraisals, I realized that the fifty thousand had been loaned to the Hamilton account by the Moreau Trust, and throughout the years, the loans had increased and diminished with the months.

I leaned back exhausted, my eyes itching from the strain of reading pages and pages of typewritten material.

Then I went back to the correspondence folders for another look. The letters to John Hamilton were all directed to an address on Rodeo Road, Beverly Hills.

So, Mr. Hamilton lived in Beverly Hills. But why?

Why on earth with all that money didn't Pauline live openly with her husband instead of only occasionally in the middle of the night in this beautiful little house? Why did she pinch and scrape and deprive her sisters when it was so totally unnecessary?

And then, of course, I got it. If she and John Hamilton had admitted their marriage back in 1927—or even possibly before that—they would have lost control of the money. The three hundred thousand would have been split seven ways, Pauline would not have been able to make the big loans from the trust to the Hamilton account, and they would not have been able to accumulate the fortune that had piled up and piled up through their judicious investments.

My head still hurt from the battering at the back entrance. But it ached even more from the impact of the knowledge I'd acquired in the last hour.

I tried to think logically without much success. I could see, of course, why Pauline and her Hamilton hadn't wanted the trust split up originally, but why not now? Why had she still refused when there was the huge sum of five million dollars to be split seven ways with plenty for all?

Finally, I thought I understood even that strange quirk in Pauline. It was probably the old business of never having enough. The more money you have, the more you want. Perhaps she and her husband wanted to hang onto the money with some wild hope of making a war fortune, which, of course, is not supposed to be possible, but which David says is possible.

I lit a cigarette and watched the smoke wind around the still, stuffy air.

We were all rich. All of us. I wondered a little about taxes and about the changes this sudden, great wealth would bring in our lives. And then I jerked myself back to the business at hand. I'd have to look through these pounds and pounds of papers and try to find the Shanley letter. When I found it, I'd stuff it down my neck and then call Cassidy and tell him about this house and the Moreaus' financial affairs. He could look for Mr. John Hamilton and for the woman—I was sure it was a woman, somehow—who'd hit me over the head in the passage way, and in due course, he'd catch the murderer. Then all of us who were innocent could settle down to the pleasant business of being rich.

What a wonderful time David and I could have after the war. Travel, a nice house in the country, lots of children with good educations assured for them, all the books and music and pictures we wanted....

I shook my head to clear it. Then I went to work after a hasty, alarmed glance at my watch. It was almost two o'clock.

The filing cabinets were, I felt, hopeless. It would take days for me to go all through them, and I was pretty sure anyway that the letter hadn't been put into the files yet. It might not, of course, have even arrived.

I tried the desk first and quite shamelessly opened some newly arrived mail. Bills, more confirmations, something about war damage insurance for the little grey house. But there was nothing of real interest.

Then I went over to the drawer marked, "Correspondence, 1942," and looked under "S." I didn't find what I really wanted, but I found enough to know that I'd better get my letter before Cassidy did.

On July 27, 1942, Pauline had written the private detectives in Cleveland ordering them to make a complete, exhaustive investigation of the life of Hilda Blake Moreau. She gave them our address and a little vague data concerning my birth, parentage, and education.

"I am especially anxious that you investigate all phases of Mrs. Moreau's life having to do with her relations with men other than her husband, David Moreau. I have reason to believe that you may find something discreditable."

I almost screamed aloud. *Discreditable!*

Instead, I tore the carbon copy of the letter into a thousand pieces and angrily flushed it down the toilet.

I couldn't find what I was after. That was all there was to it. And I knew it was quite possible that the woman who had come to the house before me had taken the letter and that in time it would find its way to Cassidy.

All right. I'd have to see what I could find that might implicate somebody else.

"O" for Oxney. Nothing doing. I went back for seven or eight years through the correspondence files. If Pauline had ever had correspondence with Gladys Oxney, she hadn't kept it.

"M" for Moreau. The only Moreau in the files was Pauline herself. Nowhere could I find any papers concerning individual sisters.

"H" for Holmes. And there I found something.

The first thing was a hand-written note scrawled on a piece of scratch paper.

"Pauline—Sorry I can't wait for you. I'm meeting Anne at six. Damned shame about David, but if he persists, I'm afraid there's nothing you can do. I don't think that even a divorce would help now if he really got tough, but you can try, and of course, there's always Elise. The Hamilton notes would have to be paid—no doubt about that. The liability for fraud still holds, just as I've always warned you.

"Janet"

"Your last check was a little stingy, Pauline."

I whistled. Janet Holmes knew all about the Moreaus' affairs. She was Pauline's lawyer. I pawed through the file. Letters about taxes, particularly income taxes. References to deeds for real estate. References to John Hamilton. My eyes felt as though they were popped at least two inches out of my head. My, my, my, wouldn't I have something nice to show Cassidy when I got around to it?

Anne's good friend, the dirty crook. Taking money from Pauline for legal assistance. Sitting by watching Anne struggle and starve. The damned shyster.

And in one of the letters, I found something particularly juicy and nice. It was a carbon copy of a letter written by Pauline to Janet. The pertinent sentence read: "Your fees are mounting with appalling rapidity. I'm wondering what the Bar Association might think. Let's discuss it the next time we meet, shall we?"

The Bar Association. Yes, yes, yes. Janet was helping to perpetrate a fraud, perhaps. She knew all about Pauline's marriage and knew that Pauline was being crooked by not dissolving the trust.

I read on and on and on through the 1942, 1941, and 1940 folders. My concentration was complete. I was shut into a tight little world of typewritten letters concerning legal affairs which were dull and dry, but with vast, unlimited willpower, I kept my mind close to the words in front of me. Too close.

I didn't hear a sound until a voice jerked me back into the world that was not a legal world of typewritten letters.

"Well, Mrs. Moreau, have you found what you're looking for?"

Cassidy's cold, skeptical blue eyes looked down on me.

CHAPTER 16

I talked. I talked for endless ages. Words poured out of me, and I felt that they were like a stream of heavy water pouring over a hard, diamond-like surface. They elicited no comment from Cassidy, and they apparently made no more impression than the water would on a huge diamond.

I told him how I had learned of the existence of the house. I told him very frankly about the reason I had come there—to search for the private detective's letter. I told him about being hit over the head in the back entrance. I told him about John Hamilton and Pauline's marriage and the great wealth of the Moreau family. I finally shoved Janet Holmes' scrawled note across the desk in his direction.

He read it without comment and put it back on the desk.

"How did you find this place?" I said urgently. "Did you follow me? How did you get in?"

"I was tipped off that you were here. I want to see your purse," he said flatly. And before I could stop him, he had picked up my bag, opened it, rooted around inside, and finally pulled out a bunch of keys which I had never seen before in my life.

"Good Lord," I gasped. "What? . . . Whose? . . . I don't understand. I never saw those. I didn't know they were there."

He held them in my direction and showed me a little gold tab engraved with the initials "P.M." Pauline Moreau, her keys.

"You stole the keys after you finished off Pauline, didn't you?" His voice was as quiet and even as if he'd asked me a pointless question about the weather.

"No, I did not," I snapped. "Marthe Moreau went back into the room while we were waiting for the police. She took the keys." Then I told him about how Marthe and I had planned to come to the house together until the keys were taken out of the chimney closet. "Listen," I said, "I'll bet those keys were put in my bag while I was lying knocked out in the back entry." I snatched off my hat. "Look at my head, if you don't believe me." I felt the bump. It was disappointingly small, and unfortunately there was no blood.

"Yeah, sure," Cassidy said. "Did you find the letter?"

I shook my head. "No, I didn't."

"You wasted a lot of time," he said. "I called Cleveland. I persuaded Shanley to give me the dope as long as his client was dead."

My throat was dry and hoarse. "What did he say?"

"He told me all about your friend, Duncan English."

Duncan English. I laughed a funny cackle. Duncan English was a nice, mild young man who'd been in summer school when I was. We'd worked together on a report for a merchandise analysis course. The merchandise was, of all things, wallpaper, and our neat, interesting report had got us both A's.

But I felt ominously uncomfortable.

"What about Duncan?" I asked.

"Suppose you tell me."

"All right." I told him—about the course and our report and the A's it brought us. Then I looked at Cassidy expectantly. "Surely Pauline didn't think she could make something of that, did she?"

"She—and English's wife—thought they could make a good deal of it."

"But *how?*" I gasped.

Cassidy's eyes sparked. "Oh, for God's sake, Mrs. Moreau, quit stalling. You and English were in and out of each other's apartments at all hours of the day and night. You lived in the same building. His wife and his mother-in-law caught you in his apartment in pajamas when the wife came to town unexpectedly." He glared at me. "Stop wasting my time. When that woman sues English for divorce and names you as corespondent, the whole thing'll come out. Pauline Moreau stirred the thing up, and you tried to stop her, because you didn't want your husband to know about it, did you?"

I closed my mouth when I realized it had been hanging open in imbecile amazement. I swallowed three or four times trying to find my voice.

"I never in all my life heard of such nonsense."

I sounded very thin and flat and unconvincing. I thought back to the hot, humid summer night over a year before when Duncan's wife and her battle-axe of a mother had walked in. I was in Duncan's apartment, all right, but I most certainly hadn't been wearing pajamas. I'd had on a pale rose slack suit. Duncan and I had put the final touches on our report and had tied it into the scrap book which I'd bought at the dimestore. We were celebrating the completion of a good job and the nearing end of the semester with a glass of beer. I had, of course, been sprawled on the couch, smoking, and I'd known at the time that his wife seemed slightly upset, but surely, surely the woman couldn't have thought . . .

But apparently she had. Cassidy went on to tell me that Mrs. English had left her husband some months before and had gone home to mother. She was now getting ready to sue for divorce with me as corespondent. She also contemplated suing me for alienation of affections.

I jerked myself to my feet and walked nervously up and down the short space between the two littered desks. "Pauline started all this?" I snapped.

Cassidy shrugged his shoulders. "I don't imagine she started it. She just found out about it. You started it."

"I never heard of anything so fiendish. Poor little Duncan." And then I laughed which was, of course, very stupid of me. Cassidy probably didn't look upon circumstantial adultery as a source of amusement. I wiped the smile off my face. "Well, something will have to be done about this. It's ridiculous in any case and rotten for Duncan—he'll probably lose his teaching job. And it won't be much fun for my husband either. But I want you to understand that this whole thing is news to me."

"I wonder."

I turned around snapping with impatience. "Oh, for the love of heaven, you're an intelligent man. Do I look like the kind of woman who'd be carrying on a little hole-in-the-corner affair with a Caspar Milquetoast like English when I was engaged to David Moreau? After all, you don't know my husband, but he's a *man*. A real one. And very attractive." I paused briefly for breath. "Besides, remember what the telegram said. Pauline undoubtedly offered those women a lot of money to start this. It said something about 'other party demanding large sum before affidavits are made,' didn't it? This is just another classic example of her dirty-work."

"Yeah, sure. You go wait in the other room. I'll talk to you again later."

I lay on the chaise longue in Pauline's beautiful little bedroom, but I was in no mood to appreciate its beauty. I was worried and apprehensive and uncomfortable. I was in a hideous mess, no doubt about that. Duncan's divorce was bad enough, but apparently Cassidy had made up his mind that I had a good strong motive for murder and was going to be very busy indeed trying to prove me guilty. Of course, the man had brains, and I knew that if he found indications that someone else was the real culprit, he'd be fair enough to exonerate me. On the other hand, I knew that the united Moreau sisters would like nothing better than to see an outsider arrested for Pauline's murder and that not only the guilty sister but all the others would do their best to hang the crime on me.

I got up and walked around the room. Perhaps movement would help me to figure some way out of my predicament. Perhaps I'd better get hold of a good lawyer, the one David told me to see about having the trust dissolved. Maybe running away might be a good plan. I'd stay hidden until Cassidy had time to find the real murderer. That, of course, was sheer nonsense, but I was tired and lonely and troubled and rather stupid.

Who had tipped off Cassidy that I was in Pauline's house? I'd have to ask him, but I thought that he probably didn't know, any more than he knew who sent him the telegram.

Where was John Hamilton? Pauline had come to the little house the night of her death. Was it to meet her husband? Could he have come home with her, followed her into the house and killed her? I hoped so.

I could hear Cassidy and a couple of other men walking around and talking and using the telephone. I shuddered. Then I cried for a while, because I was tired and missed my husband and felt horrible.

I walked over to a chest of drawers and looked at myself in the mirror above it. I certainly looked like the wrath. Then I looked at a silver-framed picture on top of the chest of drawers. It was Berthe, the dead sister. The one who had died a long time ago. Funny, I thought. Pauline must have been fond of her. Berthe's picture was the only photograph in the house. I looked around the bedroom a little more. There wasn't even a photograph of John Hamilton. Nobody except the dead sister.

She was a pretty girl in a rather mild way. Wide, light eyes and fluffy blonde hair. A weak, rather pretty mouth. She looked more like Rose than any of the others. Certainly, she was the antithesis of Pauline who was so dark and snappy and strong and sure of herself. I sighed. Well, maybe Pauline had been fond of Berthe, because Berthe was weak and malleable.

I was jerked out of my pointless reverie by Cassidy's voice calling to me. "Come back here, will you, Mrs. Moreau?"

I slumped wearily into a straight chair. Cassidy looked at me for a long, long time. He rubbed his hand thoughtfully over his chin.

"Marthe Moreau says she never had the keys," he said finally.

"She's lying," I snapped. "She went back into the room and got something. She told me this afternoon that she had the keys."

Cassidy nodded. "She says she told you that, because she wanted to find out where the house was. She never had the keys."

"All right, but I don't believe it. Did she tell you why she was so anxious to get into this house?"

"She says she wasn't. She says she just wanted to see what you'd do. She heard you leave the house. She followed you part way."

Well, it was a cinch that Marthe hadn't got into the house before I did, so she couldn't have been the one to hit me over the head, but she was lying in her teeth all right, and why I didn't know.

"Did *she* tell you where I was?"

Cassidy shook his head. "She says not. She says she didn't know where the house was. Somebody else must have telephoned me."

"Janet Holmes knows where this house is. She could have called you, and she could have been here tonight." I sat back to let that sink in.

"Yeah, I know. I'm trying to find her. She's not home."

I smiled grimly. "Listen," I said, "I don't know much about law, but I'll bet she's shaking in her boots right now, or will be as soon as she finds out that you know about this house. She's been Pauline's lawyer for a good long time, and there's probably fraud involved in this trust thing. I mean Pauline's being married and spending so much money on herself and refusing to dissolve the trust, and Janet Holmes was certainly a party to it."

"You've heard about geese and golden eggs, haven't you, Mrs. Moreau? Janet Holmes was safe as long as Pauline Moreau was alive. With her death, she'd know perfectly well that this whole thing would blow wide open."

His statement was logical but unwelcome.

"Maybe," I said. "But where's Hamilton?"

"I'm waiting for a report. I've called the Beverly Hills police to see if they can find him. I want to see that guy. He can probably tell us plenty."

I jumped as one of the telephones on the desk in front of Cassidy rang loudly. He smiled grimly and picked up the receiver. "This is probably them now." He settled himself comfortably. "Yeah," he said.

"John? Is that you?" A woman's voice crackled metallically from the mouthpiece of the telephone. Cassidy jerked himself erect.

"Yes," he said in a queer, artificial voice.

"This is Janet. You know what's happened?"

"Yes."

"I'm sorry," the woman's voice crackled. "You know that, don't you?"

"Yes." Cassidy's cold blue eyes were wary and alert.

"We'll have to do something, John. The Moreaus will land us both in jail if we don't. Any ideas?"

I was leaning forward listening so hard I hurt.

Cassidy put his hand over the mouthpiece and gestured frantically toward the other telephone. "Tell them to trace this call," he hissed.

I picked up the telephone and jiggled the buttons frantically. There was no dial on the phone. Nothing happened. I gestured helplessly, and Cassidy sighed.

"Where are you?" he croaked.

"John, what's wrong with you? You sound very queer."

Clank. Janet Holmes had hung up. I was still trying to rouse the operator on the other phone.

"I'm sorry," I said. "She doesn't answer. The operator, I mean."

Cassidy was very busy dialing, and he paid no attention to me. He gave orders for the operator to try to trace the call.

Then he looked in his grimy notebook and dialed another number. After a long while, somebody answered. "Miss Holmes there?" he said.

"No, she isn't. I don't know where she is. Is this Lieutenant Cassidy?"
"Yeah. This Doctor Moreau?"
"Yes."
"Well, tell Miss Holmes I want to see her as soon as she comes back. She can get me at Elwood 9786."

He hung up the telephone. He had barely done so when it rang again. For a long time I watched him make cryptic notes on pink scratch paper and listened to him say, over and over again, "Yeah.... Yeah.... Yeah." Finally, he hung up with a brief, "Thanks. This is good service. Do the same for you some time."

He looked over his notes. "Hamilton's not in Beverly Hills. He left there Saturday night, leaving this address with his servants. He's known in the south as a promoter—very sharp—able to get considerable amounts of capital at short notice. Supposed to be unmarried. Forty-six years old, five nine, weight around 170, brown hair...." His voice trailed off. "Well, we'll have to find him—and the Holmes woman, too." He looked directly at me. "You go back in the other room."

I went. I flopped down on the blue chaise longue again, and from sheer nervous exhaustion, I fell asleep, my mind completely blank and useless.

I was still exhausted when I felt someone shaking me and saying in a loud, disagreeable tone of voice, "Young lady, you wake up. Lieutenant Cassidy wants to talk to you again."

I was given a chance to collect myself and to wash my face in the nicely appointed bathroom. Then I went down the hall to the office.

Anne Moreau was there. The white wings in the dark hair rising from her temples were not much whiter than her face. Her dark eyes fairly crackled with anger.

"Good God, Lieutenant, do you think that if I'd known what Pauline was doing I'd have held my tongue? Do you have any understanding of the hell all of us have endured simply because *we didn't have any money?*" She stopped when she saw me. She sighed loudly. "Well, Hilda, you seem to have uncovered something very interesting. We're all rich as Croesus, and how much good it's going to do us, I can't tell you. Did you know about this or is it news to you, too?"

I was pretty unhappy when I heard the sharp antagonism in her voice.

"It was news to me, Anne. All of it, including Pauline's marriage," I said.

"I've had a couple of lovely shocks this morning. I'm a woman rich in money and extremely poor in judgment. My best friend is a cheap crook." Her voice was acrid with bitterness. She gave me a long angry look. "I wonder about this being news to you, Hilda. I wonder."

Cassidy was watching the scene with sharp interest. "What do you mean, Anne?"

"My dear Hilda, I've done a good deal of wondering about your eagerness to get your hands on fourteen thousand dollars—at Elise's expense, to say nothing of the rest of us. But with approximately eight hundred thousand each involved . . ."

"Anne! How can you say that? I never did give a damn about the money. I didn't want it for myself. *David* wanted it." There was a horrid roaring sound in my ears. It took me a minute or two to realize that it was only the angry pounding of my own blood.

"Yes, Mrs. Moreau," Cassidy drawled. "I've been doing a lot of thinking about you and your trip and your lawsuit. After all, you've worked for a living. Why the sudden need for money?"

I snapped my mouth tight shut. I wasn't going to tell that man about my 'delicate condition.' He could think anything he liked. I turned to Anne. "Use your good brain, Anne. How could I have known anything about the Moreaus' money? I've never even been in San Francisco until last Sunday."

She contented herself with a bleak shrug. She turned back to Cassidy. "If you don't mind, I'll go home and break the glad tidings to my sisters. I'll also go and look after my patients."

Before Cassidy could answer her, one of the telephones on the desk rang. It was the telephone on which I'd been unable to get the operator. Cassidy answered with his usual "Yeah."

"Hello, Mr. Hamilton. You're back, huh?" a man's voice said. "Well, here's the market. Dow-Jones up point 32 on the industrials, volume . . ."

"This isn't Hamilton. This is the police," Cassidy interrupted. "Who're you?"

"Yeah?" There was astonishment and pleased excitement in the drawn-out sound. "Gee, what's Mr. Hamilton done?"

"Never mind that. Who're you?"

"Oh, this is the order department of Merrill, Lynch. I call Mr. Hamilton every morning to give him the market openings, when he's in town, that is."

"What's Hamilton look like?" Cassidy snapped. "When'd you see him last?"

"I've never seen him," the telephone's voice answered. "None of us have. He does everything by mail."

"Okay," Cassidy said wearily. He hung up.

Anne and I spent an unpleasant two minutes of tension while I did my best to persuade Cassidy to allow me to leave the Moreau house. I hoped, unreasonably perhaps, that some hotel in San Francisco might take me in, but Cassidy was adamant.

"Nothing doing," he snapped. "You go back to Moreaus'. I'm short-handed, and I want you all in one place."

Anne dashed out ahead of me, and I gave her plenty of time to get home to talk to her sisters and to put me in as unfortunate a light as possible. Then I went out into the grey, dingy street to look for a cab. The morning was as cold and unpleasant as all the preceding days had been, and I dragged myself for five long weary blocks before I found a cab.

Fortunately I met no one in the gloomy halls of the old house. I crawled into bed and had barely time to stretch my aching legs before I was asleep.

CHAPTER 17

Late in the afternoon, I was wakened by a cheerful, gay, and friendly Elise. She chattered incessantly as she closed my windows, built and lit a fire, and handed me a tray with lots of good hot coffee and toast and scrambled eggs.

"Isn't it simply super-colossal, Hilda? We're all stinking rich, and good old Pauline done it all. Of course, she should have anted up long ago, but after all, she did make all the money, and now we can live like human beings and have ourselves a time." She flopped into a chair and lit a cigarette and rolled her eyes. "And guess what? My leftenant called last night. He wasn't on one of those ships at all, and he wanted to rush right over and do things for me, and he thinks this is all terrible, but I wouldn't let him come. I told him we were getting some lousy publicity, and it wouldn't do his Navy career any good, so he said he'd wait a couple of days." She waved the cigarette exuberantly. "Soph's not doing so well, though. Her Mr. Brown didn't telephone, and finally the poor dope called him, and I gather he didn't offer to come running, because she's been rheumy-eyed ever since."

"Maybe he'll behave better when he hears what a wad of money Soph has. He can buy six or seven drugstores with that," I said between mouthfuls of scrambled eggs.

"I hope so. Anyway, we're all happy as clams about the money. You know what Rose said when Anne told us?"

I shook my head.

"She said, 'Now we can have a forty-gallon water heater, can't we?' We've never had enough hot water in all our lives, you know."

I sighed heavily. Never enough hot water in all their lives while Pauline had her perfect little house and everything else that she needed. If Elise and her sisters could forgive that, they were a whole lot bigger and kinder than I would have been in similar circumstances.

"What do you think of dear Janet's part in this affair, Elise?" I said slowly.

Her large blue eyes turned dark with anger. "That she-bitch. I'd like to kill her with my bare hands. All these years she's been merrily blackmailing Pauline and pretending to be such a good friend. For once Nanette was right, wasn't she? *She* didn't trust Janet."

"And what has the good Nanette had to say about all this? She did a little blackmailing herself, you know."

Elise pursed her lips and shook her head in wonder. "That old hag is certainly something. 'Yes, yes, of course, I know that Miss Moreau is rich and has another house and a husband, but she paid me to take care of the house. It was not my affair to talk about it.' And that's all anybody can get out of her."

"May I have a cigarette?" Elise handed me her battered silver case and struck a match for me. I nodded my thanks. "Did they find the husband, though?"

"Not yet, baby. He seems to have gone south. Cassidy went to the bank and found that the mysterious Mr. Hamilton drew out all their money—in cash, mind you—on Tuesday, and he was in their safe deposit box, too, but of course, he didn't get any of *our* money. He didn't have access to that. And now he's gone."

I squinted thoughtfully. "Tuesday. Hmmm. As soon as he learned that Pauline was dead, he knew the jig was up, so he scrammed. Smart boy."

"Yes, and Janet's apparently hiding out, too, but she hasn't been able to get her dukes on any money. The police think she's still right here in town someplace." Her eyes glinted. "And will we have a good time sending that female shyster to jail? Cassidy says we can do it, too, he thinks." She mashed out her cigarette. "Anyway, her career's all washed up. The Bar Association will fix her for good."

We were quiet for a while, and I tried to do some thinking without a great deal of success. Who was the woman who was in the house before me? Janet? Could be. She knew about the house, and she might very well have had a key. No, that wouldn't do. Whoever had gone to the house ahead of me had stolen the keys from Marthe, and I felt very sure that Marthe had lied to Cassidy in order to protect herself at my expense. Those keys most certainly were not in my bag when I left the Moreau house, because I had filled my bag the night before and had not used it since my arrival in San Francisco.

And the woman who planted the keys on me when I was lying unconscious must have known about the little grey house in Leavenworth Street. If it wasn't Janet, that left Anne, Rose, Elise, and Sophie. Marthe was out—maybe.

And how about Gladys?

"Elise, were Gladys and Pauline very thick? Were they friends?" I asked.

Elise looked thoughtful. "Yes, I suppose they were. Of course, Pauline didn't have much talent for friendship, but she and Gladys did see a good deal of each other." Her voice dropped. "You know, it's perfectly maddening. Every time someone mentions Gladys Oxney, I have the feeling that I know something." She shook her head in irritation. "Something I can't quite remember—like a name on the tip of your tongue."

I looked at her. Then I looked away. I was trying to summon my courage to ask her a question. Finally I got it out.

"Elise, Cassidy suspects me. He's got me a fine motive, and someone planted Pauline's keys on me, and I'm afraid I'm in the soup. I think Anne's doubtful of me, too. Are you?"

She grinned widely, her large blue eyes full of impish amusement. "I can't decide, darling. Maybe you did it. Maybe I did. Who knows?"

"Well, I know I didn't do it," I snapped. "It's a pity you can't be as sure of yourself."

She looked down at her long, thin, white fingers, apparently fascinated. Finally she looked up. "Do you know what schizophrenia is?" she asked quietly.

I jerked myself upright. "Sure. It's that form of insanity that has something to do with dual personality. It's very fashionable with mystery writers these days. They're always making the murderers schizophrenics, and they don't know that they did the murdering. Why?"

"Sometimes I think I've got it," she said quietly. "Sometimes I think that things have happened, and I can't remember what they are. There's just a faint, troublesome feeling in my mind, and I connect it very vaguely." She broke off. "I don't know what it is. It's maddening."

I looked at her goggle-eyed. "Elise, you're crazy."

She smiled thinly. "That's what I'm afraid of. That's why I don't want to go to that psychiatrist of Anne's."

I snorted. "Nonsense, you're perfectly sane. You had a blackout when you were drunk. That's all that's the matter with you."

She put a long thin hand against her cheek. "I don't know. I really don't. There's this stuff about Gladys, and . . ." She looked directly at me. "There's something about Pauline. And then there's something else about a park." She sighed. "I'm scared. If I had good sense I wouldn't tell you this." She shivered miserably, and I was very sorry for her and also extremely uncomfortable.

"Look," I said briskly, "you're not crazy. I read somewhere that if you only think you're crazy, you're perfectly safe. The real insane people never think they're queer."

She smiled and shrugged her shoulders. "I hope so."

"In fact," I continued, "I think you should go to the psychiatrist and let her help you. She could tell you what's wrong, and I seem to have heard someplace that hypnotism is a useful thing in cases like yours. She could help you to remember this stuff that's bothering you, and then you'd be all right. See?"

"Well, I'll think about it." She laughed lightly. "And you're sure you didn't kill Pauline?"

I nodded with vigor. "Very sure. If I didn't do it, and you didn't, who did?"

"Janet," she said quickly.

"Why? Cassidy says that as long as Pauline was alive, Janet was safe and could get plenty of money. With Pauline dead, she's liable to go to jail."

"I don't know. I just think she did it. It's like this other stuff. I think I know something that would prove that Janet did it—and she could have nicely with Anne tramping the streets looking for me—but I can't remember anything definite."

Then I had to spend some more time trying to persuade her that she was not ripe for the loony bin. To change the subject, I said, "Listen here, why should Marthe be so anxious to get into Pauline's house? She's lying in her teeth about those keys, you know. She did go back into the room, and she certainly seemed to be telling the truth when she talked to me yesterday afternoon, and we agreed to go to the house together."

"Marthe's a deep one," Elise said slowly. "Pauline most certainly had something on her, but have you ever noticed that Marthe really never tells you anything about herself? I know perfectly well that Marthe's got a lot of friends and a lot of outside interests—besides her job—but she never lets the family in on anything."

I thought for a minute. Marthe was uncommunicative about herself, and she'd said something about coming in late but nothing about where she'd been or with whom. And she'd known for a long time about Pauline's nocturnal absences from the house and had never told anyone about them until after her sister was dead. Had she actually followed Pauline, stolen the keys, and gone to the house ahead of me? That was quite a thought, and I felt pleasurably excited. So did Elise when I told her about it.

"It's certainly an idea, isn't it?"

"Yes, it is, but I don't know how in heck I'd ever prove that she did all that. Who was home last night, Elise, or do you know?"

She shrugged. "Everybody and nobody, for all I know. I read until about eleven, and then I slept like the dead."

"You're not much help. I'd love to know, too, who telephoned Cassidy to tell him where I was. It's a cinch that whoever did it knew about the house which could, of course, be Janet. I don't see how Marthe could have, though, unless she lied about knowing where the house was." I sat up abruptly. "She couldn't have. She couldn't have. You see?"

Elise looked blank. "Why not?"

"Look. Marthe never would have told me about the keys if she'd known where the house was. She didn't have to. If she had the keys, all she had to do was sneak out and go down there. She didn't have to say a word to me."

Elise rolled her eyes and lit a cigarette. "Logic was never my strong point, dearie. You'll have to bat your own brain around. I'm afraid I can't assist you."

"You'd be able to think, all right, if you were in the mess I'm in," I said sadly. "Did you hear about my paramour, Mr. Duncan English, and his divorce?"

She laughed. "Anne told me. You're a sly one, duckie. What will David say?"

"David knows Mr. English. He'll guffaw, but it's still not very nice for him. Being cuckolded while he was engaged to me—or at least that's what people will think. I'll have to stop those people somehow."

Elise stood up and stretched widely. I liked to watch her. Most people stretching look clumsy and earthy. Elise never did. She was graceful and beautiful. "I guess I'll go down and listen to the radio. See if they've caught Janet yet."

She took the tray and started out of the room.

"Look," I said, "I'm playing invalid today. Would you mind bringing me the newspaper?"

"Not at all," she said.

The Solomon Islands could have been a figment of somebody's imagination for all the interest I had in them. I skimmed through the paper until I found what I was looking for—the report of the Moreau case spread all over the first page of the second section.

Cassidy apparently intended to continue being stingy with his news. There was nothing that I didn't already know, but some enterprising woman reporter had dug around the files and found something to print. The article said something to the effect that Pauline Moreau was not the first of her family to die violently. In the fall of 1927 Miss Berthe Moreau had fallen from a window at the back of the old house and had died of her injuries without recovering consciousness. She had been rumored engaged at the time to one Philip Pearson who collapsed on hearing the news of his fiancée's accident.

I whistled to myself. What in hell did all this mean? I thought back to the first time I'd learned of Berthe's existence when I looked at the picture in Anne's bedroom. Then I remembered the quarrel outside my door in which Pauline and Sophie had wrangled with each other and something was said about Berthe. And of course there was Berthe's picture on Pauline's chest of drawers in the little house.

Had that weakly pretty blonde girl thrown herself out the window?

Did this ancient history have anything to do with what was going on now?

I'd have to ask somebody. Soon.

CHAPTER 18

I found the Moreau sisters gathered in the downstairs living room before dinner. Anne was speaking angrily as I walked in. She had a newspaper in her hand which she waved in rhythm with her words.

"Rotten, dirty rag," she snapped. "Dragging all this stuff about Berthe out. Why couldn't they leave her alone? Let her rest in peace. The poor thing."

Sophie, wearing thick make-up that did little to disguise her splotchy skin, clucked sympathetically. "That's newspapers for you. Just sensational."

I was going to get the dope on the death of Berthe Moreau sooner than I'd hoped for.

They all turned to me as I spoke. Marthe's face was decidedly blank and unfriendly, but I had a sneaking hunch that she felt a little guilty, too, and was trying to be bland in order to conceal her feeling of guilt toward me. Sophie quickly assumed an expression of outraged disapproval. Anne raised her eyebrows. Only Elise and the infantile Rose had a smile for me.

"What happened to Berthe?" I said, only slightly ashamed of my thick skin.

"We'd rather not discuss it," Anne snapped. "It's ancient history and we were all very unhappy when it happened."

"Oh," I said airily, "then you mean she killed herself, I suppose."

Anne's eyes were black with dislike. "We don't know that at all, Hilda. We had no proof at the time, and we have less now. We were all very fond of Berthe. Let's change the subject, shall we?"

"Not quite yet," I said. "The paper said she was engaged. As Pauline disapproved greatly of any of her sisters marrying, I'd be very much interested to know how she felt about Berthe."

Sophie took over, to Anne's obvious annoyance. "She wasn't engaged, really. Philip came here to the house, and we all liked him, but she wasn't engaged."

"I see," I said. "Apparently Pauline was extremely fond of Berthe. Her photograph is the only in her house—the Leavenworth Street house, I mean."

I was thoroughly unprepared for my bombshell. There were cries of "Really?" and "Imagine!" and "Gosh!" from all sides of the room. I had to describe the photograph and the room in which I had found it very carefully.

"I'm going to ask Cassidy if we can't all go and look at the house tomorrow," Elise said. "I'm dying to see it. It sounds very ultra. Damned shame Pauline was so small, we won't be able to use any of her elegant clothes."

"Elise!" Sophie gasped. "How could you think of such a thing. Besides, we can buy our own nice things now." She looked very smug.

After dinner I stopped in the hall to examine the bookcases in the hope of finding something to read. I was anxious to get away from my husband's sisters as they had made it quite obvious that my society was not particularly enjoyable. They'd achieved their effect by talking of things that were entirely strange to me and had thereby excluded me from the conversation.

I snapped a switch at the end of the hall and spent some minutes poring over dusty old books. Finally I chose *The Moonstone* which I had not read for years. With the book tucked under my arm, I was about to turn out the light when I noticed an envelope on the table near the little heater.

It was addressed to me. Mrs. David Moreau. Well, well, I thought, maybe the girls are giving me notice to vacate. I opened it slowly and read it with dumb amazement.

"Hilda—
"I think you and I can make a deal. You need help, and I've got to get the Moreaus and the police off my neck. X marks the spot where I'd like to meet you tonight—around midnight. You can't miss if you follow the map.
Janet"

I agreed to myself that I would be double and triple damned. Janet Holmes wanted to see me, and of course, with her alluring offer to make a deal, she knew quite well that I'd want to see her. I felt pretty sure, too, that the note was genuine as I recognized Janet's distinguished scrawl, but how in the name of heaven had the note got into the house?

I went back to the living room where the girls were all sitting around the fire.

"Look," I said, "I found a note on the table at the back of the hall. It was addressed to me. Do any of you know anything about it?"

The room was full of round eyes and shaking heads. "Let's see it," Marthe said, standing up and coming toward me.

"No. It isn't necessary." I stuffed the note in my pocket. "You're sure it wasn't delivered or anything?"

"I've been home all day," Marthe said. "I answered the door. Maybe

Gladys' maids took it in before they left."

"Well, if they did, why didn't they bring it upstairs? Why leave it in the hall?"

Elise spoke up. I felt badly that her friendliness of the afternoon had disappeared. "They probably knew that you were asleep and didn't want to bother you."

I shrugged. "Well, they should have had better sense than to leave it in the hall for hours. Back there in the dark I might never have found it."

"Is it important?" Anne asked with nicely detached snootiness.

"Yes," I said, "it is. Did you get the news at eight o'clock? Have the police found Janet?"

Anne shook her head. "Not yet."

"And no Mr. Hamilton either?"

"Nope. Our brother-in-law is still missing," Marthe said.

Then I excused myself and went upstairs to think.

I pulled out Janet's note and looked at it carefully. According to the map I was supposed to walk one block west, then one block south, go up some steps, wander down a path in the park, and meet Janet at a bench. All of this was to be accomplished at the witching hour of midnight. Of course, there was the minor matter of escaping the police, but as I'd seen no brawny cops lurking around the house and had managed to escape their rather lenient vigilance the night before, I supposed that I'd have no trouble.

But I wanted to know how Janet had managed to get the note into the house.

I went downstairs and looked up Judge Oxney's number in the telephone book. The address was Larkin Street. I identified myself to the female voice who answered, and she admitted being one of the two maids who had been helping out at the Moreau house. No, she hadn't taken in any note. I waited while she made the same inquiry of her co-worker. "No, ma'am, Mabel didn't receive any note either, and we would have brought it upstairs anyway." I thanked her and hung up, with a strong smell of fish emanating from Janet's summons.

Then I went back to the living room. "Has Nanette been upstairs today?" I asked of the room in general.

"She helped to cook dinner," Rose said, "but she wouldn't serve or wash up. The knees again."

I shut the door in the face of my relatives before they could ask questions. Then I went back to the dining room and down the stairs to the basement. Nasty, cold, gloomy place.

I knocked at Nanette's door, and she muttered something in reply, so I went in. She was sitting in front of a good hot fire. She had lifted up her rusty black skirts and was toasting the offending knees. She didn't seem especially glad to see me.

"Look here, Nanette, did you put a note for me on the back hall table sometime today?" I said sharply.

"I did."

"What time?"

"Four o'clock about. After the groceries came. It was in the groceries." She turned back to the fire.

"The groceries!" I yelped. "How on earth did it get in there?"

"I'm sure I don't know. I saw it and took it out to the hall. I can't climb stairs with my knees like this." She got painfully to her feet. "Now, if you'll excuse me, I'll go to bed."

I wanted to tell the woman that she could see that messages were delivered promptly to their recipients, but I didn't. Instead I climbed back up the dimly lighted stairs, thinking that Janet was no dummy. Who on earth would ever think of getting a note delivered with the groceries? She knew, of course, that the police were watching the mailbox and that the telephone was doubtless tapped. I supposed that it had been a fairly simple matter to go to the grocery which the Moreaus patronized and to bribe their delivery boy to smuggle in the note.

Then I went into the front parlor and sat down at the desk and looked at the note again.

Janet Holmes, the false friend and crooked lawyer, wanted me to meet her in a lonely park at midnight and make a deal with her. If Elise was right and Janet was the murderer, it was also quite possible that Janet wanted me to meet her in that lonely park in order to murder me. I shivered. I most certainly wasn't that kind of a fool. I was not going to go tramping around parks at Janet's request. My solo detecting at Pauline's house the night before had not been a success. I wasn't going to try it again.

I looked in the telephone book and got the number of the police department, called it and asked for Lieutenant Cassidy. After a long time, somebody told me that Cassidy was out.

"Do you know where he can be reached?" I asked. "This is rather important."

"No, ma'am. What's it about?"

"The Moreau case," I said. "This is Mrs. David Moreau speaking."

He said he'd try to find Cassidy and have him call me back as soon as possible. I sat at the desk waiting. The room was cold, and beyond the area of the desk lamp, it was shadowy and according to my super-charged imagination, ominous. Across the room, there was a murmur of voices. The Moreau girls were very busy making plans to spend their money, I supposed, just as they had been at dinner. I'd listened to them with limitless irritation. They'd all acted as though the murder in their midst were a minor matter in comparison to being rich.

I jumped in alarm when the telephone shrilled through my thoughts. "I'm sorry, ma'am, but I can't get in touch with Lieutenant Cassidy now, but I'll have him call you as soon as he comes in."

"Well, you keep looking for him. I've got to talk to him before midnight. But if he doesn't get in before then, you call me. I'll need some help."

"Yes, ma'am," he said, and hung up. I glared at the telephone. Apparently the man didn't feel that my message was especially important. I was very much afraid that he might forget it. Well, I had about three hours to go before midnight. I needn't worry yet.

I went upstairs and got *The Moonstone* and brought it back to the front parlor. I wanted to be near the telephone, and as I couldn't make sense out of the Moreaus and their doings, I could try to read.

I read about The Storming of Seringapatam, and then I started in to read Gabriel Betteredge's leisurely and conceited account of his actions. On page 181 snapped the book shut.

I was in the midst of a mystery of my own that was, to me, a whole lot more exciting than anything Mr. Wilkie Collins had been able to invent. My watch told me that Miss Janet Holmes would be in the park in two hours and thirty-five minutes.

"If this house weren't so cold . . ." I muttered, "I might be able to think and do a little detecting that would get me out of this mess."

I then cursed the murderer of Pauline Moreau for not having left a good obvious clue beside her victim. The clues in this case lay in the unhappy, twisted minds of Pauline's sisters. There had been no revealing cigarette butts or fingerprints or bits of thread from garments worn by the murderer. All I had to think about was a fine mess of motives, any one of which would have served for Pauline's killer.

Finally, my endless and unprofitable stewing had me in such a swivet that I had visions of Hilda Moreau screaming hysterically and being carted off to an insane asylum for life.

I'd have to start doing a few constructive things and stop worrying about what I could neither understand nor change.

I called the long-distance operator and told her I wanted to talk to Mr. Christopher Bartlett, an attorney, in Chagrin Falls, Ohio, and she told me to wait and she'd get him for me. I waited. Mr. Bartlett was an old friend of my father. I wanted to tell him about Mr. Duncan English and his wife's divorce suit and see what Mr. Bartlett could do to dissuade her.

After a long, long time a very sleepy, irritable voice stuttered at me. "What's this? What's this? Long distance, you say. Do you know that it's one o'clock in the morning? I've been in bed for hours. Why don't you call in the daytime to transact your business?"

I groaned inside. "I'm terribly sorry, Mr. Bartlett. I'd forgotten about the difference in time. This is Hilda Blake, Julian Blake's daughter."

"My dear young woman, whoever you are, Julian Blake couldn't be calling me. He's been dead for three years."

"I know that, Mr. Bartlett," I shouted. "This is his daughter, Hilda."

"Well, if you know that Blake's dead, what in hell are you bothering me for at this hour of the night?" he bellowed back at me.

I swallowed and tried again. "Mr. Bartlett, this is Hilda Blake, Julian's daughter. I need your help."

At that exact moment, Sophie came pounding across the hall and stuck her head into the parlor. "Hilda, you're telephoning. Who is it?"

I glared at her and clapped my hand over the mouthpiece. "Yes, I'm telephoning—long distance. Will you get out, Sophie?"

"Blake. Blake," the telephone roared into my ear. "You're looking for Blake's daughter? How in God's name would I know where she is? She's gone away. Haven't seen the child in years. She must be eighteen or nineteen years old now."

Sophie looked injured. "But who is it?" she whined. "I guess I have a right to know about telephone calls in our house."

"I don't know where Blake's daughter is. You'll have to ask somebody else," dear kind Mr. Bartlett roared. Then he banged the receiver with all his might so that he'd be sure of cracking my ear drum straight across.

Sophie, looking more like a cretin with each passing second, continued to stand in the door. "Did they hang up?" she said.

"Yes, Sophie, they hung up. Now will you get the hell out of here?" My teeth were clenched.

"Really, Hilda, I think you have a very bad disposition. I don't imagine you make our dear brother very happy. No wonder he wanted to go to war." She sighed and rolled her eyes in their unattractive pouches. "Now, just tell me who called."

"Nobody called," I snapped. "*I* called."

"*You* called? Long distance on our phone. Well, really."

I was trembling visibly. "I'll pay. Now get the hell out of here before I strangle you with my bare hands."

Sophie yelped and fled, doubtless to tell her sisters that I was a homicidal maniac.

I tried to compose myself by walking up and down the cold, gloomy room and smoking a cigarette. Time marched on, and very slowly, too, and I waited to hear from Cassidy.

I didn't dare to leave the room and go upstairs where I could at least get warm in bed. I had to stay right by the telephone for fear Cassidy would call and Sophie or one of the others might answer and ball up everything in their characteristic fashion. That unspeakable, stupid old Bartlett. A lot of help he'd been. I tried to think of the name of another Ohio lawyer on whom I could call. No luck.

Maybe the San Francisco lawyer that David had written to about the trust could do something for me. I tried to remember his name, but I couldn't, and although I was dying to dash upstairs and get my address book, I didn't dare. The telephone might ring.

I was still marching up and down the room when the door opened to admit Anne. Her face was uncompromising and stern and frightening. She lowered her eyelids, opened them slowly, and then started to speak. When I tried to interrupt her, she gestured for silence.

"Hilda, please don't make any more threats toward my sisters. It sounds bad for you, and it frightens them. I understand, of course, that you don't like being here, and I assure you that we don't enjoy having you, but Cassidy is insistent that you stay. As long as you have to remain here, I'd appreciate your making as little trouble as possible."

She started to leave the room. I darted around in front of her and stood before the door to block her way.

"Listen, Anne, when I came here the other day, I thought that you were one person in this madhouse who could be counted on for good judgment and for kindness." I spoke as fast as I could get the words out. "Now, you're angry with me, and you've apparently convinced all the others that I'm a heel and a murderer. It's not easy to take." I wasn't making sense, but I was awfully close to tears.

"Hilda, it's not our fault that we no longer think highly of you. When Cassidy told me that you were carrying on a sneaky little affair with a married man when you were engaged to my brother . . ."

"That's a lie," I shouted. "I wasn't. It's a nasty thing that Pauline and the man's wife framed up between them. It wasn't true at all. David . . . David . . ." Then I really burst into tears and made a complete fool of myself.

I huddled into a chair and made a lot of racket and felt terribly sorry for myself. Anne, white-faced and unfriendly, waited impatiently for me to subside.

"You'd better try to control yourself, Hilda," she said flatly. "You'll only harm yourself and the child, too."

We looked at each other for a long, long time, both of us silent and wary.

At last she spoke. "I want to make my position very clear to you. I'm very glad that Pauline's dead, and I don't want my sisters to suffer for her murder. They've had all the suffering at her hands that they're ever going to have. Do you understand?"

My eyes felt tight with surprise. "Even if it means framing me?"

She looked thoughtful. "I'd hardly go that far, but if you did kill Pauline, I sincerely hope that you're caught."

Then she walked off and left me, and I got up and called Cassidy again only to be told that he couldn't be reached.

"Well, can you send someone else out here? It's very important," I said.

"Not very well, ma'am. We're shorthanded. Suppose you tell me, and I'll see what we can do." The man had a funny accent that sounded just faintly Brooklyn. I learned afterwards that it was San Francisco's South-of-Market accent.

"I'd rather not talk about it over the telephone," I said. "And if you're coming out, I wish you'd get here before midnight."

"Okay, lady. I'll try and make it." He hung up, and I could feel myself getting angry and frustrated, and I tried to beat down my feelings in accordance with Anne's advice. I wondered mildly what it was that made it possible for doctors to be able to tell....

I was at the finger-drumming stage when I heard tense mutters coming from the hall. I looked up. Elise was headed for the stairs. Sophie was following.

"I think you're a damned fool, Sophie. You shouldn't telephone the guy. It's bad policy. Maybe he really does have to make an inventory or whatever it is." Elise disappeared up the stairs, and Sophie marched determinedly into the parlor, mumbling to herself.

"Hilda, I wish you'd go someplace else. I have to use the phone—privately."

I grinned evilly. "Okay, my little lovebird, you may have your privacy, and I'd appreciate the same when I'm telephoning."

I walked out slowly and closed the door with an ultra-polite gesture. I tore upstairs and fished around in the bureau drawer until I found my address book. Then I went back and sat on one of the lower stairs, trying very hard to overhear Sophie's conversation. I was unsuccessful, but pretty soon Sophie stomped out of the parlor and almost knocked me down in her haste to get upstairs. She looked like a meat-axe.

Whistling gaily, I went back to the parlor and looked in my address book under "L" for lawyer. Aha, Mr. Philip Pearson in the Russ Building.

Slowly I put down the little book. I'd heard that name somewhere else recently. Pearson, Pearson.

Of course! He was the young man who was courting Berthe at the time of her death. How the plot thickened and such a coincidence, but perhaps not such a coincidence after all. Apparently the Moreau family had known the man pretty well, and I supposed that it was logical for David to think of his old friend when he needed a lawyer.

The telephone book had him listed in the Russ Building as "atty" and in Green Street as "r" for residence.

I was doing a little mental debating and finger-drumming when Sophie came plodding down the stairs dressed for the street. She had on a hat with far too much veiling on it and a squirrel coat that had seen better days.

"The cops'll follow you, Sophie," I said helpfully.

"I don't care if they do. I'm not a prisoner," she snapped and slammed the front door.

I looked at my watch. Mr. Cassidy apparently didn't give a hoot about help in the solution of his cases. It was nearly eleven o'clock, and no word had come from him.

It would certainly be very dumb of me to let Janet Holmes slip out of our clutches. On the other hand, I certainly could not see myself behaving like the heroine of an HIBK mystery plodding around in the dangerous dark.

Mr. Pearson seemed to be the ticket. If he was such a good friend of David, he should be willing to help David's wife solve the Moreau mystery. He could go to the park with me.

I dialed his number, and let it ring six times. Just as I was about to hang up a voice answered shrilly.

"Hello. What do you want? Mr. Pearson isn't home. You call tomorrow."

Mr. Pearson's Chinese houseboy apparently did not believe in wasting words.

Anne, Rose, and Marthe came into the hall.

"Hilda, why are you sitting here in the cold?" Anne asked sharply. "Why don't you go up to your room? I believe there's a fire laid there."

"I'm waiting for an important telephone call," I said. "Inasmuch as Pauline's room is still locked up, I have to wait here."

"Very well," she said, "but I think you're very foolish. You're not taking decent care of yourself."

Then she kissed both of her young sisters good night and admonished them to get a good sleep and left.

Rose said good night to me politely and went upstairs. Marthe asked me if Sophie had gone out, and I said that she had. Then Marthe went to the front door and opened it and went outside. She was gone for possibly three minutes.

"No cops," she said flatly. "I guess I'll go out, too."

I called her back from the stairs.

"Listen here, Madam," I said, "what's the idea of lying to Cassidy about those keys? What are you trying to do? Frame me?"

"Nuts," she said and went upstairs.

Pretty soon she came down wearing a polo coat and a stroller and went out quietly without speaking to me.

I waited for another five minutes, and then I called Cassidy again. His co-worker was very impatient with me. No, Cassidy couldn't be located and would call when he could be.

"Listen," I said, "the police are looking for Miss Janet Holmes. Do you want to find her?"

He muttered something very rude which I couldn't understand. Anyway, it sounded rude, so like the fool of the universe, I hung up violently.

All right, I thought, if they won't believe me, I'll risk my skin and go plowing around the park and maybe get myself killed. Or, maybe I'll clear up this whole thing, and will Cassidy and his henchmen feel silly, or won't they?

CHAPTER 19

Once more I put on my detecting clothes—suit, top coat, sensible shoes, and stroller. Unfortunately I couldn't find my flashlight and decided that I must have left it down at Pauline's house the night before.

As I was dressing, I heard a muffled sound that might have been the front door, but I was able to sneak out of the house without meeting anyone.

I had studied my little map carefully so that I had a very good idea of where I was going, but when I stood on the corner of Hyde and Chestnut and listened to the banshee wailing of the foghorns on the Bay, I almost had sense enough to turn back and go into the house and let Cassidy attend to police affairs. I'd waited until 11:45 for him to call back, and he hadn't done it.

Then I walked on down Chestnut Street below a high grey retaining wall with black cypresses hanging over the top. I might have been alone in the city; the streets were deserted. I turned to my left up Larkin Street and walked another block. Across the street were the stairs, a long, steep flight of them leading up into the park.

A streetlight shone up the stairs, and I hung onto the iron handrail, stopping twice on the way to rest. I had a little trouble trying to decide whether my heart was pounding from exertion or excitement.

At the top of the stairs were two wooden benches, undoubtedly vantage points where one could sit and admire the view, but I knew from my map that they were not the benches for my rendezvous with Janet. Ahead of me the path led uphill under the trees.

Ten steps beyond the benches I might just as well have been inside a cow. The night had suddenly become ink black. Only the grey concrete curb bordering the path told me that I was still on it.

I walked on slowly, still breathing like a porpoise, and once I jammed myself up against a bench containing two dark figures that had melted into one. I caught the faint gleam of a brass button, and apologized dumbly for crashing into the soldier and his girl whose affectionate embrace I had disturbed.

Finally the path emerged from the trees, and I came to the concrete steps on the south side of the park which Janet had indicated on her map. I turned to the left up the steps and peered into the dark for the path that would lead me to the proper bench. I took one last look across the street before I plunged once more into that small black world of trees and paths and lovers. Tall apartment houses loomed up on the other side of the street, and lights glowed in them reassuringly.

The path ahead of me was straight and faintly grey. Ten steps away from the street, I felt as though I had walked into the wilderness, remote from the city and warmth and lights and people.

I walked on, hoping that my eyes would soon adjust themselves to the sudden and complete darkness. Once I stopped to look up at the sky. It, too, was grey black, without the usual pinkish yellow glow that hangs over a large city. The dim-out had taken away the glow.

Finally, I called softly. "Janet, it's Hilda."

My only answer was the *Tristan und Isolde* foghorn, the blast of a freight engine's whistle in the new railroad yard down on the waterfront, and the far-off clatter of a cable car. The small park hung in a black void of isolation and silence.

At last something ahead of me took shape, and I went toward it. It was the soft gleam of a long bench. I put out my hand to touch it, to make it real. It was cold, damp, mosaic tile.

With a long thin sigh I eased myself onto the bench and leaned back. Something cold and prickly jammed into my back and I pulled myself away from it and felt the thing with my ungloved hand. It was a metal plaque of some kind.

I fumbled around in my bag for a match. I wanted to do something to keep myself busy before my chilly fear got the best of me and sent me howling from the park.

The bench on which I sat was a memorial to George Sterling, erected by, of all people, The Spring Valley Water Company. I read the inscription which said something about friendship before my match burned out in the still, black air.

Suddenly, I jumped to my feet.

Something had landed with a muffled, metallic clank against the tile of the bench. It was immediately followed by the sound of running footsteps. Pounding, crashing, down, down, first in one direction and then in another.

I stood cold and still and paralyzed, my ears tense with listening, my heart and throat pounding.

Something like a great yawn rose from my lungs. I realized that I hadn't breathed for a long, long time.

"*Janet! Is that you?*"

My voice seemed to roar back at me out of the dark.

I forced my legs to carry me in the direction of the clanking noise. I would see what had made the sound and then I'd get out, fast, with no nonsense about it. The night seemed to have gone to pieces around me. Nothing was right. Nothing had happened as I'd planned. As I'd expected it to.

My hand fumbled awkwardly with the matches. The light from the fourth match showed me the source of the noise.

It was a long, evil knife. There was something dark and sticky on the blade. I pulled back my groping hand before I could touch it.

The fifth match showed me the foot. A rather small foot in a black, low-heeled oxford with a twisted leg above it emerging from a hedge two or three feet to my right.

The sixth match flared only for a second. A long second that showed me Janet Holmes' eyes, staring and wild and unreal and just like Pauline's after she was dead.

CHAPTER 20

I ran. I ran and ran and ran for years. Through a black world that seemed to fall away beneath my feet. Toward the big apartment houses where there were lights and people.

I clung to the railing by the steps at the end of the park, my eyes glued to the lights across the street.

"I must think. I've got to think," I kept saying to myself over and over again. "I must think."

My thinking was poor and feeble and muddled. Janet was back there in that black park. I knew that all right, and the knife lay on the ground near her. And someone had thrown the knife and had run off down the hill in the dark while I stood there.

"What seems to be the trouble, young lady?"

A voice boomed in my ear, and I swung away from the railing. I couldn't answer.

"I heard you running, young lady. What's the matter?"

The voice belonged to a big policeman. A very large uniformed policeman with a lot of silver buttons on his blue coat which was stretched tight over his paunch.

"Somebody frighten you in there?" he said. "You girls ought to have better sense than to go in parks at night. With all these soldiers and sailors around—not that I'm saying anything against the services, of course. I've got two boys in the Marines myself—but it takes all kinds to make an army. Now tell me what happened."

My voice froze in my throat, and the world seemed to be dropping away from me. With effort so great that it hurt, I pointed back into the park.

"Dead," I said finally.

The policeman started. "Dead? Who?"

He looked at me for a long time, and I looked back at him, still mute. He took my arm and sat me down on the steps. "Stay here," he said and plunged into the black park.

I put my head down on my knees and tried to think.

"I'll have to get out of here, I'll have to get out." I knew that. I couldn't stay around where Janet was.

I dragged myself to my feet and started to run. The steps would take me down to Larkin Street.

Clinging with a trembling left hand to the rail, I ran down eight or ten steps. Then I dashed into a path that led back into the park. The street was too public. Through the black trees paths led up and down and around. I ran on all of them, trying to find the steps at the other end. The paths led to benches, to hedges, to drinking fountains. Around and around and around I went with a thousand little needles stabbing me in my side, my breath jerking in my throat, my ears roaring so loudly that it was a long time before I heard heavy footsteps pounding behind me and a voice shouting for me to stop.

All around me the park seemed to come to life. The policeman and I were not alone with Janet's body. The soldiers and their girls were hunting me, too, and shouting and plunging through the trees in pursuit.

I ran on blindly, hopelessly, with branches reaching out to grab at my clothes and my face and my hair. I slipped and stumbled on damp patches. Once I thought I was near the bench where Janet lay.

The footsteps and the shouting came closer. I stopped running and crouched on the ground under a heavy shrub.

I wanted to stay hidden until they got tired of looking for me. I wanted to get home before my absence was noticed. I wanted to be out of the black hell of the park. I wanted all those things with every weary, aching, pounding cell of my body. I wanted David and peace and decency and my old life.

A soldier found me.

"Here she is, Officer," he shouted triumphantly. "Under this bush."

CHAPTER 21

I was back in the blue front parlor. Shivering and damp and weary. Waiting for Cassidy to finish on the hill. The Moreau house had creaked to life when I was brought down the hill by one of Cassidy's men. I'd listened to banging doors and shouts of "What now?" and the rattle of windows being lowered.

Elise had popped her head into the blue parlor, taken one horrified look at me, and shrieked, "My God, what's happened to you?"

The policeman who was guarding me told Elise to get out and stay out. He then locked the door.

I brushed feebly at the dirt on my clothes, but it was too much trouble to do anything about it.

"Look here," I said shakily, "I think I'd better have some coffee or brandy or something. I'm afraid I'm going to be ill if I don't."

The policeman went to the door and spoke to one of his co-workers.

I must have looked pretty grim, because pretty soon another man brought a pot of coffee and poured some for me. He lit the fire, too.

I stretched out as well as I could on the Victorian settee. I do not recommend such articles of furniture for lounging.

But I must have dozed, because I had a hard time hearing Cassidy when he spoke to me.

I sat up, rubbing my face.

"All right, Mrs. Moreau," he said. "Let's have your story. Again. From the beginning."

I had talked to him briefly when he and his men had finally arrived at the park after my capture by the soldier.

"May I have some more coffee?" I asked. "I feel pretty awful."

Then I told him about finding the note, how it had been delivered to the house, my efforts to reach him, so that I wouldn't have to go to the park alone, and my attempt to get hold of the lawyer.

"Why did you go there, Mrs. Moreau?" he said, leaning toward me.

I shook my head. "Because I'm a damned fool," I said. "I was mad at your man because he wouldn't pay any attention to me. I had some crackpot idea of clearing up this thing by myself so that you'd look like a fool." I grinned very feebly. "It didn't work out that way."

He nodded. Somehow his eyes were a little less cynical than usual. He looked down at Janet's note in his hand. I'd given it to him in the park. "How about the envelope, Mrs. Moreau? Have you still got it?"

I got up and went over to the desk. The envelope was still under the blotter where I had put it early in the evening. "It was sealed?" he asked.

"Oh, yes. I had to rip it open. You can see."

He looked intently at the envelope for a long time, handling it very gingerly as he did so. Then he looked up at me. "See that?" He pointed down at the flap where it was torn away from the back of the envelope. "Looks like glue, doesn't it?"

His deduction was no surprise to me. I had long since decided that Pauline Moreau's murderer had read the note, resealed it, beat me to the rendezvous, killed Janet, and then had thrown the knife at me in the hope that I'd pick it up and mark it with my fingerprints.

"Yes, it does," I sighed.

"Now tell me again what happened in the park."

I told him about finally finding the bench, hearing the knife strike the tile of the bench, and then hearing the running footsteps.

"Listen," I said eagerly, "there were a lot of people in that park—soldiers and their girls. Did any of them hear the running or see anything?"

"Yeah. It seems you bumped into this couple on your way up there. They couldn't see you very well in the dark, but they knew it was a woman. Then a few minutes later, they said they heard someone running down the hill. That was before the patrolman found you. They heard you running all over the place later. In fact, that was the soldier who finally found you under the bush. What'd you run for anyway?"

"Because I'm a fool and because I was scared. I'd subconsciously caught on to the knife business by that time, I guess. I had a very good idea that somebody was trying to frame me. It was just a case of blind self-preservation, I suppose."

"Yeah.... Very dumb, too."

I agreed with him all right, but I didn't enjoy hearing it put into words. "But that soldier and his girl didn't see the first runner?"

He shook his head. "Nope." He grinned faintly. "Too busy, I guess. The guy had lipstick all over his face."

I thought irrelevantly that it must have been a case of true love. Otherwise why in heaven's name pick that cold, gloomy park?

"You say the maid told you the note came into the house with the groceries around four o'clock, and she put it in the hall, and you didn't find it until between eight and nine?" Cassidy said, and I nodded in agreement. He bit his lip thoughtfully and sighed. "Now what time was it when you left here to go to the park?"

I thought hard. "About 11:45. Close to it, and I don't imagine it took me long to get up there. Not more than five or six minutes."

He got out his notebook and looked at it and then at me. "The patrolman says he finally caught you at about twelve on the nose."

"What?" I squeaked. "You mean to tell me that I was only in that park for ten minutes? It felt more like ten years."

"Yeah.... Tomorrow I'd like to time you up there. See how long it'd take you to get up there and read that inscription. I'd like to place those running footsteps as close as I can. We may be able to upset some alibis that way. I'd sure like to know where Miss Holmes was before she got to the park."

I felt pretty good at that point. Apparently Cassidy was a whole lot more doubtful about my possible guilt than he'd been the night before.

He stood up. "Come on in the other room with me. I've got the whole family in there. I want to find out where they all were tonight."

Strength seemed to pour back into my weary body. I trotted along after Cassidy like an ardent and faithful dog.

The united Moreau sisters were ranged around the wood-paneled living room in varying stages of dress and undress. They all leaned forward in eager interest when Cassidy and I walked in. I looked at them one by one. Elise, in her rose flannel robe, Rose in her fluffy pink one, Anne in her black tailored suit, Sophie still wearing the worn squirrel coat.

Marthe, I suddenly realized, was missing. I wanted to call this fact to Cassidy's attention, but he had warned me as we crossed the hall to keep my mouth shut tight.

"All right," he snapped after he had closed the hall door. "I want to know where you all were from, say, nine o'clock on this evening."

"Why?" Anne asked, looking very snooty indeed.

"Never mind, Doctor Moreau. Just tell me where you were."

Sophie cocked her head on one side like an irritated bird. "I think you're being very rude," she said. "I, for one, will not account for my actions unless you give me good and sufficient reason."

Cassidy glared at her. "Come on, come on. I've got work to do."

Elise gazed up at him with doe-like simplicity. "I, Lieutenant Cassidy, was safe in my little bed all by myself, from eleven o'clock on. Before that I was in the delightful society of my sisters Anne, Rose, Marthe, and Sophie." Then she leaned back to watch the fun.

"Me, too," Rose piped. The child was obviously frightened. I wondered if it were because of guilty knowledge or because of an entirely natural fear of policemen which the most law-abiding citizens seem to have.

"And you, Doctor Moreau?"

Anne pursed her lips, gave Cassidy a dirty look, and then snapped at him that she had gone to her apartment at about eleven o'clock and had been reading when suddenly she was disturbed by the ringing of her doorbell. "It was one of your surly brutes ordering me to come over here. He refused to tell me why, and he refused to allow me to speak to my sisters after I got here."

Cassidy ignored her very pointedly and turned to Sophie. "And you, Miss Moreau?"

Sophie looked at him for a long, long time. Her eyes darted nervously away from him and then back. Then she started to cry. "I won't tell," she blubbered. "I won't tell. You can't make me."

"You'd better, Miss Moreau." His voice was without inflection.

"*I won't,*" she wailed.

Anne got up and walked over to her and patted her on the back. "Now, Sophie," she said kindly, "you must be sensible. I don't know why this man's doing this, but I really advise you to tell him. After all, if you were with your friend, the policeman isn't going to print it in the newspapers—I hope." Anne took time to glower at Cassidy before she turned back to Sophie. "You tell him."

Sophie wailed and blubbered some more, and Cassidy stood on one foot and then on the other, obviously restraining himself with a mighty effort.

Sophie was still weeping when the hall door was opened by one of Cassidy's men. "Say, boss," he said, "there's a dame here wants to make a statement."

"Come in here and keep these women from talking," Cassidy said to the policeman and stalked out of the room.

With infinite gall, I followed him. I most certainly was not going to stay in the room and watch the Moreau sisters pour forth their hatred.

A middle-aged woman with a very namby-pamby face and quite lovely white hair was sitting on the settee in the parlor. She had on a nondescript grey coat and was holding on her lap a fluffy white poodle of the most loathsome type.

She grinned to display too-even false teeth.

"I talked to the man up at the park, but he said I'd better come down here to see the man in charge." The dog squirmed and she stopped to pat it. "Be good, darling," she said, "the man won't hurt you."

"What was it you wanted to tell me, ma'am?" Cassidy sounded a trifle harassed.

The woman took a deep breath. "Well, you see, I was out walking Trixie a little after eleven. Be quiet, darling."

The dog let out a very shrill, nerve-grating bark when she heard her name. "You see Trixie and I couldn't sleep, so we decided to take a walk even if it was cold. We take lots of walks at night, don't we, darling? You see, my daughter's married, and my youngest boys are both in the service, and the other one lives in Portland, and I'm not really lonely of course, but sometimes it's nice to get a breath of air, isn't it?"

I wanted to mop my brow, but I had nothing with which to do it.

"Yes, ma'am, it is. What was it you wanted to tell me?"

"Why, about the lady," she said, looking utterly dumbfounded. Trixie yapped again.

"What lady, ma'am?" Cassidy's voice had an overtone of madness in it.

"The lady I saw going into the park. I wondered why anybody'd be going into that park alone at night. Why, I wouldn't think of it. Of course, I'm not a young woman. I'm past forty now, but not much, and I wouldn't think of going into that park late at night. I've seen all kinds of men around there. It isn't safe. No wonder that lady got murdered. I wouldn't go in that park for anything, would you?"

"No, ma'am." Cassidy's lips were clenched. "What lady did you see going into the park?"

"Why, the one who got murdered, of course. Who else?" The false teeth gleamed righteously.

"How do you know which one got murdered, ma'am?"

"How do I know? Why, it was a little one, wasn't it? The soldier told me he saw her—dead. Stabbed, wasn't she? He said she had on a suit, and the one I saw did—tweed, it was, and her hair cut off short almost like a man's. I don't like that type of haircut, do you? I like a woman to look like a woman, don't you?" The dog started squirming around again. "Be good, darling. The lady came down Larkin right straight toward me, and T-R-I-X-I-E barked at her. I have to spell her name out when she's nervous so she won't bark. Then the lady went up those stairs on Greenwich and went right into the park. I thought she was very foolish, and I was certainly right, wasn't I?"

"Yes, ma'am. What time was this?"

"Eleven-thirty," the woman said quickly. "I looked at my watch right then and there under the streetlamp. I thought to myself, 'This is no time for a lady to be going into a park alone at night.' The streets are all right, but not the park."

Cassidy was leaning forward eagerly. "Did you see anyone come out of the park? A few minutes later, I mean?"

"Oh, no," she said. "Trixie and I went home then. We just walked down Larkin to Lombard and then over to Hyde. I have a nice little apartment, very small, but nice and clean and up to date, and the landlady doesn't mind dogs. It's on the corner of Hyde and Lombard."

"This woman you saw was walking on Larkin, you say. Which direction was she coming from?"

The woman looked very thoughtful. "I don't know," she said finally. "You know I used to just about drive my husband crazy. He used to say, 'Minnie doesn't know which end is up,' he'd say. I never can tell left from right, and as to north and south and like that. *Well.*"

The sound of Cassidy's breathing was pretty loud. "I mean, ma'am, was she coming from Lombard Street or Filbert Street?"

"Why, Lombard, of course." She leaned back and Trixie squirmed madly until she succeeded in getting onto the floor. Then she yapped shrilly, and Cassidy and I could hear nothing of the woman's conversation which continued behind the yapping. Finally the woman threw up her hands in coy disgust. "She wants to go home," she shrieked. "I'm afraid I spoil her a little."

The woman finally got out after Cassidy had succeeded in indicating to her that she was to write her name and address on a piece of paper.

He turned to me. "Listen here, Mrs. Moreau. You shouldn't be sitting around listening to me interview witnesses. I had you come in the other room because I wanted to see if you could confirm or deny what those women had to say about where they were tonight, but you shouldn't have come in here."

"I know it," I said, "but I didn't want to sit in there being hated by those murdering females. I don't know which one did it, but I wouldn't put it past them to be in a plot together. By the way, where do you suppose Marthe is?"

"God knows, I don't." Cassidy sounded a little bitter.

"Look here," I said snappishly. "I'm not criticizing the police, but don't people under suspicion have *tails* put on them during a murder investigation? We've all been dashing around like mad, apparently without any surveillance at all."

Cassidy glared. "Listen, Mrs. Moreau, there's a war going on, and we're short of men. I can't assign seven or eight men to this outfit to go trailing around after you when you go to the drugstore to buy toothpaste. This isn't New York where there are 20,000 men on the force. You probably read too many books."

I grinned. "I guess I do, but if these people are going to kill their relations off one by one, I think I'll just go upstairs and lock my door and stay put."

The man grinned feebly. "That's a very good idea." He fished out a package of cigarettes, chose one carefully and lit it. He had one eye screwed up in a thoughtful squint. "That woman who was here. She's narrowed things down a good deal. Miss Holmes was alive at 11:30. You found her body at maybe five or six minutes of twelve."

The back of my mind had been fussing around with the woman's testimony ever since I'd heard it. There was a significant fact in it which suddenly came to the surface.

"Listen," I said excitedly. "Janet Holmes didn't have a hat on when I found her, and from what that woman said, I gather that she didn't have one at 11:30. The woman mentioned Janet's short hair. Do you get it?"

The man frowned and looked at the end of his cigarette. "What do you mean?"

"You people have been looking for Miss Holmes all day, haven't you? Where did you look?"

"Hotels. We checked bus and train and plane stations, of course. We also got a list of her friends from her secretary. None of them had seen her."

I was beginning to feel almost as smart as a brilliant amateur in a detective story. I was simply delighted with myself. "She must have been some place in the neighborhood. She came to the park without a hat. If she'd come from some other part of town, she would have worn a hat and probably a top coat. It was cold out. See?"

Cassidy's admiration was grudging but genuine. "Sure," he said, "that's right."

"And maybe if we could find out where she's been since last night, we might learn something. If she was with somebody, she might have told them about the deal she wanted to make with me. You know,"—I was almost, but not quite, breathless—"I've felt pretty sure since I've thought about it that she wanted to make a deal with me to tell me something about Pauline's murderer if I, in turn, would somehow get the Moreaus to agree not to prosecute her for fraud or whatever it was. From what she said in the note, I think she knew about this mess Pauline was cooking up for me back in Ohio and that you'd find out about it. She knew, of course, that if she just went to you and told you who the murderer was, you'd say, 'Thanks,' and let it go at that. If she told *me*, I'd have to agree first to do what I could to make the Moreaus leave her alone. What do you think?" I'd babbled like the well-known brook.

The front door banged back before Cassidy could answer me, and Marthe stomped in. Her face was flushed, and her eyes unnaturally bright. When she saw me and Cassidy, she made a face of uninhibited distaste.

"My God, the cops here again. What's cooking?" She leaned against the doorjamb in a loose-jointed slouch.

"Come in, will you, Miss Moreau? I'd like to know where you've been tonight."

"The hell you say. Well, it's none of your business."

Cassidy got up as she spoke, walked purposefully to the door, and took her by the arm.

Marthe pushed him away. "Let go of me, you soreheaded dick," she said, with just a faint suggestion of slur in her words. "You can't push me around, you flatfoot."

Poor Cassidy tried to get behind her and close the door to the hall. I think he was probably afraid that the entire family would come running to Marthe's rescue. Strangely enough, he didn't seem to be especially mad at her.

"I'm sorry," he said patiently, "but you'll have to tell me where you've been tonight. It's important."

She fished in her polo coat pocket, got out a cigarette, and took a good long time lighting it. Her eyes were wary when she finally spoke. "Why?" She sat down by me on the sofa, and then I got it. Marthe was as drunk as a sailor home from the seas.

"Had a drop to drink, haven't you, baby?" I said quietly.

"You're damned right I have. I feel fine." She lapsed into gloomy contemplation of her feet in saddle oxfords.

A loud sigh came from the weary cop. "Listen, Miss Moreau, Janet Holmes was murdered tonight—stabbed with a knife from the kitchen in this house. I have to know where you were."

Marthe sat up with a precarious jerk.

"Yipe! You don't say. When? Where? Tell me all."

"I can't tell you all," Cassidy snapped. "Pull yourself together. I know you're drunk, but you can make sense if you try hard."

"You're a nasty Cossack," Marthe said with a wide and generous wave of her right hand which brought her cigarette very close to my nose. "I won't talk."

And she wouldn't either. At least not until I had got her some black coffee and made her drink it very hot. When she put down the cup, she seemed a little white around the gills and quite a lot soberer.

She closed her eyes. "I feel horrible. I never did this before. The eight hundred thousand went to my head. The liquor too." She started to get up very slowly. "I think I'd better go to bed. How does Elise stand it?" She wavered over to the door with my support, then she turned back to Cassidy. "I was at Izzy's. Oh, my God!"

She tore up the stairs, and I let her go. I had no desire to play nurse to a drunk after all I'd been through.

"That was a very fine act, wasn't it?"

I swung around to face Cassidy. "What do you mean?"

He shrugged his shoulders just faintly, not Gallicly the way the Moreaus did. "She wasn't that drunk."

"Well," I said, "maybe not. And she wasn't particularly upset about Janet Holmes' death, either. I tell you that girl's a deep one. I'd certainly give my right eye to know what she wanted from Pauline's house, wouldn't you?"

"Yeah." He got up. "What time did she leave here, do you know?"

"Well, maybe five or ten minutes after eleven. Around there."

He nodded. "And Miss Sophie Moreau?"

I frowned in thought. "It's hard to say. Quite a while before Marthe and before Anne left. Maybe a quarter of eleven." I brightened up a bit. "Look, I just remembered something. Sophie has a beau, and I think she called him up just before she went out. He's a Mr. Brown who has a drugstore somewhere around here. She was probably with him. She's kind of coy. She probably doesn't want to drag him into this mess."

Cassidy wrote in his notebook and muttered thanks.

Then I followed him back to the living room and listened to him break the news to the family.

The women all looked up when we came in. The atmosphere was definitely sullen.

"You're undoubtedly wondering why I want to know where you all were tonight. Janet Holmes was murdered—stabbed with a knife from this house—sometime between 11:30 and midnight." He spoke matter-of-factly.

And the Moreau sisters all gasped and chirped and said "Really?" and "My God!" and made a lot of other exclamations.

I wondered just how much of a surprise the announcement was.

Then I went upstairs and locked my door and went to bed. I made timetables and alibis in my sleep all night long.

CHAPTER 22

I was on my way downstairs the next morning when I heard Cassidy's voice coming from the front parlor.

"You'll have to do better than that, Miss Moreau," he said with decided irritation. "Izzy says he remembers seeing you, but he doesn't know what time you got to his place. Why don't you tell me the names of your friends?"

There was silence. I sat down on the stairs to listen.

"Because I don't have to," Marthe said finally. "I've told you that I walked down to Izzy's from here, and it's a good long walk and that I got there at about 11:30 and stayed until the place closed at two."

"You can't prove it, can you?" Cassidy said sharply.

"No," Marthe snapped back, "and you can't prove that I didn't."

"What did you do when you went back to Pauline Moreau's room after she was dead?"

"None of your business."

"The keys."

"No!"

I toyed with the idea of buying Marthe the complete works of Mr. Dale Carnegie for Christmas. She certainly was going out of her way to make an enemy of the hard-working Cassidy.

"All right. You can go. Please send your sister Sophie down here."

Before Marthe came out of the parlor, I stood up and tried to look like an innocent woman walking down a flight of stairs. Marthe's eyes blazed indignantly in a very pale, washed-out face.

"How's your hangover, baby?" I asked sympathetically.

"Mind your own business, eavesdropper," she snapped, passing me on the stairs.

I went into the parlor and said good morning to our ever-present policeman. "Look, Lieutenant Cassidy, may I go downtown this morning? I want to go see Philip Pearson, a lawyer in the Russ Building."

"What about?"

"Well, he's the lawyer my husband wrote to about dissolving the trust. I thought maybe I could get him to do something about Duncan English's wife and her crazy divorce."

He muttered thoughtfully. "Okay. I'll take you down after I talk to Sophie Moreau."

I thanked him and went down the hall and sneaked into the back parlor so that I could listen to Sophie.

"Miss Moreau, I talked to a friend of yours, Mr. Harold Brown."

Sophie let out a yelp. "You had no business bothering him. You had no business talking to him."

"It's my business to find out where you were last night. If you want to tell me, I won't have to bother your friends."

Sophie, the cretin, then took refuge in tears. She bawled and carried on for a long time, and I had a pretty picture of Cassidy mopping his brow.

"I was on the corner," Sophie moaned through her tears.

"Corner? Corner? What corner?"

"The corner of Union and Larkin across the street from Harold's store," she bawled.

"Well, why didn't you say so? What were you doing there?"

Her voice broke on a high note. "Harold said he had to work late on the inventory." She stopped to blow her nose. "He said he couldn't see me, but I *had* to see him. I was waiting for him to get through."

Cassidy made a noise indicating irritation. "All right. All right. What time did you get to the corner, how long did you stay, and what time did you get home?"

Sophie sobbed and bellowed and carried on, but she finally managed to tell Cassidy that she'd left home at 10:45, had got to the corner where she waited at around eleven and had stayed there until maybe ten minutes after twelve. She'd got home at 12:30.

"Brown says he left his store at twelve," Cassidy said. "Did you see him then?"

"No," Sophie wailed. "I saw the lights go out. I think he sneaked out the back way. So I decided I might as well come home."

"You see anybody while you were standing there? Anybody you knew?"

"I was in the doorway of a vacant store," she said between sniffles. "People were getting on the Union Street cars when they came past, and once a man asked me when the next car would be there. I told him I didn't know." She blew her nose vigorously. "Listen, please don't tell my sisters where I was. *Please* don't."

"Okay. Okay. You can go."

I whipped out of the back parlor and into the dressing room at the end of the hall where I put on my hat and gathered up my bag and gloves. I also took a brief minute to admire my nice black suit and white handmade blouse which I wouldn't be able to wear much longer.

Cassidy was waiting for me by the front door, so we went out to his car and drove downtown. He was being awfully nice to me in a sort of social way, so I thought I'd do him a good turn when he finished telling me about the North Beach district and a dreadful-looking thing sticking up on a hill which he said was the Coit Tower. A long time afterwards David told me the colloquial name for the tower which was obscene, and funny.

"Lieutenant Cassidy, this lawyer I'm going to see is a man named Philip Pearson. He's the man who was reported engaged to Berthe Moreau, the one who fell out of the window a long time ago."

"Yeah? Well, that's interesting." He looked pretty perky, and I thought that when he wasn't working, he was probably a nice man. "I'd like to talk to him. I think I'll come up with you."

Mr. Pearson's office was on the 28th floor of a very tall, elaborate building with fast elevators which reminded me that I'd had no breakfast. His handsome red-headed receptionist muttered into a little box on her desk after she had flipped some levers, and pretty soon a very well-groomed, efficient-looking girl came out and ushered us into Mr. Pearson's office. He was a man of middle-height with most of his weight carried under the buttons of a beautifully tailored oxford grey double-breasted suit which matched his hair. His eyes were sharp and grey, too, and his bright red mouth made a pleasant contrast.

"Mrs. Moreau, how nice to meet you," he said, smiling and ushering me to a comfortable leather sofa. "I was going to call you this morning to see if I could be of assistance."

I introduced Cassidy, and they shook hands.

"Dreadful business. Dreadful business. I'm terribly distressed about it."

He sat beside me on the sofa, and Cassidy sat in an armchair, and we all lit cigarettes and smiled at each other. We might have been in a pleasant house rather than in a business office. I felt just fine.

I grinned, and then I laughed aloud. "You know, Mr. Pearson, the only man I've seen in nearly a week is Lieutenant Cassidy. I'd begun to think that the world was entirely populated by women."

He laughed back at me. "I would have called you much earlier, Mrs. Moreau, but I've been in Los Angeles. I just returned this morning. Of course, I've had a good deal of correspondence with David, and I've been looking forward to meeting you." He smiled to show a lot of nice sound teeth.

"May I offer my sincere congratulations? David's written me your good news."

I could feel myself blushing. "Thanks very much," I said and tried desperately to think of a change of subject. Pearson beat me to the draw.

"When does this great event take place," he asked, "if I may be so impertinent?"

"February," I said, writhing inside.

Cassidy's eyes were round. The blue ice in them seemed to be thawing. "You going to have a baby, Mrs. Moreau?" he said avidly.

"That's right," I said.

Cassidy's long Irish upper lip crinkled into a smile. "Well, why didn't you tell me?"

I blinked. "It seems sort of silly to talk about something that's five months in the future, but now that you know, that's the reason I came out here to try to get David's share of the money. He wanted me to have it in case something happened to him in the war."

Mr. Pearson looked very unhappy. "Please forgive me, Mrs. Moreau. I'm sorry to have told your news before you wanted it known. It was very tactless of me."

"That's all right," I said smiling. "Now Lieutenant Cassidy won't think I'm just gold-digging. He wanted to know why I didn't just go back to work when David went into the Navy, and I was too stubborn to tell him. Now he knows."

Then we got down to business. Cassidy told Pearson at length about all that had happened. Pauline's murder, the complete absence of decent alibis, the great fortune which was managed from the Leavenworth house, Pauline's marriage to John Hamilton some fifteen years before, my discovery of the house, everything.

And all the time that Cassidy talked, Pearson listened attentively and asked intelligent questions. He was also told about Janet Holmes' murder, and my discovery of her body, and the note.

"They're a tragic lot, those Moreaus," the lawyer said thoughtfully. He turned to me. "You must get out of that house, Mrs. Moreau. It's certainly not good for you to be there under the circumstances. Will you let me see what I can do about finding an apartment for you?"

I turned to Cassidy. "You're the boss," I said. "You're the one who's made me stay there."

The policeman sighed. "Well, I guess you'd better leave." He colored just slightly. "On account of the baby, I mean."

I was laughing very loudly inside. Cassidy was an arrant sentimentalist. "Have you children?" I asked.

"Five," he said. "The three oldest go to sisters' school—St. Bridget's." He looked as though he might whip out snapshots with the slightest encouragement. Then he jerked his mind back to business. "Mr. Pearson, the newspapers have been carrying a story about you being engaged to Miss Berthe Moreau." He pronounced the name "berth" instead of "bairt." Apparently he hadn't had the advantages of instruction in the French language. "I looked up the police records on her death, and I see that you were interviewed at the time to see if you knew of any reason why she might have taken her life."

Mr. Pearson's face was glazed with unhappiness. I was very sorry for him. "There was no reason at all. I never could understand it. It must have been an accident. That was what the Coroner's inquest decided. I agreed—to some extent."

"What do you mean? To some extent?"

He stroked his firm chin thoughtfully, and I noticed that he had fine, well-shaped hands. But after the dose of women I'd had in the last week, I probably would have thought a deformed midget attractive, as long as said midget was male.

"Well, Lieutenant, I hardly know what to say. As you undoubtedly know, Berthe was supposed to have fallen out of one of the windows in that big bay in Pauline's room. Pauline said she was downstairs at the time, and that she thought Berthe had probably lost her balance trying to get the window down—it was stuck in the frame and the rain was coming in." His forehead was lined with a thoughtful frown. "The window somehow didn't seem large enough. The accident occurred late at night. There were a whole lot of things that just didn't, well, 'click.'"

Cassidy nodded and leaned over to mash out his cigarette in a big copper ashtray.

"You're a lawyer, and I know you want evidence," Cassidy said slowly, "but I wish you'd tell me what you think happened."

"I think Pauline killed her," Pearson said firmly. "I thought so at the time, and I think so more than ever now. I'll tell you why."

He leaned forward with his hands clasped rigidly before him. "At first I wasn't really engaged to Berthe. I was a very young man just getting my start working in a big legal firm for the princely sum of a hundred dollars a month. Naturally, I couldn't marry on that, but I had prospects, and I hoped that in a year or two I could marry. In the meantime, I didn't want to make my intentions too obvious. I used to just call at the Moreau house with the idea of being pleasant to all of the girls. I suppose I more or less wanted to keep an eye on Berthe, and yet not commit either one of us."

"I see." Cassidy looked interested and thoughtful.

The lawyer grinned wryly. "Well, that was what I intended, but I was young and ardent, and it didn't quite work out that way. I, well, weakened, and told Berthe I was in love with her and asked her if she'd wait for me. She said she would, and we were both very happy—all alone in that terrible Victorian back parlor on a Sunday afternoon." Pain had come into his grey eyes. "That night, she died. But in the evening after I'd gone home, she telephoned me. She was crying, and she told me there'd been a terrible row and that Pauline was furious and didn't want her to marry a man with no money."

"Pauline didn't want her to marry. Period," I said.

Philip Pearson sighed. "From what you've told me today, I've come back to believing that Pauline killed her. I think she got into a rage because she could see control of the money slipping out of her hands and she managed to get Berthe by the window and give her a good push." He stopped for a minute, gesturing for silence. "I'm trying to remember something else. Something about that telephone call. You see, at the time this thing happened, I was afraid that Berthe might have taken her life, and I felt terribly guilty. On the other hand, if she was murdered, I had no possible means of proving that Pauline had killed her. I didn't tell about the telephone call at the Coroner's inquest, because I wanted to do a little investigating on my own. I knew that if I told about the call, Pauline would forbid me the house, and I had to go there." He shook his head slowly. "I know I wasn't being a good citizen, or a good officer of the court, and finally when I didn't get anywhere with my investigation, I just drifted away from the Moreaus. I decided that I'd been over-imaginative. Now, I'm not so sure."

"Why?"

The lawyer pressed one of his long hands to his forehead. "When you were telling me about Pauline's marriage and all the money involved, I had a fleeting thought about something that Berthe said on the telephone." He closed his eyes in deep concentration. "I can't remember the exact words, but it was something about 'how Pauline couldn't do this to us.' Berthe said she'd meet me for lunch the next day and tell me, but she had to hang up then. She had been excited about something when I came in that Sunday afternoon, and I know that Pauline had been away for several days. In Los Angeles looking at some property that the Moreaus owned, she said."

"You think, then, that maybe Berthe had learned that Pauline was married?" Cassidy asked.

Philip Pearson nodded. "You say that Pauline married Hamilton in Las Vegas in October of 1927, don't you? Well, Berthe died on October 25, 1927. I remember that very well indeed."

I'd listened to the conversation with great and eager interest, and now I was ready to put in my two cents' worth. "She killed her all right," I said simply.

The two men jerked their eyes around to look at me.

"How do you know, Mrs. Moreau?" Cassidy gasped.

"Look," I said, "this Mr. Brown of Sophie's, the druggist? Well, Sophie came home last Sunday night after she'd been up to the drugstore to call on her friend, and Pauline caught her in the hall and gave her the devil. Sophie said she and Mr. Brown were going to get married, and Pauline said, 'Oh, no, you're not.' Then Sophie let out a loud yell and said something like, 'You mean Berthe?' and Pauline said yes, and then Sophie yelled some more and went into her room." I paused briefly for breath. "The next night I was playing Russian Bank with Sophie and I said, 'Why don't you marry the guy? You're over age.' Sophie said that Pauline wouldn't *let* her and that as long as Pauline lived, Soph would be an old maid." I leaned back.

"Then Sophie was afraid that Pauline would kill her the same way she did Berthe if she insisted on marrying?" Pearson's eyes were wild with anger. "My God, I don't know who killed Pauline Moreau, but she deserved it, all right. She was the most inhuman, vicious monster . . ."

"Maybe Sophie killed her," I said. "She could have all right because she didn't have any more of an alibi than any of the rest of us. Maybe she killed Pauline in order to save her own life and because she was hell-bent to marry Mr. Brown."

Cassidy shushed me. He was apparently trying to think something out. Finally he spoke.

"I can see why Sophie would kill Pauline, but why Janet Holmes?"

"Yes," Pearson said, "why Janet Holmes?"

"Well," I said, "Janet Holmes undoubtedly knew something about Pauline's murder that she was going to tell me in exchange for favors. Sophie had just as good a chance to read that note as anybody else." I turned to Cassidy. "Is Union and Larkin very far from that park?"

"Two blocks, exactly."

I spread out my hands, palms up. "There you have it. I'll put my money on Sophie."

Cassidy shook his head. "It won't wash," he said. "It won't wash. Why on earth would Sophie Moreau keep still if she knew Pauline had murdered Berthe? Why wouldn't she just go to the police and tell them what she knew? That way she'd get rid of Pauline and be perfectly free to marry, all at the same time." He smiled lightly. "Miss Sophie Moreau is probably one of the dumbest women I've ever met in my life, but she's not so dumb that she'd just sit around waiting for Pauline to murder her when she got around to it."

"She's not so dumb," Pearson said. "Of course, I haven't seen her in years, but Sophie was a very attractive young girl fifteen years ago. Intensely feminine, of course, but she wasn't stupid." He wrinkled his forehead. "In fact, Sophie was rather shrewd in some ways. She used to manage Pauline in a quite remarkable manner. I mean, she'd get clothes when the others couldn't and things like that."

"Well," I said, "maybe it's middle-age or something, but she's dumb as hell now. She drives me mad."

"I don't know," Cassidy said. "I really don't know. I never saw such a pack of women in my life. I can't get anywhere with them." He twisted his mouth in a grin. "I sometimes wish I had a rubber hose when I'm talking to them."

"Why, Lieutenant Cassidy. I'm shocked." I made my face serious. "Anyway, I'm glad you don't suspect me anymore."

"What makes you think I don't?" he said blandly.

"Now, Lieutenant Cassidy, you know perfectly well that mothers-to-be don't go around murdering their sisters-in-law. It isn't done."

"Did you ever really suspect Mrs. Moreau, Cassidy?" Pearson said seriously.

"Yeah, I did." Then he told Pearson about Pauline's antics with the Shanley Investigators and Mr. Duncan English's good wife. Pearson was shocked.

"My God," he said, "was there nothing too vile for that woman to do?"

"Well, there's nothing much worse than murder, Mr. Pearson, and if Pauline Moreau killed her sister fifteen years ago, she wouldn't be squeamish about framing her brother's wife now." Cassidy got to his feet. "Well, I'm due in court in an hour, so I guess I'd better go. I'm getting an order to open the Moreaus' safe deposit boxes. If you're representing Mrs. Moreau, maybe you'd like to be there when we open them."

"I most certainly would," Pearson said. "When and where?"

"Shall we make it two o'clock this afternoon?" He told Pearson the name of the bank where the boxes were located. He picked up his grey felt hat from Mr. Pearson's desk. "I'm very much afraid Berthe Moreau's murder—if it was a murder—hasn't got anything to do with Pauline and Janet Holmes. I'll have to look elsewhere. What a case! All those women . . ."

"Wait a minute, Lieutenant," I said. Then I turned to Philip Pearson. "Was Pauline fond of Berthe? Fonder of her than the others girls, I mean?"

"No," he said slowly, "I don't think so. In fact, Pauline was anything but affectionate with any of them."

"That's interesting," I said, "because the only family photograph in Pauline's house was one of Berthe." I described the photograph, and the two men looked puzzled, and Cassidy said he'd check up or something. Then he left, and I settled down for a nice chat with lovely Mr. Pearson.

He agreed that we'd have to do something about Mrs. English and her fantastic divorce case. "I can probably get her present address from her husband and the name of her lawyer, too. Don't worry about it anymore."

I said I wouldn't, and then he called for his secretary and had her get in touch with some real estate people so that they could get me an apartment.

I felt fine and cherished and free from trouble. He turned to me, smiling. "How does it feel to be suddenly rich?"

"I don't really know," I said. "I suppose I'll have to spend some money before I actually find out. Will it take a long time to untangle this thing?"

He shook his head. "Not too long. I'll petition the court for dissolution of the trust right away. Then the court'll appoint an administrator, and we can go right ahead. I imagine that Pauline's probably been pretty conscientious about income taxes. She'd have to be."

"Why?"

"Well, she'd have the Bureau of Internal Revenue on her neck and that might get in the papers. That, of course, would let her sisters in on her secret."

"Oh, I see. Well, I wish they'd find Mr. John Hamilton. If he didn't kill her himself, I'll bet he could tell us plenty."

He said uh-huh.

"And, of course, Janet Holmes undoubtedly could have blown the whole thing wide open if Nanette had delivered the note directly to me instead of leaving it on the table for hours."

"She certainly could have. Of course, I haven't seen Janet in years, but in a way, it's probably just as well that she's dead—for her sake, I mean." He looked very ethical and full of integrity. "She would have been ruined professionally, you know."

I smiled inside at Mr. Pearson's feeling that death was preferable to dishonor.

"It'd be awfully interesting to know where she was the other day when she couldn't be found. That might lead to information." I told him my reason for believing that she'd probably been in the neighborhood. Then a loud bell rang in my head, and I asked him to give me the telephone book.

Triumphantly, I pointed to a name and address. "Judge Oxney's house," I said. "Larkin Street. Would that number be near Lombard?"

Pearson smiled and nodded. "Probably between Lombard and Chestnut. Come on. Let's go see Gladys."

In the taxi on the way to the Oxneys' house, I told him that Gladys and Pauline had been pretty thick and that Gladys' maids had been at the Moreau house looking after us all during the day that Janet was missing. "Gladys could have hidden her out, couldn't she?"

"She certainly could have."

The Oxneys' house was a good-looking three-story building of half timbered, faintly Tudor style set behind a high brick wall. The small garden was full of well-tended shiny green shrubbery planted on either side of a neat, red-brick path, and the brass door knob, mailbox, and knocker shone brilliantly.

The maid who answered our ring ushered us into a small walnut-paneled study and said that she would see if Mrs. Oxney were in.

The little room where we sat on a comfortable gold velvet sofa was richly attractive. The limestone mantel was nicely carved, and the fireplace had costly-looking oak logs set on heavy wrought-iron fire dogs. The whole effect was one of warmth and comfort and no expense spared twenty years ago.

Mr. Pearson and I lit cigarettes and he put the burnt match in a large onyx ashtray. Then Gladys, plump and well-groomed and covered with expensive tailoring, bustled in.

"Dear Hilda. Philip. I'm so glad to see you. So you know each other. Philip, you've neglected us. It's been years. How are the girls, Hilda?" Her face got a trifle pinker under her carefully applied rouge. "I suppose you've come about Janet. Isn't it hideous—and practically on our doorstep? The park's right across the street. Don't you think it was some tramp? Surely the Moreaus couldn't have had anything to do with it." She settled herself in a small red brocade chair.

"I'm afraid it wasn't a tramp, Gladys," Mr. Pearson said very seriously. "The police have established beyond a shadow of a doubt that the knife used to kill her came from the Moreau house."

Gladys Oxney was shocked, so shocked that she was actually speechless. "Oh, no. How ghastly." She was scared as hell, too.

"Mrs. Oxney," I said evenly, "did Janet tell you anything about what she was doing? I mean, when she was here yesterday at your house."

Gladys' blue eyes darted with apprehension.

"Why, Hilda, what on earth do you mean? I haven't seen Janet for ages. Since I saw her at the Moreaus' the other night, I mean. What do you mean when she was here? I can't imagine what you're talking about."

"Gladys, I think you'd better tell the truth, don't you?" Mr. Pearson's voice was chilly and definite.

Mrs. Oxney's face paled beneath her rouge, and she seemed to melt with fear. Her body slumped lower in the chair, and she put her fine hanky to her mouth.

"Oh, God. Oh, God," she sighed. "How did you find this out?"

Of course we hadn't found it out. We'd merely jumped to conclusions, but there was no point in telling Mrs. Oxney that she'd spilled the beans.

"Never mind that, Gladys. Just tell us what she said and did while she was here and how long and everything." Mr. Pearson certainly knew how to handle witnesses. He was bullying Gladys into talking but in a very nice impersonal manner.

Mrs. Oxney leaned back and shut her eyes. "Janet came over here night before last—at about eleven, I think. She said she had to make some telephone calls, and she was afraid that the apartment house wire might be tapped. She stayed here until last night at eleven-thirty. That's all I know." She pursed her lips tightly.

"Gladys, she must have told you something. Something about why she was here or something about Pauline's murder. You must tell us. You realize that, don't you?"

Mrs. Oxney's grey curls bobbed slightly as she shook her head in negation. Her eyes were still shut as though open they might tell more than she wanted them to.

"No, no, Philip. I don't know anything. Anything at all."

"But, Gladys," the lawyer snapped, "you certainly knew that the police were looking for her yesterday. You also knew that it was your duty to tell them where she was. Why didn't you?"

Her blue eyes, round and frightened, opened at last. "She *begged* me not to, Philip. She was an old friend. I had to help her. She *begged* me to let her stay here until she arranged something. I kept her hidden in my dressing room all day, and last night she left. I didn't know where she was going or if she was coming back or anything." She shut her eyes again. "Then this morning I saw in the paper that she was dead. I tell you, I nearly died myself." She opened her eyes and sat up. "Philip, you mustn't tell the police this. You mustn't. The Judge.... The Judge.... You don't realize. He's so law-abiding and formal and everything."

"Yes, he is, and I'm very much surprised that you aren't also, I must say. You certainly know enough about the law to know what you're doing, Gladys." Mr. Pearson was very stern and all over ethics.

"Whom did she call, Mrs. Oxney?" I asked.

Gladys swung around to look at me. "Anne."

"Anne?" I squeaked.

"Yes," she said, nodding hard. "I didn't hear the conversation, but she told me that the Moreaus would be happy to see her in jail and that she wasn't going." Gladys' face was the color of library paste. "She said she knew too much. That they couldn't prosecute her. She said she could make a deal with the Moreaus."

I was sitting on the very edge of the sofa. "But she didn't tell you what she knew?"

The curls bobbed again. "No," she said lifelessly. "No."

"Whom else did she call from here?" Mr. Pearson asked.

"I don't know. I wasn't around when she called and she didn't tell me. Philip, you've got to keep this quiet. I don't know a thing that would help the police. If the Judge finds out that Janet was here, I don't know *what* he'd do."

"Gladys, I'm certainly no smarter than the police. They'll figure this out just as I did. I can't do anything for you."

The smell of fish figuratively assailed my nostrils. What did Janet have on Gladys which made her willing to let Janet hide out in her house? The threat of the Judge's anger didn't seem to account for Gladys' fear very adequately.

"How long have you known about Pauline's marriage?"

Philip Pearson's question seemed to split the air with the force of a bomb. Mrs. Oxney actually leapt out of her chair and walked rapidly to the other end of the room.

"I didn't know a thing about it," she said rapidly. "Not a thing. It was all news to me. You'll have to excuse me now, Philip. I'm afraid this is a busy day for me. I have a lot of telephoning to do—AWVS, you know."

"Why did you endorse those notes over to Pauline, Gladys? You knew better." Mr. P. was persistent.

She shook her head. "I didn't realize what I was doing. I was busy at the time. Pauline just came over and paid off the notes and the interest and told me what to sign so I did it." Her plump hands were tight as she clutched the back of a chair and leaned toward the lawyer. "The Judge doesn't know about that. For God's sake, don't tell him, Philip. I tell you I'm nearly crazy. Don't tell him. *Don't tell him.*"

A look of bleak distaste flashed over Philip Pearson's nice face. He got to his feet slowly. "Gladys, I don't know what you've been up to, but you're certainly behaving very strangely, and I've known you for over fifteen years. I wish you could bring yourself to be honest with me."

Mrs. Oxney was angry, but her nervous apprehension was greater than her anger. "Philip, you've no right to talk to me this way. No right at all."

There was a light knock at the door followed immediately by the entrance of Mabel, the young maid who had helped out at the Moreau house. She was obviously excited.

"Excuse me, Mrs. Oxney, but Wu just told me something I think you ought to know," she said. "Right away."

Gladys' gaze was irritated. "Never mind, Mabel. I can talk to you later. I have guests, as you can see."

Pearson and I had caught the maid's excitement, and we watched the girl's face set in stubborn lines. "Very well, Mrs. Oxney, I guess I'd better telephone the police. It's my duty."

Gladys hesitated for the fraction of a second. Apparently she decided on our hearing the news as the lesser of two evils. "Very well, Mabel, what is it? What did Wu tell you?" She turned to Pearson. "Wu's the cook, you know."

"He said that Miss Holmes came into the kitchen yesterday afternoon when the boy brought the groceries, and she paid him five dollars to put a note in the Moreaus' grocery box. That means she was here, right in this house, doesn't it?" The girl's eyes were wide in astonishment at the obvious. I realized, of course, that the maids had been over at the Moreau house and had therefore been unable to learn of Janet's presence at the Oxneys'.

Gladys cast a pleading glance at Pearson. "All right, Mabel," she said. "Thank you for telling me. I'll see that your information gets to the right quarter. You may go now."

The girl left the room considerably deflated.

"Nasty little wretch," Gladys muttered. "Poking into things, and besides she's leaving me high and dry the first of the month to go and be a welder in the shipyards. I've told her very definitely that she needn't come running to me for a job after the war's over. There's such a thing as loyalty, after all. And what's more, she's infected Wilma with her crazy ideas too."

"Well, anyway, we know how the note got over to the Moreaus', and that's been bothering me. Do you all patronize the same grocery in this neighborhood?" I asked.

Mrs. Oxney nodded faintly. "Yes. For twenty years, and now I suppose that wretched boy will go to the police, and the cat will be out of the bag. I imagine that Janet sat in here until she saw the wagon out in front, and then went in the kitchen to bribe the boy. Of all the rotten luck."

I stood up. We'd probably got all we were going to get from Gladys, but it had been quite a bit at that.

The maid had left the hall door open, and as I stood pulling on my gloves, I heard the front door open and close emphatically.

"Gladys. Gladys," a quavering old voice called. "Where are you?"

Gladys stepped into the hall. "Here I am, Henry. What's the matter with you? Are you ill? Coming home at this hour, I mean."

"Certainly I'm ill," the old voice said with rasping anger. "Ill inside. I want to see your check book immediately. The Retail Credit Association called me this morning."

I couldn't see the Judge, but I could see Gladys standing in the hall.

Slowly, haltingly, she crumpled onto the floor. She had fainted a good genuine, real McCoy faint. It took the combined efforts of the maids, Philip Pearson, and myself to bring her around. The Judge, very ancient and wobbly, had been quite useless. When Gladys finally came to, she demanded to be helped to bed. She also demanded her doctor.

CHAPTER 23

Mr. Pearson took me to the Palace Hotel for luncheon and recommended that I eat a delicious concoction called Palm Court salad.

"This is marvelous," I said, chewing happily. "This fresh crab is much better than canned, isn't it?"

Mr. Pearson smiled and said yes it was and told me something about the hotel. I was suitably impressed with the great Palm Court and promised to read a book called *Bonanza Inn* which would tell me the history of the hotel before the fire, as Californians are pleased to call the 1906 earthquake.

We'd been very careful not to interfere with the pleasures of the table by discussing the Moreaus but over our coffee we got back to the business at hand.

"What do you make of Gladys Oxney's antics, Mr. Pearson?" I asked.

"Well, I don't know," he said, "but I think it would be nice if we'd stop this Mr. and Mrs. business, don't you? After all I might have been your brother-in-law, and I'm very fond of David."

I said that would be fine, Philip, and grinned.

"I'm looking forward to seeing what's in Pauline's safe deposit boxes, aren't you? There may be something there that would help us to understand Gladys," he said.

"She's certainly scared green," I said. "Elise told me the other day about the Oxney marriage and other assorted bits of gossip."

He nodded. "Yes, I suppose so, and there was some other talk about Gladys some years ago, but I can't remember what it was. None of my business. By the way, how's Elise these days?" His face clouded slightly.

"She's planning to reform," I said. "She's met an attractive man, and Anne's going to take her to a good psychiatrist. Pauline wouldn't let her do it when she was alive." I could feel myself scowling. "Pauline was certainly an inhuman monster."

I told him what Pauline had done to Rose in order to keep her from getting married, and he clucked and frowned. "She was certainly rotten, and I was always particularly sorry for Elise. I used to see her around town occasionally, and she's such a lovely looking thing that it seemed especially sad for her to be, well, uh, an alcoholic." He sighed. "It's a shame, of course, that she and Dennis Russell didn't marry. He might have helped her. But he was a prig, and didn't want to take a chance. It was very sad."

I agreed and told him about Elise's final fling and her fear that she might have been the murderer. His mouth hung open in astonishment.

"Good Lord, Hilda." He swallowed. "It's possible, you know."

"She's afraid she's crazy, too, because she can't remember things. She thinks maybe she's schizophrenic. Isn't there something that can be done for her?"

He looked thoughtful. "Hypnosis, I suppose."

He paid our check and then we got up and left to walk across Market Street to the bank where we were to meet Cassidy. On the way across Market Street I died a thousand deaths when we got caught in a traffic signal change and had to stand between two madly racing street cars. I thought to myself that it was a good thing that the Moreau heir wasn't expected until February or he might have got clipped.

The sky was a clear, pale blue, and a brisk wind blew dust and newspapers and other debris all over San Francisco's main street. I was glad to get inside the bank and go down into the vault where the atmosphere was stuffy but warm.

Cassidy and some other men were standing around, and after we arrived, he muttered a lot of names at us, and we went into a small room and waited until three big black tin boxes were placed on the table and ceremoniously opened by a man wearing correct banker's grey.

Philip Pearson took a lot of interest in the proceedings, but I soon felt myself getting very bored. The black boxes were stuffed with brown envelopes containing crisp, nicely engraved bonds and stock certificates and all kinds of receipts and cancelled checks, but there were no mysterious letters or other documents that would throw any light on who had killed Pauline and Janet.

I was about to ask if I might go home when Cassidy hit the jackpot.

"Well," he said, "looks like we've got something."

He had all right. In a plain brown envelope, there was a brief note signed by Marthe Moreau. It was very interesting indeed. It said, "I confess that I stole $50 from my sister Pauline and gave it to—" The words, "Russian War Relief," had been scratched out with the pen, and in their place above the line of writing, "the Communists" had been filled in. In turn these latter words were scratched out until the little piece of paper was a messy lot of blots.

I had a very clear picture of Marthe writing at Pauline's dictation and scratching out and being forced to change her confession under the pressure of Pauline's browbeating.

"Well, now we know a lot of things, don't we?" Cassidy asked. "We know what Marthe Moreau wanted out of her sister's house and why she stole the keys, but Good Lord, murder for a thing like this?" He sighed and looked at the little piece of paper.

"I can't believe it," I said firmly. "Marthe may be a secretive wench, but I can't see her committing murder in cold blood for a thing like this. After all, she's a strong enough character that I think she'd probably be willing to go to jail if Pauline insisted on prosecuting."

We all talked at once for a few minutes and finally agreed that Marthe herself was the one to explain this little document. Cassidy gave orders for one of his men to telephone and find out where Marthe was. "I want to finish with these boxes before I talk to her."

Then he and Pearson went back to the business of listing securities and looking at papers. After a while I went out into the main room of the bank's safe deposit department and had a cigarette and did over my face and otherwise fooled around.

Then I went back into the little room and watched Philip and the policeman. "Quite a lot of stuff, isn't there?" I said, bored and obvious.

"Yes, Hilda. You're all nice and comfortably rich. I'm glad," he said.

I was glad, too, and I thought about the long, complicated letter I'd have to write David. The poor thing, I thought. There'd be ten thousand questions he'd want answered and there he'd be out in the middle of the Atlantic, shocked, stupefied, and unable to find out anything. He'd be glad about the money, though, because there were lots of things that he could do with it. I could see him having a wonderful orgy of book buying, and from the interest he'd shown in the selection of simple but attractive things for our little apartment, I knew that he'd have a wonderful time planning and building a house. Dear David. Slim and gentle and kind and intelligent. All this gory mess would be a dreadful thing for him to take, but some day, after the war, he'd be happy again....

I was pulled out of my reverie by the sound of Cassidy's voice. "I don't know what to make of it," he said. "Show it to Mrs. Moreau. Maybe she'll have ideas."

Philip Pearson handed me an old calendar for 1931. I took it and looked at it carefully. Plain white cardboard with all the months of the year on it in four rows of three months. Black and white printing with Sundays and holidays in red. There was nothing in the world to distinguish it from ten million other calendars except some pencil marks on a few days of the fall months. Some of them were little "L's" and others were "S's." The back of the calendar was slightly soiled but otherwise unmarked.

I shook my head. "I don't know," I said. "I can't make anything of it. Why on earth keep a thing like this in a bank box. Do you suppose it got in by mistake?"

"I don't know," Cassidy said. "It seems silly, doesn't it? Well . . ." He put it aside, and he and Pearson went back to work, and finally we were able to leave.

One of Cassidy's men reported that Marthe Moreau had gone with her sisters to the Leavenworth Street house—Cassidy had given permission for this jaunt which was chaperoned by his men—and as far as he knew, the girls were still there.

Philip Pearson and I rode there in Cassidy's car. One of his men let us into the house, but the girls had left.

I pointed out some of the luxurious phases of the house to Philip Pearson who was properly impressed. He shook his head and said it was very elegant and that he'd give a great deal to meet Mr. Hamilton face to face, Cassidy said. "Same here. That guy's certainly holed in."

We were about to leave when I asked to go upstairs to Pauline's bedroom. "You come, too, Philip. I want you to see that photograph of Berthe. There's something funny about it."

He and Cassidy followed me upstairs to the bedroom, and I walked over to the carved chest of drawers.

"Maybe I'm crazy," I said. "The picture's gone."

Then we started looking for it. We looked all over the bedroom and poked around in the drawers and cupboards and closets. Finally, Cassidy had two of his men help, and we searched the entire house without success. The longer we looked, the stranger and less confident I felt.

"I don't know," I said. "I'm beginning to think I'm out of my mind, but I'm sure I saw that picture the other night. Who could have taken it and why?"

The small, dark policeman who had been on duty in the house swore roundly that no one had touched a thing.

"Of course," he said, "one of them women might of taken it. They were all in this room together yelling and talking."

"Well," Cassidy said disgustedly, "we'll have to ask them. Come on. We might as well go."

"It probably doesn't mean anything anyway," I said. "I just thought it was queer because it was the only family photograph in the whole place."

"I think I'll go talk to Miss Marthe Moreau now," Cassidy said. "You want to come with me?"

Pearson and I did want to.

Marthe's voice, urgent and excited, was the first thing we heard as we walked into the hall of the Moreau house.

"I tell you she did it deliberately, Anne. She isn't lost. She ran away."

Anne, Sophie, Marthe and Elise were in the living room.

The house looked cold and messy and shabby, and so did its inhabitants. They still wore their street clothes and were all standing around looking white and nervous.

"What's the matter, Miss Moreau?" Cassidy said clearly.

The four women all started at the sound of his voice.

"Nothing," Anne said decisively. "Nothing at all." Then the four women saw Philip Pearson, and Cassidy had to wait impatiently while they greeted him and exclaimed over the long period of time since they had seen him.

Cassidy finally managed to get Anne's attention.

"Oh, come now, who's run away?" He looked around the room as though making a mental check. "Miss Rose?"

Marthe glared at him. She shrugged her shoulders. "Intelligent deduction, isn't it?"

"Quite obvious," Cassidy snapped. "We'll find your sister, but first I'd like to talk to you."

"The same way you found John Hamilton?" Sophie sneered.

Or Janet? I thought to myself.

Cassidy didn't answer her. "Incidentally," he said, "did any of you take the photograph of Berthe Moreau out of Pauline Moreau's house?"

They all solemnly shook their heads in negation.

"I saw it, though," Marthe said and then clapped a hand on her mouth in a gesture of regret for having spoken.

"On the chiffonier?" Cassidy asked.

"Yes."

"And you were all in the room together?"

She nodded. "Yes, admiring our sister's possessions." Her words were bitter. I watched Sophie's eyes glint. Cassidy looked very puzzled.

"Well, maybe Miss Rose took it. It doesn't seem especially important anyway. When did you lose your sister, Miss Marthe?"

"Hell," she snapped. "You're the world's biggest snooper. I lost her in the White House. We went down there to shop after we left Pauline's about three quarters of an hour ago. She said she was tired and wanted to come home. She didn't. That's all there is to it."

Cassidy's blue eyes were icy. "Well, if she disappeared less than an hour ago, why did you say she'd run away?"

I watched Anne's long white hand clench and unclench. "The child is very distressed and unhappy, Lieutenant. We don't want her to be alone. That's why Marthe thinks that Rose deliberately got away from her."

"What's she distressed about?"

Anne's shoulders lifted and dropped. "Her fiancé is being, or has been, sent overseas. She only learned this fact Sunday night. Naturally she's unhappy."

The policeman looked unhappy, too. "You mean you're afraid she might do herself harm?"

Sophie spoke up. "Certainly not. It just isn't good for her to brood, and she might be absentminded and get run over or something."

I sighed very loudly. Sophie's brain was certainly something out of this world.

Elise had eased herself into a chair early in the conversation and had sat quietly looking from Philip Pearson to me and then back to Cassidy. She blew out a long plume of smoke and poked at it absently with her left hand to break up the pattern.

"Philip," she said slowly, "are you the lawyer David wrote to? Is that why you're with Hilda?"

"Yes, Elise. That's why."

The conversation died on the damp, smoky air. "Speaking of lawyers," Cassidy said, "you'd better hire another one to look after your affairs. We opened the safe deposit boxes at the bank this afternoon. You'll need somebody to help you out now."

Sophie let out a yip. "You opened our boxes? Why of all the nerve. You had no right to do such a thing."

"Yes, I did, Miss Moreau. I had a court order that said I could." He turned to Marthe. "That's why I want to talk to you, Miss Marthe. I found an interesting little document which you signed."

Marthe's face was brick red. She took a deep breath and finally spoke with a lot of phony bravado. "My neat little confession, I suppose. Well, what are you going to do about it?"

"Just keep it for evidence," Cassidy said blandly.

"What confession, Marthe?" Anne said shakily. She sat down on the couch as though unable to stand. Elise looked amused, and Sophie looked outraged.

Marthe was very scared and very embarrassed. She tried hard to be flippant. "My confession that I borrowed fifty dollars of the housekeeping money. Pauline found out about it before I could put it back, and she raised hell with me and made me say I'd given it to the Communist Party. I hadn't. I gave it to Russian War Relief," she said speaking very fast as though there were no time to waste in putting herself right with her sisters. "You see, I went to a party and pledged fifty bucks for the War Relief fund, and then I couldn't pay it, so I just dipped into the grocery money and charged things, and of course, Pauline got the bill and raised hell. She found my receipt for the donation, too."

She laughed, and it didn't sound very funny.

"Marthe, how could you have done such a thing? Such a *stupid* thing." Anne sounded pretty tired.

"I was going to pay it back, Anne. I went to work the very next month. I could have paid it nicely, but Pauline saw a chance to get something on me, and she took it."

I remembered suddenly that Marthe was pretty young, and probably she'd pledged the fifty dollars in a rash moment in order to make a nice impression on her friends. The poor young idiot.

"And you *did* take the keys after your sister was murdered?" Cassidy asked.

She nodded, her face still flushed and hot-looking. "Sure, I did. You would have too. I'd looked all over the house for the thing, and I'd found out about Pauline's tootling around at night. I hoped to be able to find out where she went and maybe get the thing back." She grinned. "But somebody else pinched the keys, and I didn't have the nerve to break in the way Hilda did. I thought the damned confession was probably in the safe deposit box anyway. That isn't the kind of thing you leave lying around, is it?"

"No, it isn't," Cassidy's voice was quiet and even. "After your sister made you sign this thing, what did she threaten to do with it? Prosecute you?"

Marthe shook her head. "No, not that. She wouldn't have done that. It would reflect on her. She just said that she'd like to have it." Marthe spoke rapidly. "I was afraid she'd show it to the girls. She used to make a lot of cracks to me about being a thief." Her dark eyes were black with resentment. "I wasn't really. I wasn't."

Pearson's well-modulated voice jerked the room to even deeper attention. "She didn't threaten to turn it over to the FBI, did she, Marthe?"

The color drained out of Marthe's face. "Why, why, of course not. Why would she do a thing like that?"

"She might have imperiled your shipyard job by doing that, you know," the lawyer answered. And I knew he'd struck home. Marthe was a whole lot more worried about her 'little confession' than fear of her sisters' disrespect warranted.

"That's ridiculous," she snapped. "I'm not subversive, or whatever you call it. Besides, the Russians are perfectly respectable now, and you know it." She grinned feebly.

Anne and Elise and Sophie had sat in shocked silence.

Apparently Marthe's action was pretty distressing to them. Perhaps I lack proper moral sense, but I couldn't really take it seriously, especially in view of Pauline's life of crime and selfish ambition.

"Oh, hell," Marthe said, standing up. "If you're trying to make out a murder case against me, you're crazy. I'm fed to the teeth."

She started to walk out of the room, but she stopped when I spoke.

"Did you go into Pauline's room to talk to her about your confession, Marthe? I mean Sunday night around one when you went in and found her gone."

"You damned, eavesdropping busybody!" she shouted, coming toward me.

"What's this? What's this?" Cassidy yelped.

I had the good sense to hide behind Philip Pearson. I think Marthe was really mad enough to take a poke at me. And actually I didn't blame her. I was being pretty snide, also curious.

"Shut up, Marthe!" Elise yelled. Then she turned to me.

"Mind your own business, Hilda. I can settle this whole thing anyway." She gestured for Marthe and me to keep still. Then she faced Cassidy. "Look here," she said, "you lay off this family and go after Gladys Oxney. She's your real culprit."

The whole room was supercharged with excitement. We all asked silly questions at once which kept Elise from talking at all. Finally we all shut our months and waited, listening.

"Look, Constable, I told you the other day that I'd drawn a blank. Remember?" She smiled all full of attractive female charm. Cassidy was taken in by it, too. "Well, I'm beginning to remember things. When Janet got done in in the park, I remembered that I'd been in the park Monday night swilling my little bottle of liquor."

"Elise, have you no shame?" Sophie chirped.

"Shaddap, Soph," Marthe said.

Elise rolled her eyes in an expression of mock patience.

"When I left home and weaved down the hill, I retired to the flower bed and then, guess what?"

"What?" Cassidy asked, and he didn't snap at all.

"Gladys, dear, fat, rich, silly Gladys came down the front steps and marched up the path and out the gate. There!" She smiled broadly. "Aren't I wonderful?"

"Yeah," Cassidy said. "I'll ask her about this." He turned back to Marthe who'd had a reprieve but not for long.

"Now, Miss Moreau, you tell me about Monday night. This is the first I've heard of this." He looked very mad, and I was momentarily sorry that I'd forgotten to tell him before.

Marthe glared and set her mouth. Then she opened it. "Hilda told you. She told you I was in Pauline's room. What more do you want?"

"Why?"

"Because I wanted to talk to her. That's why."

"But what about?"

Marthe groaned out loud. "It's none of your business, but you'll probably grind it out of me anyway. I wanted to tell her that I wanted the confession back and permission to take Rose away. I was going to threaten to tell the rest of the family about Pauline's running around at night. I thought maybe she'd give in about Rose."

Cassidy leaned forward. "And why did you want to take your sister Rose away?"

Oh, oh. Here it comes. Marthe was certainly going to tell more than she wanted to. She spoke fast before she had a chance to think.

"Pauline had raised hell with her, and she was terribly unhappy. I didn't want any more of it."

"In what way did she raise, well, hell?"

Marthe sighed. "About Rose's beau, Bill Everett. She didn't want Rosie to marry him, and he got sent overseas, and naturally the child was heartbroken. Have you had enough?"

Cassidy gave Marthe a long, detached look. "Almost," he said ominously. "Where was your sister Rose during this time?"

"In bed! Right in bed asleep. I saw her. She didn't move an inch all night. You can't think . . ."

Marthe had got herself well into the soup, all right.

Cassidy got up and stalked out of the room, and we heard him at the telephone giving directions for Miss Rose Moreau's apprehension. Then we heard him make another call and ask to speak to Mrs. Oxney. He said yeah a few times and then he came back.

"Perhaps Miss Rose can tell me something interesting when she comes home," he said. "Mrs. Oxney's in bed and her doctor says she can't see anyone."

"Gladys is no dummy," Elise said. "Let's all go to bed and have doctors."

Philip Pearson had been sitting quietly taking in everything. I was looking forward to hearing his ideas on a whole lot of subjects.

"Anne," he said quietly, "this is perhaps very indiscreet, as well as unkind of me, but do you remember some old talk about Gladys and some man?"

Anne's dark eyebrows shot up, and her face was a rigid mass of disapproval. "No, Philip, I don't. And it's scarcely our affair anyway, is it?"

Marthe was still glowering and glaring. "The hell with Gladys. You find Rosie." There were actually bright tears in her eyes, but she was careful to keep her eyes wide open so that the tears wouldn't run over. "You find her. The poor little thing's sick with unhappiness."

Then she walked out of the room and went upstairs. Cassidy turned to Elise. "You're quite sure you saw Mrs. Oxney on Monday night?"

"Very sure, my man. Very sure indeed. It's that park business that started me remembering. The park's a very nice spot for a solitary drinker, also for a murderer."

I gulped. "But why on earth would Gladys want to murder Pauline?" I asked.

"Why did Gladys endorse those notes when she could have merely marked them paid?" Elise said quickly. "She knew better, certainly. Pauline must have had something on her so that she had to do as Pauline asked. See?"

It made sense all right, and Gladys was worried as hell and had sheltered Janet. I turned quickly to Cassidy. "Look here," I said, "Mr. Pearson and I must be out of our heads. We forgot to tell you that Janet Holmes hid out at the Oxney house for twenty-four hours before her death."

"Yeah," Cassidy said. "I know. I was up there this afternoon. I talked to the maids. Mrs. Oxney was already in bed. They told me about the cook and the note, and Mrs. Oxney's faint too."

Anne was very green around the gills, and I was sorry for her, but I let her have it anyway. "Janet telephoned you, didn't she, Anne? She tried to make a deal with you, didn't she?"

"Yes," Anne said emphatically, "she most certainly did. She telephoned me Thursday afternoon and said that if I would promise not to prosecute her for fraud, she'd keep her mouth shut about some of the things she knew." Anne got a trifle greener. "At the time, I thought she just meant something about Pauline, and I told her I'd send her to prison if it were the last act of my life. She didn't say a word about knowing who the murderer was. Not a word."

Elise whistled, and Sophie humphed.

Anne took a few short paces up and down the room. "Really, I doubt very much if Janet knew who the murderer was. I think she sent Hilda that note in order to get Hilda to help her out of her own jam in return for Janet's help." She gestured with her long right hand. "Gladys probably killed her."

"That would be nice, wouldn't it, Doctor Moreau?" Cassidy's tone was bland. Anne glared at him, but he ignored her. "In fact," he continued, "you people have been very consistent in your policy throughout this investigation, haven't you?"

"What do you mean?" Sophie asked.

"I mean, Miss Sophie, that you people—you Moreau sisters—have been very lavish with your information when it concerned someone outside the family and that you have lied or failed to tell me about anything that concerned yourselves."

Elise's laugh was light and musical. "And why on earth not? It's no secret that we all hated Pauline. You can't expect us to be glad to hang for her murder."

Cassidy turned to her quickly. "Yes, Miss Moreau, that's just the kind of thing I'm talking about. To begin with, you couldn't remember a thing about where you'd been on Monday. Today, you suddenly tell me that you have recently been in the park where Janet Holmes was murdered and that you saw Mrs. Oxney coming out of this house at a critical time. If you want to convince me that you're telling the truth, tell me where you were before you saw all these interesting things."

"All right, chum," she said. "I saw a casualty list in the paper Monday morning, and I went down to Palo Alto to call on the widow of one of the men who was killed. I came back with another friend who was calling, had dinner, and then headed for home." She cocked her head on one side. "Instead of coming straight home, I bought a bottle and retired to the park. That's the works."

"The name of your friend in Palo Alto?"

Elise shook her head. "Nothing doing. You leave her out of this."

"All right, the name of your friend you had dinner with?"

"Nope." She shook her head slowly and emphatically.

"You're being very foolish, Elise, aren't you?" Philip Pearson asked. "The name of the woman you called on in Palo Alto was Mrs. Dennis Russell, wasn't it?"

Elise's face was dead dull white suddenly. I watched a pulse hammer in her long, graceful throat. "So what?" she whispered. "So what?"

"Who's Mrs. Dennis Russell?" Cassidy asked.

"You tell him, Elise," Pearson said. "I read the paper Monday morning, too. I recognized the name."

Elise was breathing hard. Suddenly she put her hands to her face and stared out wildly above them. "My God! My God! I . . . I don't know . . . I'm scared."

Anne walked over to her and put her hand on Elise's shoulder. "Try to pull yourself together, Elise. You've done nothing. You'll be all right." She turned back to Cassidy. "Dennis Russell was a man whom Elise loved very deeply at one time. He refused to marry her when he learned that she was an alcoholic. He married somebody else, and he was killed in the Solomon Islands. I don't know why Elise went to see his widow, but I daresay she had reasons."

Elise nodded. "I was sorry for her. He was such a swell guy. I wanted to tell her that I was glad she'd had a chance to make him happy. I wouldn't have...."

Cassidy sighed loudly. "Good Lord, I'm not going to print this in the papers, you know. Why not tell the truth occasionally? Now, tell me who you had dinner with and what time you left him—or her?"

"Marsh Russell," Elise said jerkily. "Dennis's brother. He's a lieutenant in the Navy, too. I rode in a cab down to his ship with him. He left me about 10:30 or so. Then I rode in the cab as far as Post and Sutter. I got out there and walked—I wanted to think—and then up at Hyde and Pacific I finally bought the bottle. I guess I was in the park for a long time." She shook her head in bewilderment. "I don't know. I don't know anything except that I did see Gladys."

Cassidy looked very thoughtful. "Who told this Dennis Russell that you were an alcoholic? Your sister Pauline?"

Elise nodded slowly. "She did. She did."

I looked down at my hands wondering what made them hurt so. I had clenched them as tightly as the well-known vise all the time Elise was talking. I could see the whole thing much too vividly for comfort. Elise going to Palo Alto, full of bitterness of her own battered, broken life, meeting her dead lover's brother who might very well have resembled him so that she was able to place him in her affections easily, coming back with the hope of some new, decent life ahead of her. I could see her taking her long, long walk, thinking about what Pauline might do. Commitment to an asylum for the chronically alcoholic, no decent medical or psychiatric treatment, nothing but blank despair. No chance. No chance at all. Except with Pauline dead.

A bottle for Dutch courage and a knife from the kitchen. The rest of the bottle out in front. Blank, peaceful oblivion for almost twenty-four hours.

Cassidy had walked slowly up and down the room. Finally he turned and gave Elise a look full of regret.

"How about it, Miss Moreau? You kill your sister?"

She put a shaking, clenched fist up to her mouth.

"No, no, no! I didn't. I've wanted to often enough, but I didn't. I know that now. For a while when I couldn't remember about the other night, I thought I might have."

Everybody in the room heaved sighs of relief. Heaven knows the word of a drunk is not especially reliable, but no one really wanted Elise to be the murderer.

The doorbell rang, and as I was nearest the hall, I went to answer it.

A young girl, blonde and scrubbed-looking and neat in her tweed coat and saddle oxfords, stood on the front porch. She smiled and showed some nice even white teeth.

"Hello," she said, "I'm Sally Stephenson. Is Doctor Anne here? I want to tell her about Rose."

CHAPTER 24

Marthe came plunging down the stairs as I ushered Miss Sally Stephenson into the living room.

"Sally, for God's sake, have you seen Rose? I called you and your telephone's disconnected," she shrieked.

Sally laughed. "I know it. Mother forgot to pay the bill again. Father's furious. But Rose is at our house."

I introduced myself and Philip Pearson and Cassidy, and Miss Stephenson acknowledged the introductions with fine manners and a great deal of poise.

"Rose is having hysterics," she finally said. "Very loud ones, and she doesn't want to come home, but Mother said I'd better tell you where she was so that you wouldn't worry." She turned to Marthe. "She managed to tell us between yells what Pauline had done to her and Bill. No wonder Pauline got murdered."

Cassidy's ice blue eyes were watching everything with great interest.

"And just what did Pauline Moreau do to Rose and Bill?" he asked.

Sally turned to him. "Didn't they tell you?" she said with admirable calm. "I guess they forgot. It seems that Pauline intercepted all Bill's letters and wires and things, and then Bill got ordered overseas, and it was too late for them to get married. Rose has been in hell for weeks. She's nothing but a bag of bones. Have you seen her?"

"Sally, really," Anne said sharply. "There's no need to discuss this in front of strangers. I don't think Rose would like it."

Sally's sherry-colored eyes were very wide and innocent. "Oh? Well, maybe not." She turned to Cassidy. "You see Rose and I went to school together—Girl's High—and she's my best friend. I hated seeing her so unhappy, but she wouldn't tell us what it was. Anyway, she wants to stay at our house, and Mother says we'd better let her, she's in such a state."

"Very, well, Sally, I'll come up and see her later," Anne said, looking very pinched around the mouth and irritated.

"Rose says she doesn't want to see any of you for a while, so maybe you'd better not come. She says she's scared." The young girl was still maddeningly calm with each little bombshell she exploded for Cassidy's edification. She turned to the policeman. "My mother's Susan Greathead. She forgets to pay the bills, but she's really marvelous with people. I think she'll be good for Rose right now, don't you?"

I swallowed. Susan Greathead was a very famous writer. I hoped I'd have a chance to meet her some time.

"Yes, miss," Cassidy said. "And what is your address?"

She told him the number in Vallejo Street and then stood up. "Well, I'll go back now. Don't worry. We'll take care of Rose."

She said goodbye to everybody and marched out of the house. Anne looked as though strangling were a whole lot too good for Rose's young friend, but everyone managed to keep still while Cassidy walked up and down the floor.

The silence was too much for Anne. "You don't actually think that Rose, a child of twenty, could have had anything to do with Pauline's death, do you?"

Cassidy looked at her for a long minute. "Age has very little to do with the character or kind of murderers, Doctor Moreau. You may remember that a seventeen-year-old girl shot her mother here in San Francisco some years ago. Then she went out dancing and acted in a perfectly normal fashion. She was a pretty nice-looking girl, too."

"Good God," Anne said violently. "You're a monster. You can't believe Rose did it. You can't!"

"Frankly, I don't know," Cassidy said quietly.

Sophie spoke up. "Well, how about Hilda? You're so friendly and all with her, but she's got just as good a motive as anybody else. Carrying on with a married man."

Dear Sophie, huddled inside the old squirrel coat. I fondly hoped that she'd spend some money for a new one soon, also keep her mouth shut at the right time.

"Look," Cassidy said, "the driving force in Pauline Moreau's life was to make money and to do that she had to keep control of the Moreau trust. Right?"

I nodded solemnly and so did everyone else.

"All right," the policeman continued, "the only way she could do that was to keep you people from getting married. When one of you did marry—I mean David Moreau—she resorted to blackmail and to cooking up a scheme for getting David Moreau to divorce his wife." He sighed. "Now, today I've learned that there were three prospective marriages in this house that she prevented—Miss Rose's, Miss Elise's, and Miss Berthe's. I knew a couple of days ago that she didn't want Miss Sophie to marry Mr. Brown. Marriage, marriage, marriage. I keep coming back to that. It seems to be the theme."

Anne gave Philip Pearson a very dirty look indeed. "Did you tell Cassidy all the old business about Berthe? I should think you'd be ashamed of yourself."

"Not at all, Anne. I told Lieutenant Cassidy that I thought Pauline Moreau had murdered Berthe fifteen years ago."

Marthe screamed. The rest of us jumped out of our skins—almost.

"Marthe, what's the matter with you?" Anne had run to her sister's side. "What is it?"

Marthe was nearly shaking to pieces. "Really?" she said urgently. "You really believe that, Philip?"

I turned quickly to Sophie. "You believed it, didn't you?"

Sophie's eyes were round with horror. She shook her head from side to side. "No. I don't know. I thought she might have. I never really knew."

I leaned toward Sophie. "Then what did Pauline mean when she said something to you in the hall Sunday night about Berthe? Why did you say that as long as Pauline lived you could never marry?"

I thought Sophie was about to faint. She pulled herself together valiantly. "Berthe killed herself. Pauline didn't kill her." Her breath came hard and with violent jerks. "Pauline told her she couldn't marry Philip because . . . because our mother was insane."

Anne swung around on her heels. "Sophie, Sophie! When did she tell you that?"

"Years ago," she said. "A long time ago."

"But that wasn't true. Not a word of it, and you know it. You remember our mother. She was perfectly normal and decent. Judge Oxney's told me lots of times that she was charming. You were eight years old when she died. You must have remembered her."

Sophie's eyes were closed. The brownish lids were wrinkled and unhealthy-looking. She nodded her head. "She seemed all right. She did. Our mother, I mean." She dragged herself to her feet and stumbled out of the room as though drunk or suddenly blind. I was sick all over, inside and out.

Cassidy looked pretty sick, too. This business was probably wearing him down as well as the rest of us. One bit of horror piled on top of another.

"Doctor Moreau," he said, "why don't you get the maid up here and ask her about your mother? She'd know, wouldn't she?"

I liked him for that. All of us were feeling pretty awful about the possibility of the insane parent in the family.

Nanette came stumping in at long last. She looked blacker and fatter and dingier than ever. She was as sullen as ever, too.

"Nanette," Anne said calmly, "did you ever see anything in Mrs. Moreau to indicate that she was insane? I mean Celeste Moreau, my mother."

Nanette looked back at her for a long, long time. My stomach was doing a lot of unlovely things.

"No," she said at last. "She was not insane. She was sick from having too many children, but she was very intelligent. That is where you get the brains to be a doctor. Your father was a nice man, as you know, but not at all serious."

She did not make her statement in a manner that could be construed as flattering or complimentary. It was just plain fact. Then she turned on her heel and went back to the kitchen.

"Well, that's that," Cassidy said firmly. "Pauline Moreau didn't stop at anything to keep her sisters from marrying, not anything."

Elise looked up at him. She looked her age—thirty-five—at that moment, or perhaps older. "Why don't you find this Hamilton? You know what she did to the rest of us. It's a cinch that he probably had plenty of reasons to kill her. And he knew Janet."

"I'd like to find him, Miss Moreau, but strangely enough he seems to have been very fond of his wife. I found some letters there in the little house. They were a combination of shrewd business and love letters. And you have to remember, too, that he stood a much better chance to make money as long as his wife was alive. The Hamilton account owed your trust a lot of money. I think that's why, when he learned of his wife's death, he took what securities and cash he could get and lit out." He sighed. "He and your sister had just put a lot of money into a big nightclub down in San Diego near the aircraft factories. He stood a good chance to clean up. With Pauline Moreau dead, he'd have to pay the notes to you people."

As he talked, one half of my mind was listening to him. The other half was thinking that Sophie had given herself a good cast-iron motive for murdering Pauline—the insane mother. I also thought about Elise's fears that she might be insane. Perhaps Pauline had told her something of the same sort. It was all a mess any way you looked at it, and I was tired enough to lie down on the floor and sleep.

"Very well," Anne said. "I suppose that sounds like good reasoning to you, but what do you intend to do—to us, I mean."

"I'm not doing anything to you, Doctor Moreau, or to your sisters either. There have been two murders committed by a member of this family, and it's my duty to investigate them and find out who committed them and to present my evidence to the district attorney's office. You're glad enough to have me badger outsiders, but I should think you'd want this thing cleared up so that only one of you will have to suffer instead of the whole family."

"You're ready enough to be decent to Mrs. Moreau," Anne said, looking at me as though I were overripe cheese. "After all, nothing happened in this house until Hilda came here."

I was good and mad. "Things have been happening in the house since the day Pauline was born. Don't try to tell me that everything was fine until I came along. I'd never been in such an unhappy, chaotic place in my life until last Sunday. No wonder David appreciated a pleasant, peaceful home life."

Cassidy sighed. "Doctor Moreau, I'm not exonerating any of you of complicity in this thing. Not you, nor your sisters, nor Hamilton, nor Mrs. Oxney, nor Mrs. Moreau. But there's such a thing as horse sense. After all, Mrs. Moreau didn't mail the telegram from the detective agency. Somebody else did it to tip me off, and I think it's quite logical to assume that the murderer found the telegram in Pauline Moreau's room right after the murder." He shrugged lightly. "You've all denied sending it. Why?"

"Perhaps, Lieutenant Cassidy, because one of us has the decency enough to be ashamed of pointing the finger of guilt where it belongs." Dear Anne, my former friend.

"Perhaps, very perhaps. But who telephoned my office Wednesday night in a phony voice and told one of my men that Hilda Moreau was in Pauline's house? Did you?"

"Of course not," Anne snapped.

"You've all denied knowing of the existence of that house. Somebody knew it. Somebody was in it before Mrs. Moreau got there." He turned to Marthe. "How about it? Was it you?"

She shook her head slowly. "It was not me."

"Well, it's a cinch it wasn't Mrs. Moreau who telephoned, and I'm willing to believe that she did get knocked on the head and that the keys to the house were planted in her purse." He stood up. "I'll be back later."

The telephone rang just then, and Marthe answered it. Cassidy was halfway down the front steps when she ungraciously called him back. "It's for you, copper." Her old spunk seemed to be returning.

Cassidy came back into the living room when he had finished telephoning. "That was a lawyer representing John Hamilton. He phoned from my office. I told him to come out here."

"You mean Hamilton's been found?" Elise asked excitedly.

"No, but apparently he wants to talk or make a deal or something. This lawyer wants to see me." He beckoned to Marthe who was on her way out of the room. "Look here, Miss Moreau, you said that your sister Rose ran away from you deliberately in the White House. Her friend says she's scared and doesn't want to see any of you. Will you explain those two things?"

Marthe made a face full of disgust. "She's just a kid, and she's unhappy. I don't blame her for being sick of us. I'll admit she ditched me in the White House, but it's all right. She's probably tired of all this muck going on around here. You, too. That's all."

Cassidy stared at her.

"Lieutenant, why couldn't it have been Janet who tipped you off about Hilda's being in Pauline's house? She certainly knew where the place was," Anne said brightly.

"Because Miss Janet Holmes was at the Oxney house from eleven o'clock on Wednesday night. She had no way of knowing that Mrs. Moreau was there." He turned to me. "What time did you get to the little house?"

"It was nearly midnight," I said, "and I didn't answer any mysterious telephone calls and give myself away, either."

"You see?" Cassidy said with an eloquent gesture involving both hands.

Anne muttered and said that she and her sisters would be upstairs if they were needed. Apparently, they couldn't stand the contaminating atmosphere with me around.

"Hilda," Philip Pearson said, "I'll telephone my office to see what luck we've had getting you a place to live. Perhaps you'd like to begin packing your things."

"Would I not?" I said with feeling. "But I'd like to stay here at the house until after Lieutenant Cassidy talks to this lawyer fellow. Then we can go."

As I passed the door to Marthe's room I heard the murmur of several female voices, and thanked my stars inwardly that I would soon be where I didn't have to listen to a pack of antagonistic women heckling me.

I put my bags on the bed without caring a hoot about what I did to the Moreaus' candlewick spread and started to put things into them. I only hoped that Philip Pearson wouldn't come upstairs and tell me to take the things out as I had no place to go.

My toilet articles were neatly fitted into my make-up bag when there was a tentative rap on the door, and I called "Come in."

Elise came in, her face fine-drawn and very serious.

"Look, Hilda, I've come to apologize. I hope you'll accept it." There was nothing gay or light about her tone.

"That's all right," I said. "We're all pretty wrought up and excited, but as a matter of fact, you seem to be the only one of the family that isn't doing her best to hang me."

"I know. I know. We've all behaved like unmitigated bitches, and when Anne told me just now about the baby, I could have died." She shook her head from side to side, and tried to help me lift my big fortnighter off the bed.

"Don't bother," I said. "I'm anything but delicate or I'd be dead by now." I even managed to smile a little.

"Well, it's all a nightmare, and I'm sorrier than I can say that you've had such an introduction to us." She paused for a second as though searching for words. "Actually, if it weren't for Pauline's getting herself murdered, we'd probably all be good friends. We really like you. You're a swell gal. I wish there was some way we could make it up to you."

It was a fine speech, and it sounded almost as though Elise might be speaking for the family, but I wasn't having any, thank you.

"You can make it up to me by not accusing me of murder anymore," I said. I was sorry to be snippy, but I felt that way and with reason. "Anyway, I'm leaving and as soon as I can. I'll go back to Chagrin Falls where I came from. I have friends there who'll be glad to help me bring forth." I was uncomfortably close to tears, and I wished that Elise would get out and leave me alone.

Philip Pearson called to me from the hall, and I told him to come in. He was beaming, and I felt wonderful—for a second.

"Well, Hilda," he said cheerfully, "I think we have you fixed up."

Elise sat down on the bed and gazed at him silently.

"Yes? That's wonderful," I said.

"My secretary says that she's going to be able to get you a small apartment on the Marina the first of next month. Some Army people have it now."

I felt like telling him to wipe that smile off his face. "But that's almost three weeks off, or anyway two," I said with false gaiety. "How about now?"

Then he sobered. "In the meantime I'm going to insist that you take over my apartment and my house boy. I can move down to the Bohemian Club. I like to stay there, anyway, and I'll be very comfortable."

I sat down on the bed next to Elise. "Oh, Philip, I can't let you do that. It's really too much."

We did a lot of protesting back and forth, and finally I told him I'd do it if he'd make sure first that his club wasn't filled up. He agreed and went back downstairs to telephone.

"That Pearson's a right guy, isn't he?" Elise said thoughtfully. "I've always been sorry that we didn't get him in the family."

I said yes he was a very right guy.

"And he must have loved Berthe like mad," Elise continued, "because he's never married. Of course, I could have batted him one when he dragged the Russells into this, but I've always been a little self-conscious about them anyway." Color began to mount in her face and she shook her head as though to clear it of unwelcome thought. "Dennis was wonderful in his quiet way, but he also was a bit of a prig."

"That's what Philip said this morning," I said.

"He should talk. He's a prig himself."

"A little maybe, but no one can say that he doesn't do his best for his clients. I'd hate to have been downstairs with all you girls slugging away at me and no Pearson to protect me."

Elise grinned a little, "Aw, Hilda, come on. Forget it. Let's part friends or something."

Philip Pearson came back into the room, his face very sober and sad. "Well, Hilda, now I have bad news for you. The club can't take me in until tomorrow."

I almost screamed aloud. "Well, maybe we can find me a cot in a hotel until then." Again I was falsely gay.

"This is the weekend, Hilda. It's worse then."

I had to stay another night in the damned old Moreau house. That was all there was to it. For a few seconds I toyed with the idea of making a shakedown for myself in Janet's park, but the idea hardly seemed practicable, especially as a gale was blowing outside, and the fog was pouring past the windows down Chestnut Street.

Elise said that she was very glad that I had to stay another night. "I was going to beg you to do it anyway. We want a chance to show you that we can be decent so that you won't leave us with too rotten a taste in your mouth." She turned to Philip Pearson. "You stay and have dinner with us, too. It'll relieve the strain."

He agreed, and I thought that he'd be a comfort to me. Maybe I'd be able to persuade him to stay late and then there'd be only a few hours of the night to get through and those I could pass in solitude behind my locked door.

Later after I had unpacked my things, Cassidy sent for me and Philip Pearson.

The detective was pacing up and down the blue parlor, quite obviously excited.

"You saw the lawyer? Hamilton's, I mean," I asked.

"Yes, and he gave me a very good lead, and I can't do a thing with it," he answered. "That's why I want to talk to you. This lawyer is a man named Ernst from Los Angeles. I don't know anything about him, but I'm checking. He swears by all that's holy that he has no idea where Hamilton is and I couldn't shake his story. Anyway, he says that Hamilton communicated with him via a third person—over the telephone. He also swears that he doesn't know who the third person is. Didn't recognize the voice or anything."

"All very mysterious, isn't it? It sounds like a gangster movie," I said.

Pearson flicked his eyes over me as a polite method of telling me to shut up. I shut.

"Well, anyway, this third person told Ernst that Hamilton wanted him to go to the San Francisco police and tell us that Pauline Moreau had a telephone call from Mrs. Oxney last Monday night at the Leavenworth Street house."

"Wow!" I yipped.

"Mrs. Oxney was very angry, and she insisted that Miss Moreau come home at once as she wanted to see her immediately. Miss Moreau left Leavenworth Street a little before two which means that she undoubtedly took a cab—no street cars at that hour—and arrived here probably about quarter after two."

"Then Elise wasn't lying," Pearson said, his voice full of excitement. "She did see Gladys."

"Yes, that's right. At least, it's quite likely, but here's the trouble. Mrs. Oxney is under a doctor's care, and she won't see me." Cassidy's blue eyes were hard and cold.

"But she can't keep that up forever," I said. "She'll have to see you some time."

"Have you seen the papers this afternoon?" Cassidy asked.

I shook my head.

"It's the same old stuff. Two murders, one of them probably directly due to police carelessness. Nothing being done." He shrugged wearily. "I've got to get going on this thing. All I've been able to do so far is to uncover a lot of motives. I haven't one single shred of evidence. This Oxney thing is the first lead I've had that looks as though it might develop favorably. That's why I want you to do something for me, Mrs. Moreau."

I looked at him eagerly. "Sure. What?"

"I think there's a faint possibility that Mrs. Oxney might be willing to see you. I want you to go over to inquire how she's feeling. If you can send a note up to her hinting at this Hamilton business, I think she might talk to you. How about it?"

I nodded vigorously. "Yes, I'll do it. It's worth a try anyway."

The atmosphere of the hall in Gladys Oxney's house was hushed and subdued. The maid, Mabel, wide-eyed and curious, said that she'd take up my message, but that Mrs. Oxney was pretty sick. I had written a little note saying that I had very important information from "J.H." which I wanted to discuss with her, and I felt like a low snake. The woman had been frightened and ill and under terrible strain earlier in the day, but I had to blunt my own feelings with the thought that if she'd had anything to do with Pauline's death, she deserved to have her privacy violated by any means possible to us.

The maid came back quickly and said that Mrs. Oxney would see me.

Her husband, thank heaven, had not appeared.

I had judged Gladys to be about forty-five. When I saw her propped up on a mass of lace pillows against the bulging, shiny peach satin of her bed, she looked nearer sixty. Her attractive curly grey hair was neatly arranged, and she'd made the effort to put on lipstick, but her rather prominent blue eyes were red-rimmed, and the pouches beneath them were blue black. She looked like a bitter caricature of the woman who had come bustling into the Moreaus' house last Tuesday.

"I'm glad you came, Hilda. I've been nearly out of my mind. I had to talk to someone." Her mouth twitched uncontrollably. "What's John Hamilton done? Sold me out?"

I sat down on a luscious blue and peach striped chair and felt myself enfolded by its down cushions. In the over-luxurious atmosphere of Gladys' bedroom, nerves and suffering and fear struck a false note.

"Something like that," I said. "He had some lawyer tell the police that you called Pauline last Monday night and demanded to see her and that Pauline dashed home around two in the morning."

Gladys' bosom rose and fell rapidly under the fine lace of her bedjacket.

"Damn the man. He . . ." She started to cry.

I shrugged my shoulders. I was feeling pretty tough. "Elise said this afternoon that she remembered seeing you come down the steps. That was when she was tight in the flower bed."

Gladys grabbed a wad of Kleenex out of a pretty painted box on the bed table. She blew and sniffled and made a lot of noise.

"My God," she wailed, "my God. It's all over. Everything. It'll all come out now. They know I was there."

CHAPTER 25

As Gladys spoke, I had a pretty vision of myself handing Cassidy his case complete with confession on a figurative silver platter.

I was never so disappointed in all my life.

I leaned forward eagerly waiting for Mrs. Oxney to tell me all about the two murders she'd committed. Instead, she wailed and sniffled and sobbed out a story of illicit love and blackmail and an elderly husband and social ambition. The tale followed a dull and time-worn pattern, and it included nothing of murder. I was wild with frustration.

"Look here, Gladys," I snapped. "You'll have to stop crying. I can't get this straight. You're incoherent." Snapping at her was unkind, but effective in treatment of hysteria. "You say that you had an affair with somebody named Jim Ramey and that he's dead and that Pauline knew it."

The grey curls bobbed. "That's right. He died over five years ago. I heard it at a nightclub Monday night." Sob. Sob. "Some women were talking. I asked them about it even if they were strangers. We were powdering our noses, and they said that everybody knew Jim was dead. *But I didn't.*"

"But what did this have to do with Pauline? Where did she come into it?"

Gladys looked as though I didn't have good sense. "I told you. She introduced me to him down at Caliente, and we used to meet in her house. That was way back in the fall of 1931. Then in 1932 Jim started asking me for money. He was a gambler—a really dreadful person, but exciting—and he was broke."

I remembered the calendar in Pauline's safe deposit box. 1931. That was it. Pauline had kept it so as to be sure of the dates of Gladys' indiscretions!

"Then you knew all along that Pauline was married?" I asked sternly.

She nodded. "I was in Caliente with some friends for the races, and Pauline and her husband were there, and she asked me to keep her secret a little while longer." Her chin trembled helplessly. "She introduced me to Jim for just one reason. I realize that now. She wanted to get something on me so that she'd be sure I kept still. That's why she never told me Jim was dead. She wanted to keep on having a hold on me, and *she blackmailed me for five long years herself!*"

Pauline certainly ran true to form. She at least had the virtue of consistency.

"Then you mean that first this Ramey person blackmailed you, and then after he died, Pauline carried on?"

Gladys nodded. "You see, the affair didn't last long. Just two or three months, and then I got scared and broke it off. It was next June that Jim called me up and asked for money, and I had to give it to him." She wailed again and it was some time before she could speak. "Hilda, you don't know the hell I've lived in for ten long years. Just sheer hell."

She explained at some length that it was pretty tough to be married to a man thirty-five years older than she was. "Although Henry's a fine man, and that's no excuse for my behaving like any other damned fool woman with an old husband." She also explained that the Judge, in common with other old men, was extremely jealous and lived in mortal terror of being made ridiculous by his wife's behavior. "But the worst fear I had," she gasped, "was of his damned, snooty children. My God! They would have given their eyes—all of them—to get something on me."

The Judge, it seemed, had three children two of whom were older than Gladys, and all of them, especially the daughter, had been furious when the Judge married his youthful secretary scarcely a year after his wife's death. "They've never accepted me. They've never introduced me to their friends. They've treated me like a damned pariah. I'm a nobody, and I always will be as far as they're concerned. None of the Judge's old friends would have anything to do with me, and it was all on account of those damned children of his. *I hate them! I hate them!*"

I sincerely hoped that the Judge was deaf. Gladys was making a lot of noise, and I had to talk fast to get her to stop bellowing any longer.

She calmed down finally and did a lot of blowing and sniffling. "The only people who ever accepted me were the Moreaus, and that turned out to be just plain bad luck. Lately, though, I've met a lot of nice women in AWVS, and they like me, because I'm competent, and it really looked as though I might have some decent friends. Now this whole mess will come out, and I'll be worse off than ever."

"Look here, Gladys, I still haven't got this straight. How did Pauline work her racket?" I asked. "How did she make you pay her?"

Gladys' blood pressure must have shot up twenty points. Her face was an apoplectic red. "That dirty, low snake! I'm damned glad she's dead. I just hope she suffered good and plenty before she died." She clamped her mouth shut viciously. "She used to call me and say that Jim had called her and wanted money. I'd give it to her, and I supposed that she was turning it over to him. You see there were letters."

I had a hard time to stop myself from guffawing vulgarly. Letters! That was really too much.

"You wrote letters to this man?" I gasped. "How on earth did Pauline get hold of them?"

She shook her head. "How should I know? Anyway, she got them, and maybe once or twice a year, I'd get one back." Apoplexy looked like a real possibility. "And they kept getting more and more expensive. She got two thousand dollars from me for the last one. My God!"

I was beginning to feel a little more intelligent. "That's why you couldn't pay your bills, then? Is that why the Retail Credit called up the Judge?"

She nodded hard. "That's it. You see, he's never settled any money of my own on me. I just get an allowance for clothes and things and running the house. I didn't know where to turn or what to do. Everything's gone up so, and I'm always in debt anyway. I have been for years, but never as bad as this, and when I realized that it wasn't Jim, but my friend Pauline who was doing this to me, I tell you . . ."

I tell you, I was so mad that I told her what I thought, dashed out to the kitchen, got the knife, and plunged the whole twelve-inch blade . . .

But she didn't tell me that.

"You see, Hilda, Monday night Henry and I had to go to a nightclub with some political friends of his. I hate nightclubs, and I know that smart people don't go to them here in San Francisco, but we had to go, and then in the dressing room, I heard those women talking about Jim Ramey. He was sort of a prominent figure in his own world." Her mouth was bitter. "The underworld—almost. When I got home, I couldn't sleep. I was wild with rage, so I called Pauline in the Leavenworth Street house. I knew she'd be there, because I'd seen John on the street Monday. I made her come home, and I sneaked out of the house and walked over there. She opened the door before I could ring, and we had a dreadful row in the front parlor. We didn't even turn on the lights, but I called her everything I could think of. I told her she wouldn't get one more red cent out of me—it wasn't as though she needed it—and she could turn over the letters or I'd tell the girls about Hamilton. She was wild, but she promised finally, and I left." Gladys had talked as though wound up to top speed. "*And I left her alive.* We didn't even go upstairs. Understand that!"

I shook my head in amazement. It was some story. "Did Janet know about this?" I asked finally. I was doing a lot of thinking.

"Yes. I told her Thursday. She said she'd try and help me get those damned letters. There's only two or three left, but I don't care now." She started to cry again. "The whole thing'll come out now. I'll have to tell Henry, and he'll probably divorce me, and I'll have to leave all this . . ." She gestured with a plump hand to indicate the fancy bedroom full of ruffles and soft comfort.

"Look here," I said firmly, "pull yourself together. What kind of a man is

Hamilton?"

"Decent." Sniff, sniff. "Not a gentleman, of course, but the poor idiot was crazy about Pauline. I'm sure he had no idea what she was doing to people. He thought she was terribly smart, and he admired her taste. He thought she was aristocratic, too, but of course, the Moreaus aren't." She darted a guilty glance at me. "I'm sorry. I didn't mean to be rude or critical."

"That's all right," I said. "I've met people who were better bred than the Moreaus, God knows. I don't understand how David . . ." Then I stopped myself. "You'd better see Cassidy, Gladys. If you can convince him that you left Pauline alive, maybe he'll help you. About the letters, I mean. After all, blackmail is illegal."

"But what about all this money I owe? Even if I get the letters back, what am I going to tell Henry?"

I shrugged callously. "You'll have to think up your own lies. I can't help you there. I'll tell Cassidy that you'll see him."

She wailed again. "I can't bear it. I can't bear it."

Oh, nuts, I thought, but I didn't say it. I made a few polite remarks and left. I wasn't at all convinced that Gladys hadn't killed Pauline and Janet, too—Janet could very nicely have known about Gladys' little affair—but if she did kill two women, why had she talked so freely to me? And all through the interview, her principal concern seemed to be getting thrown out of the peach satin bed because she'd committed adultery. She apparently hadn't worried at all about being thrown into a death cell because she'd committed murder. May and December, I thought, with hopeless lack of originality.

CHAPTER 26

I walked the two and a half blocks back to the Moreau house very slowly. I wanted time to think. Gladys admitted she'd been with Pauline a very short time before her death. Gladys had Janet at her house before the murderer made Janet the second victim, and she could very easily have followed Janet to the park, and stabbed her with a knife which she'd had the forethought to steal from the Moreaus' kitchen during the two preceding days, but what about the note?

Whoever threw the knife at me in the park must have known about the note. According to the maid's story, Janet Holmes had come into the kitchen alone, and I'd had the feeling that Gladys was out of the house when the grocery boy arrived. Well, maybe. Maybe Gladys had been able to get at the note earlier in the day, steam it open, and make her plans to frame me.

Back in the house, I told Cassidy that Gladys would see him. "But I'll let her tell you the story. You don't want it secondhand," I said. "And, incidentally, I'm not going to tell anyone in this house about it. It's none of their business anyway, and if Mrs. Oxney is innocent, there's no point in scandal-mongering about something that happened a long time ago."

Cassidy thanked me for my help and left. I went down the hall to the dressing room and took off my things so that I could join the family at dinner.

I tossed my hat up onto the shelf, but it fell back before it lit firmly. I threw it again, and the second time it fell down it brought something with it that hit me a good crack on the forehead.

I jumped to get out of the way of the falling object, and blinked from the sharp little stab of pain. I looked around to see what had hit me.

An oval silver picture frame lay on the brussels carpet of the dressing room. The frame which I'd last seen in Pauline Moreau's bedroom in Leavenworth Street.

"What the hell?" I said, right out loud.

After all frames do look alike, but this one was enough like the frame around Berthe's picture to warrant further investigation. I dragged over the straight chair and stood on it so that I could get a good view of the high shelf.

There it was. Berthe's photograph and the velvet pad for the back of the frame. The thing that held it in. And the small oval of glass, too.

All pulled apart up there on the shelf.

"What the hell again?"

I started to reassemble the various parts of the photograph and its frame. Then I changed my mind. I'd leave them there for Cassidy to look at. As I had already picked up the velvet pad, I looked at it closely. On the part which would be against the back of the picture, the nap of the velvet had a mark on it about two inches square. I peered at the shelf again. There was nothing there except the oval of glass and the sepia-toned photograph of a blonde girl with a wind-blown haircut (circa 1926). If there had been something in the photograph recently that made the mark on the velvet, it was gone now.

I put the frame back up on the shelf, mentally apologizing to Cassidy for any fingerprints I might have smudged and carefully adjusted my hat to cover the things.

Then I crawled down off the chair and did a little thinking. Somebody in the Moreau house took the photograph out of Pauline's bedroom, pulled it hastily apart, and threw it up on the shelf.

The thing that made the two-inch mark could have been cardboard or folded paper or another small photograph. The plumbing fixture before me gave me a pretty good idea of where it had gone.

Well, well, well.

When I had washed my face and hands and tidied my hair, I went into the dining room.

Philip Pearson got to his feet at my entrance and pulled out a chair for me, and I sat down amid smiles and questions and a certain amount of self-consciousness on all sides.

"Did you see Gladys?" Anne asked pleasantly, just as though she hadn't tried to do me all kinds of dirt.

"Yes," I said briefly. "She's probably talking to Cassidy right now."

"What'd she tell you? Did she admit she'd been over here?" Elise asked eagerly.

I stalled for time by taking a big bite of avocado. I shook my head until I managed to swallow. "I'd rather not talk about it until Cassidy says what's what."

"Nuts!" Marthe said with finality.

Anne and Elise and Sophie smiled and raised their eyebrows, and the conversation turned to the war. Throughout the rest of the dinner I was preoccupied and quiet and not very receptive to the obvious efforts of the Moreaus to include me in the talk and to make me feel less like a leper.

Nanette, fat and sullen, came in to take away the plates—my own was still full of good food—and to bring the dessert and coffee. When she had gone back to the kitchen, Elise hissed in a stage whisper, "She's leaving. Isn't that God's blessing? I was scared to death she'd insist on staying."

I nodded and looked at the elaborate embossed wallpaper and the big center fixture that had obviously been built for illuminating gas, not electricity, and at the heavy walnut sideboard laden with massive silver. I looked at everything except these women, one of whom I was pretty sure was a murderer.

After dinner, when we were settled with cigarettes in the living room, my husband's sisters continued to be nice to me.

They were, of course, back to their pet subject. Their money and how much there was and how soon they'd be able to get their paws on it. I didn't blame them for their interest, but it was still pretty difficult for me to understand how they could so easily ignore the fact that they were all suspected of murder.

Sophie turned to Philip Pearson. "Look here, Philip, you can help us with all this, can't you? You can arrange loans or whatever we need so that we won't have to wait too long for our affairs to be settled, can't you?"

Pearson smiled tolerantly. "I'm afraid not, Sophie. After all, I'm representing David and Hilda in this, you know."

Sophie pouted. She looked pretty unattractive. "You were our friend long before you ever heard of Hilda. I don't see why...."

"Hush, Sophie," Anne said with emphasis. "There are other lawyers. After all, Philip's known David for a long time."

It was heavy sledding, but Anne seemed determined to keep things as pleasant as possible.

After an hour of desultory and uninspired conversation, Philip got up to go. When we were saying good night to him in the front hall, Cassidy came up the front steps, looking cold and unfriendly. He said that he wanted to see Nanette.

Marthe took him down to the maid's quarters in the basement, and I waited in the frigid blue front parlor so that I could tell him about the mysterious picture.

The rest of the family went upstairs to bed after a lot of polite good nights to me. Anne had said that she would stay in Rose's room as her own apartment gave her little comfort or pleasure any more.

When Cassidy finally came back upstairs, his expression was still bleak and unfriendly.

"That old hag," he said bitterly, "is a blackmailer from the word go. She undoubtedly heard Mrs. Oxney around two o'clock quarrelling with Pauline Moreau. She's been trying to blackmail Mrs. Oxney, and that's why Mrs. Oxney finally decided to talk. To you and to me. I guess Mrs. O. has had enough of that kind of thing. In a way, I'm kind of sorry for her."

I nodded in agreement. "Yes, I am, too. Of course, she's been an awful fool, but I can't help sympathizing with her. Does Nanette admit what she was doing? Does she admit that she came upstairs and heard the quarrel?"

Cassidy snorted loudly. "Of course not. She says they're all lying. She also says she wants to leave this house early tomorrow morning. I suppose we might as well let her. She can do more harm than good around here."

Then I told him about the picture and took him down the hall to the dressing room to see it. He got up on the straight chair and lifted up my big black hat and looked at the things. He tsk-tsk-ed in bewilderment and picked up the silver frame after he had wrapped his hand carefully in a giddy blue cotton handkerchief. He turned the frame slowly from side to side beneath the light. "Can't see any prints, but I'll take it downtown just to be sure. You say it hit you on the head and you picked it up?"

"Yes, I did. I wish I'd remembered the handkerchief trick, but I was so startled I didn't think. Have you looked at that velvet pad thing?"

He looked at it for a long two minutes. "There's a mark there all right. Somebody went to a lot of trouble over this thing. I'd sure like to know what was in it."

I pointed to the toilet. "Whatever it was, I'll lay money on the line that it went down there."

Slowly and carefully he assembled the various parts of the photograph and wrapped them gently in the blue hanky and then put the whole works in his pocket.

I saw him to the door, and then I went upstairs to try again to write a letter to David at the little marble-topped table in my room.

I made four or five false starts. Never in my life had I faced such a difficult task. I had to tell my husband, far away on the Atlantic, that his eldest sister had been murdered and that quite possibly one of his other sisters had done the murder.

At last my pen began to work. I wrote on and on and on, trying to tell him completely but as briefly as possible all that had happened in the six days I had been in San Francisco.

I told him, too, about the scheme Pauline had cooked up with Duncan English's wife, but I made a great effort to emphasize that I was in no danger and that Cassidy seemed fairly sure of my innocence, and that I was really all right.

When I had written for a couple of hours, I realized that I was dead tired and cold and cramped and starving hungry. I thought for a minute or two about the good dinner I'd sent back untouched to the kitchen, and the more I thought the hungrier I became.

Finally I finished my letter, reread it, put it in an envelope, and sealed it. Then I undressed and put on my warm robe and went down the hall to the bathroom. After I had brushed my teeth I drank two glasses of cold water which was a great mistake. The pangs of hunger fairly tore at my vitals under the impact of the icy water.

With the light still on in the bathroom, I stood in the open door looking into the dark hall. At the front of the house, the door to my room was ajar, and a narrow shaft of light came through reassuringly. I wanted something to eat so that I could go to sleep. My problem was quite simple. All I had to do was to turn on more lights and go down in the kitchen and eat and come back upstairs.

It would be stupid to wander around the creaking old house in the dark, but I didn't have to do that.

I tied my bathrobe around me more tightly and went over to the switch by the stairs and snapped on the light.

I walked down the stairs with no special effort to be quiet, and in the lower hall, I snapped another switch and had more light. As far as I could tell from the sound, the house and its inhabitants were asleep. In the dining room, I groped for the chain on the center fixture, gave it a yank, and then went on to the kitchen.

I had to grope in there for a few chilly seconds, but at last I had light pouring around me, and I quickly went to work on the ice box. There was half an avocado and a piece of lemon which I arranged on a large dinner plate. Then I sliced some lamb and debated a second or two about making a sandwich until I investigated the bread box and found some nice English muffins. I lit the oven and cut a muffin in half and put it in to toast. Then I put water on for coffee—this was before rationing so that I had no qualms about helping myself to four fat tablespoonfuls of the now precious bean.

My little feast tasted very fine. In fact, so fine that I cut more lamb and toasted another muffin and put plenty of butter on said muffin, too. Oscar and I were really very hungry, and I was having a good time feeding both of us. At last I sat back with a large sigh and lit a cigarette and prepared to enjoy my third cup of coffee. I was warm and sleepy and comfortable, and I knew I'd sleep well.

Suddenly I put down my cup. The coffee slopped into the saucer, and a rackety pulse beat somewhere in the region of my muffins and lamb.

There was a noise of some sort in the dining room. "Hey," I yelled. "Who's there?"

The ordinary everyday smell of the coffee and my cigarette were somehow incongruous. I felt that it was out of place to be excited and scared when I was doing something as commonplace as drinking coffee and smoking a cigarette.

Slowly I got to my feet and forced myself over to the swinging door into the dining room. Halfway to the door I heard another muffled noise. I put the cigarette in my saucer. No sense in dropping it from my trembling hand and burning holes in the Moreaus' linoleum.

Very reluctantly I pushed open the swinging door. The dining room was dark. Absolutely black dark without any light in it at all. I sighed heavily, in reaction to my self-imposed tension. Somebody had seen the light on, and had turned it out. Quite simple. I'd do the same.

I propped open the kitchen door and turned on the dining room light and went on to the hall.

"Who's there?" I hissed. No sense in waking the whole house.

The hall was dark and so were the stairs and the upstairs hall. There was no answering voice.

Now what? Should I yell and wake up the house so that I could find out who had gone around turning off my comforting lights? Or should I just get the hell up the stairs as fast as I could and get behind my locked door and into my big cold bed?

Upstairs for me, baby, I muttered.

I had a very clear feeling that I was acting like an overly apprehensive fool, but I was also extremely uncomfortable.

But how about the lights? I'd have to go back to the kitchen and the dining room after I got the hall lighted and then I'd have to come downstairs again after I turned on the light in the upstairs hall. It was getting very complicated.

I was no longer hungry, but at what a price.

The closed doors leading into the hall were somehow ominous.

Suddenly I turned and ran for the stairs. The hell with the lights. I'd leave them on. The Moreaus had the money for the electric bill all right.

Stumbling awkwardly I forced myself up the stairs. With a muttered curse I pulled my robe out from under my clumsy feet and grabbed the railing of the baluster. At the top I swung myself around to go toward the front of the house. There was no bright shaft of light coming from my own door. Somebody had turned off my light too. Somebody. *Somebody.*

A dry scream froze in my mouth. I made a wild, strangling sound. I had bumped into somebody.

"Good God, who is it?" Anne's voice spoke irritatedly from the dark. I was absolutely mute with terror.

Finally the lights went on.

"Hilda," she snapped, "what in God's name are you doing? I heard you running and crashing around." Her huge dark eyes blazed in her white face. The white wings in her black hair made her look like a charcoal drawing.

"The lights," I stammered. "Somebody turned them all off."

"I should think so," she said tartly. "What's the matter with you?"

"I was hungry," I said painfully. "I went down and got something to eat and while I was still in the kitchen somebody turned the lights off. Was it you?"

She shook her head angrily. "No, it wasn't. And why shouldn't somebody turn the lights off? Now for God's sake, go to bed and let the rest of the household get some sleep."

She gave her robe a yank and marched downstairs to turn off the lights. She acted very injured and put upon, and I felt like the world's prize ass.

I shrugged and went into my own room and carefully locked the door and got into bed.

CHAPTER 27

In the morning at breakfast I inquired about who had turned out the lights. My question met with blank stares and shaking heads. No one had turned off the lights. Neither Marthe nor Elise nor Anne nor Sophie.

"Then the pixies must have done it," I snapped. "The same pixies that stole Berthe's picture and pulled it apart and left it in the dressing room."

There were cheerful female chirpings to greet my statement. There was no information forthcoming, however, so I allowed Anne to take charge of the conversation, and I tried to answer her conversational gambits civilly.

"David's on a transport, I think," I said in answer to her question. "He didn't tell me exactly, but I gathered from a few hints that that's the kind of ship he's on. At least that means he'll be in a convoy."

David, David, David, where art thou? And how did you manage to grow up to be such a nice man when you were born and reared in this booby hatch?

During the morning Philip Pearson's secretary telephoned to say that her employer would be in court most of the day but would be around to pick me up late in the afternoon and take me to his apartment.

When I told Elise about the arrangement, she smiled and asked if she could come and call. Inwardly I said no, that I had no desire to see any or all of the members of the Moreau family. Actually I said that I'd be glad to see her.

"I think I'll learn to make wee garments," she said. "I'm really very thrilled about being an aunt. What will you call it if it's a boy?"

I shrugged. "I don't know, Maybe John after my father. David likes that name. But I do know that I most certainly won't call him Michael or Peter. Why do names go in cycles? Every woman in the world has named her child Michael or Peter in the last five years."

Sophie spent the morning on the telephone calling all the domestic agencies trying to get a retinue of servants on short notice.

"We can certainly afford decent service now," she said, trying to look like a competent chatelaine.

"Nanette go?" I asked.

She pursed her mouth. "I suppose so. She didn't cook breakfast. I had to help, and I hate housework."

Marthe went out before lunch and came in, looking very depressed and tired, at about three. When Elise asked her where she'd been she snapped that she'd been up to see Rose who was still having the vapors. "Can you imagine, Elise? She wouldn't see me. Sally told her I was there, and she yelled and cried. Susan told me not to come back for a day or two."

Elise and I had been hugging the fire in the living room for a couple of hours and had been talking about fixing some tea for ourselves when Marthe came in.

Elise stood up. "Let's make tea. It'd do us good. This lousy, rotten weather. I don't know what the world's coming to. We're supposed to have our summer in September, and here it is the 12th and still as foggy as July."

We drank the tea and ate what was left of the English muffins which we spread liberally with strawberry jam.

"I'd still like to know who turned out those lights last night," I said. "I don't see the object in lying."

"Maybe Gladys came calling," Elise said with a mild grin.

I snorted. "Or maybe Rose did it."

"Pooh," Marthe said. "That baby."

Then Elise started to talk about my baby. She made a lot of extravagant prophecies about its beauty and brains and charm. She seemed to be having a good time, and I hoped that she might someday have one of her own.

Finally we took the tea things back to the kitchen and washed them, and Marthe and Elise talked about what we were going to have for dinner.

I started toward the dressing room to wash my hands, but as I passed the door to the basement, I remembered the hobbyhorse I'd seen down there several days before. I thought I'd like to take another look at it. If it was in decent enough condition, I'd ask the girls to let David and me have it for Oscar. The first grandchild and stuff.

A blast of cold dusty air hit me in the face as I went down the splintery stairs. Pale, dull grey light filtered through the dirty windows, and it was really hard for me to get a good look at the hobbyhorse. I pulled several other bits of junk away from it, and at last was able to drag it out into a cleared space on the floor. It was very dusty, and the paint was worn through on the once bright red saddle. One of Dobbin's eyes was missing, and his mane looked slightly moth-eaten, and his leather harness was rotten, but he had possibilities. I smiled to myself. It'd be pretty nice to repair this old toy, and perhaps by the time Oscar was eight or nine months old, I'd be able to hold him on the horse, and David could be there to admire. I could see the whole pretty family picture. Bright sunlight streaming through very full dotted Swiss curtains. A nice baby with a handsome father and a mother who'd get her figure back....

The clear blue linoleum of the imaginary nursery floor disappeared to be replaced by a dusty wooden floor with brownish tracks on it the shape of a woman's shoes. The tracks led from the foot of the stairs.... Why, right over to my own feet. Right to where I was standing.

I walked over to the foot of the stairs and leaned down and looked. There was a sticky puddle of something brownish. The puddle came across the sloping, crooked floor that had settled in odd lumps and bumps during the ninety years of the house's existence. The puddle came from under Nanette's door.

I put my right forefinger in the puddle and then held it up to my nose and sniffed. It smelled sweetish and unpleasant, unlike anything I'd ever smelled in my life before. I stood up with an involuntary jerk. Run, my mind said. Run fast. You don't know what this is, but run. Before you find out.

The basement, the whole house was full of evil, full of terror.

Three times more I put my finger in that dirty brown puddle. It always smelled the same. Sweetish and unclean and ominous.

I wiped my left hand on my skirt. It was wet and sticky and cold. I couldn't wipe off my right hand. I couldn't have that terrible brown stuff on my clothes.

I turned and stumbled up the rickety wooden stairs and slammed the door and leaned against it panting.

Elise looked up from her work of setting the table for dinner.

"What's cookin'?" she said. "You look as though you'd seen a ghost. What were you doing down there anyway?"

I swallowed the sandpaper that seemed to be lining my throat. Slowly I shook my head and walked out of the room without answering.

Blindly, almost without feeling I crashed into the damned little heater. I ignored my own muffled yelp of pain and went on into the front parlor and telephoned to Cassidy. I don't remember to this day what I said to him, but he must have understood the urgency of my summons. He came within a very few minutes, his arrival heralded by the excitement-producing wail of sirens.

Somehow I managed to keep the jittery family out of the front parlor as I told him about the puddle in the basement.

"Did you try the door?" he asked quickly.

I shook my head. "No," I said. "I was too scared."

"Good," he said and went off with his men.

Nanette was, of course, dead. Stabbed by another knife from the Moreaus' kitchen. But this was a smaller knife which had not brought death as quickly as it had come to Janet or even to Pauline.

Cassidy told me that it looked as though the old woman had crawled from one end of her Victorian sitting room almost to the door with that sharp, dreadful knife sticking out of her back, only to die at last in front of the door that might have led to help.

The pattern of his investigation was by now familiar routine. It had lost much of its terror, and at times I was bored and weary with waiting, numb with experience.

I told him, of course, of the extinguished lights and of my meeting with Anne in the upper hall. I told him about going down for something to eat with the lights ablaze and coming back in the dark.

"You say you called out?" he asked eagerly.

I nodded. "But no one answered. No one spoke until I crashed into Anne upstairs."

"What time was this?"

"Around one, I suppose. I'd been writing to my husband. A long letter."

He let his lids fall over his icy eyes. "What was this noise like? The noise you heard in the dining room?"

I shook my head. I tried to move back in time, to reproduce in my mind the two noises I'd heard the night before, but it was no use. "They were just noises," I said inadequately. "Maybe bumping into a chair or something." Then I jumped. I'd almost had the noise, the second one, but it trickled away, lost in my tired mind.

"Has the doctor looked at her?" I asked. "Does he say when she died?"

Cassidy nodded. "Yes. She didn't die right away, you know. Lived maybe an hour or two. I think you probably heard the murderer come upstairs around one right after she'd stabbed the woman. The doctor says he thinks she'd been dead maybe fourteen or fifteen hours."

I shuddered without wanting to. I was thankful that I'd stayed in the kitchen until the lights were safely out and the murderer hidden in the dark. I had little hope that she would have spared me in her escape back to the safety of her own room.

"But *why?*" I said. "*Why* kill Nanette?"

Cassidy shrugged. "She tried to blackmail Mrs. Oxney, didn't she? Well, I think that when she failed there, she tried it on the murderer and got killed for her efforts. I've had the feeling all along that the maid knew a lot more than she was willing to tell. If she heard Mrs. Oxney in the house, why isn't it reasonable that she might just as well have heard the murderer upstairs?"

I had disliked the maid thoroughly, and I had no sympathy for her as a blackmailer. I certainly couldn't mourn her, but it seemed somehow horrible that the old woman had lain there dying for an hour when help was so near. If we'd got her in time, she might have been able to tell us who killed her.

But we had got to Pauline before she was dead, and she hadn't been able to tell us anything.

I jerked myself up in my chair and looked hard at Cassidy. "I've been thinking about something. I've been thinking that if we'd got to the maid before she was dead, she might have been able to tell us who . . ." I stopped in thought.

"Well, what, Mrs. Moreau?" Cassidy was impatient. His nerves were frayed and thin, too.

"Pauline," I said very slowly. "She wasn't dead when I went in there. I think she was trying to tell me something."

"Think," he said. "Think very hard."

I closed my eyes and thought. "Pauline lying in my arms. A long whistling sound, a sibilance. Sssssss. And then the bright red bubbles," I said.

"Elise? Sophie? Gladys? Rose?" Cassidy said the names slowly, drawing out the s's.

I sighed from the tension. "I don't know. I don't know," I said. "But why would Nanette be such a fool as to let the murderer in her room? Didn't she know she was in danger?"

"Greed has often been known to triumph over caution," he said bitterly. "You may go now. Please ask Doctor Moreau to come in."

I went into the living room and gave Anne Cassidy's message. She nodded silently and walked out.

For the first time the Moreau sisters were taking a murder hard. Sophie and Anne and Elise and Marthe looked white and scared and completely washed out. There were no wisecracks, no Gallic shoulder shrugs of dismissal. It had taken three murders to jar their complacency, but at last it was really jarred.

A policeman sat on one of the small rosewood side-chairs and kept us from talking even if we'd wanted to. We all smoked and moved about restlessly and just looked at each other.

Anne came back, and the other three followed in turn.

They looked no more white and scared when they came back from talking to Cassidy than when they had gone.

I looked from one face to the other, searching desperately for some sign of guilt, the mark of Cain, anything that would end this frightful, bloody massacre that had taken place in less than a week.

Three women had died. None of them was a particularly desirable human being, and I could not feel that the world would suffer their loss. Too many good young men were dying in too many corners of the world for the deaths of these three women to matter greatly, but I thought with dread of the ghastly effect these murders must have had on the mind of the killer. How could any human being live with that terrible load of blood and death on her mind?

I rubbed my shin distractedly where I had banged it on the heater and looked from one face to another.

Anne's great eyes told only that she was sick with horror. Elise's nervous movements with her long, thin hands seemed to say that she was dangerously near to cracking. Sophie's mouth sagged and twitched. Marthe's furtive eyes belied the calm of her facial muscles.

When Cassidy came to the door, I stood up.

"You cannot make me stay in this house another night," I said. "Philip Pearson ought to have been here by now. He's lending me his apartment, and you can put a policeman in every room if you like, but I simply am not going to stay here." My voice was shaking perilously. There were dammed-up tears in it. "You'll have to let me go."

"All right," Cassidy said flatly. "Go upstairs and get your things. Mr. Pearson's waiting on the porch."

I walked out of the room. In the hall, after I had closed the door, I turned to Cassidy. I gestured toward the living room. "What do they say?" I asked.

"Nothing. They were in bed asleep. Doctor Anne says she was wakened by your racket and came into the hall to investigate. She didn't see anyone else. The lights were out."

"It doesn't seem possible," I said. "There wasn't enough time for the lights to be put out. I think she saw something. She's so terrified. Can't you see?"

"I can't prove anything, Mrs. Moreau. Not anything. I'll be talking to Pearson for a few minutes. Come down when you're ready."

I threw my things that I had unpacked the day before back into my overnight bag. Then I gathered up my bag and gloves and coat. My hat was downstairs. I put my things in the upstairs hall and went back to get my other large bags.

Thank God, I said over and over again. Thank God I'm getting out of this house. Forever. All my life. I'll never come back.

I was shaking clumsily and dropping things and doing an altogether bad job of trying to get my things downstairs when Sophie came up the stairs.

"May I help you, Hilda?" she said in a shaky voice. "You shouldn't carry all that stuff."

"Thanks," I said hastily and turned back for the rest. Then I stopped in my tracks. "Good Lord, Sophie. What's that?"

Outside the night sky was full of long, brilliant shafts of clear yellow light. It was magnificent and amazing.

"The searchlights," Sophie said dully. "They're practicing. They shine all those lights in the sky so that they can find airplanes, and then the antiaircraft can shoot them down. That is Jap planes, not ours, but they practice."

I could see very little from the hall window. "It's beautiful, isn't it?" I turned away from the window. Right in front of me were the stairs leading to the cupola and the roof. "Look, I could see better from the roof, couldn't I?"

"Yes," Sophie said flatly. "You could. I'll take your things down. You go look. They don't last long."

She turned away, and I ran quickly up the stairs and out onto the roof.

From every corner of the Bay the great long shafts of light stabbed the clear night sky. The beams swung and crossed each other and went on and off, stretching their beautiful pattern. I thought almost guiltily that here was one phase of war that was wonderful to watch, not ugly or grim or deadly.

I stood there in the brisk wind blowing from the west, sucking in great breaths of clean air, until I was almost dizzy. The air and the waving, groping, swinging lights. Something clean and beautiful to take away from my husband's old home. Something decent, too, in its implications of protection.

High up, miles above the earth, I saw three long fingers of light converge on a plane. They caught it tight in their net of illumination. These men with their wonderful big searchlights would be able to catch enemy planes in that net, too.

My eyes swept the sky all around me. I must remember this, I kept saying to myself. I must remember this to tell to my grandchildren. The big searchlights on San Francisco Bay a few months after Pearl Harbor.

Then I turned. Just slightly. Just enough to see the wild, haggard face of a woman. Just enough to see her long, flabby arm holding something heavy. Something that was coming down, down, down closer to my head.

There was death in the woman's hand and in her heart. I knew that.

"Hilda! Look out! Jump!"

Jump? How could I jump? I was frozen there on that windy flat roof. Dizzy from cold air and searchlights. Paralyzed in the face of death.

The thing in the woman's hand fell heavily on my shoulder.

She screamed at me, and little bubbles formed at the corner of her tight, agonized mouth. *"You saw my leg, didn't you? You were going to tell!"* Then she ran.

Marthe tore past me after the other desperate running figure. A terrible scream of death anguish split the night into a million ugly pieces.

The searchlights went out. The night and the city were dimmed-out once more.

Three stories below Sophie Moreau's body lay on a hard bed of concrete.

CHAPTER 28

It is December now, and I am still in the Moreau house in San Francisco. At first I didn't want to stay, but it seemed somehow inhuman to go off safely and comfortably and leave David's sisters alone with their dreadful grief. Later I stayed because I wanted to, because the girls were kind and interested and after all, my family.

The house isn't dreary and cold and dingy anymore. With an adequate heating system and refurbished upholstery and carpets, it's an interesting, comfortable old house. And even with its tragedies still so close to us in time, we all know that what happened wasn't the fault of the house, but of its inhabitants.

Basically, I think that the fault lies in the rather whimsical will of an old man who foolishly and lazily gave one of his children too much power.

It was not easy to answer all the "whys" of Sophie's and Pauline's behavior, but yesterday when I was going through Sophie's massive walnut desk, I found the answer to the last question. We had all avoided Sophie's room until the rest of the house was done over, but after my nap yesterday, I went in to start clearing out her things. It had to be done, of course, and I felt that it would be easier for me than for any of the others.

Deep under a pile of old letters, I found a yellowed newspaper clipping. It came from the *Los Angeles Times* for October 21, 1927. It gave a list of marriage licenses issued in Las Vegas, Nevada, and included, of course, the names of Pauline Moreau and John Hamilton. Sophie had known for years of Pauline's marriage, and only the terrible hold which Pauline had over her had kept her silent.

That hold was, of course, Berthe's murder in 1927. Berthe didn't fall out of a window. Sophie quarreled with her and threatened her with physical violence. Poor silly Berthe ran to the roof to get away from Sophie. She couldn't have chosen a worse place, because Sophie followed her and pushed her over.

Elise helped us to figure this point out. She told us that at the time of Berthe's death, she had come home from a party, a little the worse for alcohol, and had fallen into a heavy sleep. And poor Elise was only twenty then.

A terrible scream had wakened her, but she was slow about getting up, and by the time she went into Pauline's lighted room, Sophie and Pauline were leaning out the open window looking down below.

"I asked them what had happened," Elise said. "Sophie looked more dead than alive, but Pauline seemed to have the situation in hand. She said that Berthe had fallen out the window. I was still pretty tight, of course, and nothing really sank in very well, but later I noticed the water on the stairs."

We were talking in my room the morning after Sophie's death. Elise sighed and sat down on my bed. Rose and Marthe were on the other side of it, and Anne sat in an armchair. She looked ghastly, even after the drug-induced sleep which she'd had the night before.

I shook my head from side to side. One week. Three murders and one suicide in one week. And I myself lucky to be alive.

"Water on the stairs, Elise? What do you mean?" I asked.

"I saw some wet footprints on the stairs that go up to the cupola. It was raining that night, and I asked Pauline about it, and she said I was drunk and to keep my mouth shut. Sophie got that water on the stairs after she'd pushed Berthe off the roof. That's why she'd never go up on the roof. Not until she had to, of course, when she thought she could push you off."

I pulled the covers a little tighter around me and put my hands on the hot water bottle.

"I knew last night that she'd killed Berthe," I said, "but I still don't understand why. Was she crazy?"

Anne shook her head, her dark eyes clouded with grief. "Only man crazy, Hilda. I guess poor Sophie thought that Philip Pearson was her beau. When Berthe told her she was engaged to Philip, Sophie must have been wild with jealousy." She turned to Marthe. "You were a little girl then, only ten years old, but you told me once that Sophie, as well as Pauline, had had a fight with Berthe that night. Do you remember?"

Marthe nodded and tightened her hand over Rose's. "Yes," she said, "I heard them and after a little while I heard the scream, but I was very young and sleepy. It wasn't until the next morning that Pauline came in and told me that Berthe had fallen out the window."

"You see, Hilda, Pauline was so anxious to hang onto the money that she concealed the murder of her own sister all these years," Anne said sadly. "I think maybe Berthe had told Sophie that Pauline was married, and Pauline agreed to cover up for Sophie if Sophie would promise never to reveal the marriage."

I groaned and shuddered at the same time.

"Finally, Sophie saw her last chance to get a man slipping out of her hands. She decided that she was going to marry Mr. Brown, and the only way she could do it was to kill Pauline. Your being here made the time ripe for it. There was an outsider in the house for the first time in years, and Lord knows she tried hard enough to throw suspicion on you."

I nodded. The wire she'd sent to Cassidy, the keys she'd planted on me after she knocked me out in the back entrance of Pauline's Leavenworth Street house, the telephone call to Cassidy to let him know that I was in the house, the knife she'd thrown in the park in the hope that I'd mark it with my fingerprints. It all stacked up very neatly. I was lucky that she'd overdone it a bit so that Cassidy didn't think me guilty.

"Where were you and David when Berthe died, Anne?" I asked.

"I was a senior over at Cal. David was away at school in Menlo Park." She shrugged her shoulders. "When we came home, Pauline had her story all fixed. The only doubt was whether or not Berthe had killed herself or fallen accidentally as Pauline said she had. Naturally, we kept still."

Marthe looked at me. "Pauline dearly loved a nice confession all down in black and white. Look what she made me do, all on account of that fifty bucks' worth of housekeeping money. You can bet your last dollar that that was what she had hidden in the back of Berthe's picture."

And a very neat hiding place, too. "Sophie must have been nearly crazy when she couldn't find that thing in the Leavenworth Street house," Elise said, exhaling a long plume of smoke that was blue in the morning sunshine. "She was terribly jittery before we went down to Pauline's house, and after we came back, remember how calm and stuffy she was? Telling me I ought to be ashamed of myself for admitting I was a drunk and stuff."

I remembered. "But do you think that Janet knew that Sophie had killed Berthe? I doubt it," I said. "After all, Pauline kept Sophie's confession hidden in a picture. That looks to me as though Pauline was keeping it hidden from her husband and therefore probably from Janet. Otherwise, she would have kept it in the bank box with Marthe's little paper. After all, they told us at the bank that John Hamilton used to come down there with Pauline to clip coupons and get things in and out."

"Janet knew," Elise said. "Janet was no dummy, and she was here for the weekend when Berthe died. If I, in my drunken condition, saw that water on the stairs, you can bet that Janet did, too. She and Pauline were undoubtedly tied up in their criminal-legal-whatever partnership away back then. She probably just kept her mouth shut, but when Pauline was killed, she drew a few well-chosen conclusions and was going to tell you about them in exchange for making us lay off her. Not prosecute, I mean."

I didn't want to talk about Janet. The mention of her name made the pain in Anne's eyes deepen. It was still a bitter blow for her to be reminded that her friend hadn't been a friend at all but a spy from the enemy's camp.

"And Nanette tried her blackmailing tricks just once too often," Marthe said. "First she blackmailed Pauline into keeping her here at a hundred dollars a month, then she tried it on poor old Gladys, and finally on Sophie."

I was thoughtful for a minute. "Remember when Nanette said she heard somebody come in the kitchen at one-thirty? She said something about how they probably came to get the knife. I'll bet anything she actually saw Sophie do it—get the knife, I mean. She was obviously wandering around the house that night, and she could have stood at the top of the basement stairs and watched."

Anne and Elise nodded soberly. "That's right," they said in chorus.

"And Nanette is certainly no loss," Marthe said callously. "She scared the pants off of Rose the other day. That's why Rose left."

"Really, Rose?" I yipped. "What'd she do?"

Rose's infantile face was a little less infantile. The child had done a lot of growing up in the last week. "She said she knew who did it, and that the Moreau family would have to take care of her the rest of her life or she'd do something awful to us. I was terrified. I was sick, too. I didn't want to know. I was so afraid . . ."

Marthe snorted. "She was afraid it might have been me."

Marthe. Funny, difficult, bitter Marthe who had saved my life. I squeezed the hot water bottle nervously. I had a hard time bringing out the words which needed so badly to be spoken.

"Marthe, how on earth did you happen to come upstairs last night?" My voice shook.

She shrugged her shoulders. "I don't really know. Sophie just looked sort of sly when she went into the dining room, and then a few seconds later, I heard someone go up the stairs. I . . . I was just nervous. When I saw her heading for the roof, I knew there was something up. I . . . I saw her pick up that loose brick where it had fallen from the chimney." Marthe's face was paper-white. My own probably was, too. "I damned near died."

"Last night, Hilda, before you passed out, you kept talking about your leg and the heater," Elise said. "What'd you mean?"

Icy little drops of perspiration formed on my forehead.

"One more murder was no skin off poor old Sophie's nose, I guess. It was certainly a silly reason to try to kill me. Of course, I might have remembered later, but I didn't then."

I paused to light a cigarette. "You see, I've run into that damnable little heater downstairs two or three times, and it makes a frightful welt on the shin. Friday night when I was in the kitchen, I heard a couple of noises, and I knew subconsciously, I guess, what the second one was—somebody bumping into the heater. Ouch." I started when the match I'd forgotten to blow out burned my finger. "Yesterday afternoon when we were all in the living room talking to Cassidy I kept rubbing my leg. From what Sophie said on the roof, I think she was afraid I'd ask to look at everybody's shins, and then I'd say 'You're it' to the one who had a welt."

I turned to Anne. "Did you see anyone in the hall Friday night just before I bumped into you? I really have to know."

She got up and came over and sat down beside me on the bed. I was so close to hysteria that I almost laughed at the idea of the entire Moreau family in bed with me. But I didn't, because Anne took my hand and looked at me with very wet, shiny, dark eyes.

"If Sophie had killed you, Hilda," she said jerkily, "I don't know what I would have done—to myself. I didn't see her, but I heard footsteps, and I knew they weren't yours. They could only be Sophie's going to the front of the house. When we learned of Nanette's death, I knew." Her mouth was a thin greyish-white line. "I was going to talk to her, to make her confess. I had some hope of a plea of insanity. I somehow couldn't bear the thought of turning her over to the police before I talked to her. I make no excuses for her, but try to imagine what that poor, foolish creature has suffered all these years."

I nodded and blinked back my own tears. "It's all right, Anne. I'm alive, and Sophie's out of this. Don't reproach yourself, please."

We all had a good cry then, and David's four remaining sisters made a lot of fine speeches about how they would take care of me and Oscar and keep us both safe for David's return. They have taken care of me, too. I'm rotten spoiled.

EPILOGUE

I am hurrying like mad to finish this because Marthe, jiggling with impatience, is hanging over my shoulder. We are going out in her car, its four-gallon gas ration safe in the tank, to comb the town for a little butter.

We need the butter because we're having a party tonight—a party with men. Philip Pearson is coming, although he might not if we'd been cruel enough to tell him of his innocent part in the Moreau tragedies. Judge and Mrs. Oxney will be here, too. Apparently they've managed to iron out their troubles, because when I saw them last week, Gladys looked and acted like a nice woman who was very fond of her elderly but distinguished husband.

Elise's friend, Lieutenant Marsh Russell, got in yesterday from Pearl Harbor, so he'll be at the party, too. We're always glad when he's in town, because he's so encouraging to Elise about the treatment she's getting from Anne's psychiatrist friend, Doctor Henry.

Another of our male guests will be Rose's fiancé, Lieutenant William Everett, just home from North Africa with a slight, but impressive wound.

The party is in honor of Lieutenant (j.g.) David Moreau, USNR, recently detached from the North Atlantic Patrol, now stationed at Twelfth Naval District Headquarters, Federal Office Building, San Francisco, California.

THE END

Masterful mysteries and chilling crime novels from
Elizabeth Fenwick

"Miss Fenwick has employed the dagger of the mind to stab her readers with pity and suspense—and real horror."—*San Francisco Chronicle*

Two Names for Death as by E. P. Fenwick $9.99
"Simply and subtly written, with knowable characters and plausibly complex motivations, this won't disappoint..."—Anthony Boucher, *NY Times*

The Make-Believe Man / The Friend of Mary Rose $17.95
"This Fenwick is a real chiller, the more so because it is based on a familiar dream, that of being unable to keep an evil intruder out of your house."
—Dorothy B. Hughes

Poor Harriet / The Silent Cousin $17.95
"...a psychologically intricate, adeptly plotted, eerie, and wry mystery that takes sharp aim at misogyny."—Donna Seaman, *Booklist*

Disturbance on Berry Hill / A Night Run $17.95
"Strange and terrifying... not to be read late at night."—Houston Chronicle

And coming soon: **Goodbye, Aunt Elva / The Last of Lysandra**

"The contrast between menace and domestic life is Miss Fenwick's specialty."
—Peter Phillips, *The Sun*

"[She] can describe the best and worst of a character in one sentence, and can make a single gesture tell of years of accumulated pain or madness... Fenwick's novels are all beautifully plotted in human intimacy."
—*Twentieth-Century Crime and Mystery Writers*

STARK HOUSE

In trade paperback from:
Stark House Press, 1315 H Street, Eureka, CA 95501
griffinskye3@sbcglobal.net / www.StarkHousePress.com
Available from your local bookstore, or order direct via our website.

Made in the USA
Middletown, DE
04 May 2025